Slicers

By: Bonnie Baraka

Table of Contents

Modern Life

My first Monday of High school ever, and I was stoked. The first couple of days last week were like a test to see if I fit in at this school or that class or this group, and I wasn't sure if I did. I found my niche, and I was happy to finally relax and be myself, but I wasn't sure if I fit with the rest exactly. *I'm in high school,* I thought. The thought made my stomach flip.

Jess and I were in most of the same classes, aside from a couple. Physical Education (P.E.), Art, and Music. Stuff we didn't necessarily share that made us be 'Best Friends Forever' much more interesting. I'd changed my outfit 17 times now. I even woke up in the middle of the night from a nightmare where I couldn't find anything to wear. I felt like that dream was coming true right here before my eyes because I sure was having trouble making the decision. *Pink, white, blue, purple? Ahh, purple, isn't that the color of royalty?* Well, in this house, that was me, so I guess that was why the purple fit so well with my deep brown curls dusted with blonde and sweet hazel eyes. *Finally!* The anxiety had been literally killing me. But I was ready now.

I let the color wash back into my face as I grabbed my gold, sparkling backpack and headed for the door. I stopped dead in my tracks as I noticed something shift under my bed. "Trey, why aren't you dressed for school? We have to leave in 20 minutes to be there on time!" I shouted to the shadow under my bed that was trying so hard to be invisible.

"I am dressed for school," he whined as he slithered from his hiding spot. Lucky for him, my bed was fairly high from the ground since that was quickly becoming his favorite place to hide these days. I probably would have squished him by now if it weren't. Big hazel green eyes filled with torment and grief looked up at me from the darkness under my bed. He wiggled his arm out and grabbed my ankle, stopping me in my tracks. "I don't wanna go to school without you."

I knew this was coming. 'The Great Divide' was what I liked to call it when talking to Pops. I was excited, no longer a child, but a young adult, a teenager. Trey, on the other hand, was no more excited for this change than a snowman was excited for summer. I was on to the next chapter, and Trey would be left behind to fend for himself in Elementary School. We weren't always close or together because I had been in middle school, of course, but Rose Middle and Stafford Elementary were connected by a long hallway, and I had seen him every day outside playing when I took my lunch. All the teachers knew he was my baby brother and boy did he get lucky with that one. They gave him more chances with his temper, more tolerance of his arrogance, and more attention to his educational needs than was allowed for any one student. Just for the sake of hoping that he would, one day, blossom into the 'joy to have in class' that his big sister was. He hated when they mentioned that last part, but he knew it kept him out of trouble, and for that, he appreciated and milked it.

"I'm sorry, Trey; it's just the way the cookie crumbles. You gotta grow and learn, and you need to work on being nicer to others," I told him with a pointed finger. "I mean it! You have to treat others how you want to be treated, and not just the ones you think are smart," I added, bracing for an explosion of vulgar remarks. None came.

The realization that he would, in fact, have to be nice to people for the simple fact that he was all alone with no one to protect him at school now was evident on his face as he took a deep breath and slid closer to the edge of the bed. "Okay. I will try, but you have to promise to be there to pick me up AS SOON AS you get out of class," he whined.

"Okay," I said, bending down so we were eye level and ruffling his loose curls, "Pinky Promise."

He grinned, snagging my outstretched pinky tightly as he slid the rest of the way out from under the bed, before running off to get his backpack. I beamed at his back as he ran. Today was going to be a good day. I could just feel it.

"Star-la. Star-la King?" My new History teacher was hilarious to me in her odd way. My name was by no means hard to say and pronounced just as it read, but she insisted on pronouncing it like there were extra syllables somewhere that you couldn't see.

"Present," I said coyly as I looked over at Jess and rolled my eyes. She was busy preparing her dramatic correction for when her name was called.

Jess was always right after me, coincidentally. Always there, always ready to correct them when they called her by her full name, like a panther stalking its prey, waiting for the perfect time to pounce. One time, a boy laughed at her when she started her spiel. She spun around and punched him in the face so fast that neither he nor the teacher knew what happened. Mr. Coolly just turned back to the chalkboard to finish taking roll and wipe away the lesson from his last class. They never laughed at her again, and I know why!

Jess had been my best friend since 7. My Jelly Belly. Sweet and squishy in the center for sure but to the outside world: thorns and barbwire. She was the queen of thorns if you asked anyone at our school. Well, as long as you asked them in private. Jess was different; always changing, always trying something new, always inquisitive about things happening around us and in the world. With her love for all things competitive and the muscular physique to prove it, she was rough like a pineapple, and she didn't care if they knew it. She probably wanted them to. Right now, she was going through one of her changing phases, but this one felt different, like it may stick. It felt personal, like real, and I wasn't sure how much I was enjoying it.

I was just saying to myself that I hoped this one wouldn't last long when she decided to address Miss Pentiwether before she could finish her last name and let her know that there would be no 'Justina's' here.

"You can call me Jay, you can call me Jess, and you can call me Student. But I will not answer to Justina, I do not know HER, and I will not answer for her," Jess said with confidence as she swiveled in her seat, making eye contact with anyone looking to make sure everyone else got that memo as well.

The teacher continued the roll as if she didn't hear the tone of Jess' voice or feel the icy stare she gave, daring her to challenge. She merely put her head down to the page and continued with the next name on the list, "Susan Mendoza?"

Bonnie Baraka

Satisfied with herself, Jess turned to me to start our normal morning banter of ignoring the rest of the class as they whispered around us. Before she could ask the question burning in her eyes, I heard a guy from behind us clear his throat and lean in. It was Ken, one of the guys from her BFS gym class. All the athletes took the BFS gym; it stood for *Bigger Faster Stronger*. They did a lot of weightlifting and cardio during class instead of the 'fun' stuff like kickball and running the mile. I personally thought they made this class for the kids who were athletically challenged. If they took all the really good kids out, maybe the scrawny ones would have a chance not to get clobbered and actually play in the gym instead of forming a line at the nurse's office with their heads tipped back so the blood in their noses would clot faster. Thinking of this made me laugh, *that is going to be Trey. Either that or he will be up a rope somewhere yelling obscenities at others to let him down and not to hit him or he will get his dad.* That thought made me chuckle out loud.

I quickly checked around me to see if anyone had heard, but Jess and Ken were now deep in an argument about who was going to the league from the draft this year, and who should probably stay in college another year. A topic that was getting boring fast. I was an athlete for sure, but pops was not allowing me to 'ruin my muscle tissue' at my age. He said I could take BFS when I was a varsity player in whatever sport I decided to get serious about. He was probably right. Slimming down for volleyball, and then turning right around to get 'ripped' for softball was actually harder on me than just picking one and focusing on that. Even worse than that, no one wanted a cheerleader with her quads popping out. My guidance counselor said it was good to be well rounded, and I ran with it. My Daddy followed it up with, "Be what you want, but know what you want to be. No one likes an indecisive woman, little star." He would then pat me on the head as if that would help shake some sort of decision into me.

To be fair, I do hold that sentiment close to me when I get nervous or anxious. *Focus on what you want, don't get distracted.* Distracted—that's what I was right now. Turning to join the conversation, I froze when I heard the next question.

"So why do they call you Jus anyway? Cause your daddy 'Just' wanted a boy?" Ken chided in his joking voice, elbowing the frozen boy next to him for crowd participation.

There were no jokes in Jess' eyes as she stood to retaliate on her friend. I launched into action.

"Maybe because she's 'jus' right for kicking your butt. Or 'jus' the person to beat you in an arm wrestle. Ever thought about that?" I kept my voice steady and low. I made sure the words had the right amount of bite in the areas to alert Ken that his questions weren't funny. Not to Jess. I felt my eyebrows rise as I stared at Ken, telling him to proceed with caution. She slacked her grip on my arm, which I had thrown out in front of her before I chimed in.

Ken immediately realized his mistake and tried to brush it off with a small laugh. Knowing that he would lose if he subjected Jess to any physical contact in her current state, he said, "You know what? I will take that offer. Today in BFS, let's arm wrestle!" He smiled as big as he could, with his dark eyes that seemed apologetic, and held out his hand for Jess to shake.

Jess finally calmed enough to realize what was happening. With her face dead set and ready for war, she took his hand and shook it firmly, backing Ken off quickly with a yelp. I could see the gears turning as she realized what almost happened. Her temper was boiling, and she almost let it out on a friend. After a glance over to me with understanding and thanks, she looked Ken over and replied, "Sounds like a bet."

Ken, clearly still trying to keep the situation as light as possible, smiled again and chided, "Alright then, we're on! See you in 4th period!" With that, he went back to his seat before Miss P could catch him by the ear and drag him there.

Turning my attention back to the front of the class, I noticed that Mrs. P had not skipped a beat for our little gathering in the back of the class. *What exactly was she talking about? Was this what happened in High school? The teachers just pretended you weren't there when you misbehaved?* Maybe it was because of Ken, who was getting big on the popular side, being the new Varsity QB back up and all. To ignore us completely when there was about to be a real fight didn't sit well with me, though. I couldn't put my finger on it, but it seemed wrong.

I brushed it off completely. It was probably something extremely boring anyway. I tuned in for a second to see if my thoughts were right—they were. I put my head in my arms and was on my way to dreamland when something she said snapped me back to reality.

"Centuries ago, the Mayans created the Sun Dial to tell time and a Calendar to tell us when the world would come to an end if a certain chain of events weren't altered through our history or their future. Our Studies show that they were given this information by a member of their tribe that was an Astral plane Traveler."

I tilted my head up slowly, raising my eyebrows. Susan had beaten me to my next question.

"ANNNDDDDDD, WHEN WILL THAT BE??" She asked, sounding a little angry that they hadn't already taught us this information.

"December 21st, 2012" was all Miss P said before she turned to continue her reading on Blackhawk and Cherokee Native Americans.

Jess, seeming just as curious as I felt retorted, "Umhmm. Hasn't that already passed?"

Miss P, now looking irritated with the sudden pause in the lesson and checking the clock to make sure we could get through everything, decided we were wasting time and snipped out a stern 'Yes. Now Let's Move On' and continued to read without answering any more questions.

High school was getting more and more interesting by the minute, and just as I was about to ask for more details on the Mayans, the bell rang. Still confused about the topic, but happy that the tension seemed to evaporate, I headed off to Choir. I picked up my books and ran for the door. There would always be tomorrow, and I guess my explanation would just have to wait until then.

I was relieved when I realized I had the next couple periods to myself, only to realize that meant I would coincidently miss the scheduled Arm-Wrestling match in BFS. I knew Jess could handle herself in the match. She was fearless in her own right. The only help I offered these days was to help others avoid her bad side. I was there to cool some of the Lava that occasionally sprouted from her ears, and I was totally fine with that. On the other side, when my usual misty attitude needed a little spicing up, I knew she would be there to lend a match and burn it down if necessary.

Jess and I had been inseparable since the day we met in Kindergarten. My mom had just come back from her 4-year-on-again-off-again vacation, and she was pregnant with my little brother, who would be with us any day. At that time, we didn't have much. It was just me and my daddy before she decided to come back and ruin it. *Now another mouth to feed?* I could see the tension in Pop's eyes clear as day like I was standing on the banister listening to them fight all over again. But I wasn't. I was standing in the rafters belting out some song about a purple cat and yellow leathers. I knew this was supposed to help with enunciation when singing, but it just made me giggle. I saw Jess walk by the door, urging me to get a bathroom pass, and I obliged.

In the hall, she told me what the big deal was. "I need you to come watch me arm-wrestle Ken in case he tries any funny business, and I have to punch him. I can't get any more suspensions, in school or out. My dad will freak. You gotta be there." Jess belted out as if we were alone.

As quiet as it was in the halls during class, we were never alone, and even I knew that. So, I replied much quieter to remind her of what we both knew. I brought my hands from the top of my head to the middle of my torso, to remind her to breathe and calm down a smidge and to rally her for her match.

"Okay, but Ken is your friend, he didn't mean any harm in what he said, I don't think. You need to keep thinking that. Repeat it in your mind, but not too much. Don't get all squishy and forget that this is an arm-wrestle to the death of your reputation if you lose!" I gave her solid shoulders a little squeeze, and we walked to the BFS training room where a group had already started to gather in anticipation of the match.

"Great. Thanks. Am I supposed to be calm or clobber him!? Now you've got me all confused," she retorted with a glare.

"Both," I said with a sideways shrug.

"Had to go get your coach, did you?" Ken smirked as he leaned coolly up from the doorpost, ready to take his position at the matted table. He was 5 feet 4 inches of pure Quarterback talent with the JV record to prove it. The contrast of his straight white teeth on his deep smooth coffee brown skin could melt away any thoughts of anger I could muster. I could tell he thought he was sure to win. I looked away with a smile of my own. *Boy, was he in for a surprise?*

"No, but I thought you might want someone who can tie a bandage pretty well once she rips your arm off, and I knew it would be over soon, so I figured a bathroom break would do." I gave an icy smile as I shook the bathroom pass at him. *Was that shock or nerves I saw in his eyes?* I couldn't tell.

He sat down at the table and placed his arm in the correct position. Then looked up at Jess to see if she had followed. She hadn't; she was standing there clearly holding back rage and muttering something to herself.

I knew she was muttering the mantra I had just asked her to remember. "Ken is my friend." Deep sigh. "Ken is my friend."

I rolled my eyes and looked at Ken again. "Oh, hell with that! Rip his arm off!" Jess immediately snapped out of the trance, looking like a hellhound bracing for the pounce. A couple of people in the crowd cringed, but Ken stood firm. She wasn't going to give him any slack. She sat down and got right to business.

"Alright, this is a wrestling matcchhhh! There will be no use of the other arm. No Standing, no use of vulgar language or intimidation tactics during the match, and most of all, NO QUITTING," Ken's best friend Johnny called out the rules.

"Do both parties understand the rules?" Nods from both.

"Okay, Let's Play Ball!"

I must have looked confused at the last statement because he clarified himself.

"Not actual ball, it's just a term... you know, to start the... Never mind, just go on my whistle."

TWEEEET! And they were off.

Jess was looking cool as a cucumber at Ken flushing under her grip. What Ken didn't know was that all Jess' cousins were boys, and their mother died in childbirth with her youngest cousin, who was 16. She was literally the only girl besides her mother who almost always opted to stay home in bed on family outing days. Beyond that, Jess' father's favorite sport was proving how his little girl was tougher than any boy, any day, and that included all of her cousins who were at least two years older than her. At first, she wasn't particularly good at this whole arm-wrestling thing. One time in 2nd grade, she came over after one of those family outings, and I legit thought her arm was going to fall right off her shoulder. It was like putty. She couldn't tell my Pops it wasn't broken enough times for him to believe her. He drove her straight over to the family clinic and got X rays. When they asked what happened and she had shared her story, both the nurse and Daddy asked the same thing at the same time. "Where was your father?" She lied and said he was in the other room. That he didn't know. It was at that point that I knew something was not right. After they said she would be okay, that it was just a sprain and that thankfully nothing was broken but that she would need rest and a couple of protein shakes to build the muscle back up in her arm, I decided to call her 'Limp Biscuit' for the rest of the month. She actually tried to punch me after I annoyed her enough about it, but with that gimpy arm tissue healing like it was, she couldn't even get close enough to connect.

That was when I first stood up to Jess. I felt confident in the timing to say what I needed to say without the fear of a pounding. Hands on my hips bracing for her to try and take me out anyway, I used my 'I'm calm, but you better listen up, or I won't be' voice and my stern face when I said, "The Justina I know would never allow anyone ESPECIALLY a pack of filthy boys to boss her around or corral her into doing anything she didn't want to or wasn't PREPARED to do. I am not saying that you should not arm-wrestle with them anymore. I mean, it IS a family tradition. I get that. HOWEVER, if that's what your gonna do, then you better get some muscle on those arms, and you better find a strategy that makes sure you win EVERYTIME. Because if you win once, they are going to come back harder. They are not going to let you have it or leave you alone, and if you win by luck, they WILL break your arm next time." She only scowled, which caught me off guard. That was when Justina Matthews shared something so important to her with me that I could barely stand.

"I know," she said, sounding defeated. "I just want to fit in. At school, I have you. You don't care whether I'm popular or not. But at home..." she paused, and my gut knotted looking at how upset she was and how hard it was for her to say this to me.

"I hear my parents fight all the time. How upset my dad is that my mom can't conceive any more kids. How she's worthless because she can't give him a junior. How I will never get a scholarship to his Alma mater for football and carry on the Matthews Tradition. How I will get married and be a worthless childbearing woman just like she is." The tears began to fall at that point. Not hers, though—mine. Not with sympathy, but with anger.

I looked her in her eyes and said, "You are an Amazing PERSON, Boy or Girl, Big or Little, Fast or Slow. You will be an amazing whatever you want to be! When people step up to you, you knock them down, and not just with your fists. You outsmart them. You sidestep them. You play them like a fiddle! And by golly, if that's what you have to do to shine in your house, that's what you do for the brief time that you're there. Then you bring your ass RIGHT back over

9

here and live a normal life like a normal girl's best friend." I stomped my foot down so hard it stung, but she got the memo. She took what I said to heart and started lifting weights, drinking protein shakes, daily workouts, the whole 9. She practically lived at my house, and well, she developed an arm-wrestling strategy that worked every time if you knew what you were doing, and you could bet she knew what she was doing at this point.

Ken's seat slid across the floor slowly, catching my attention and bringing me back to the current match. *Poor Ken. It was over before he could blink.* She grunted and pretended to struggle for a good 5 seconds before she laughed in his face. Before he could comprehend what was happening, she was slamming his fist down and yelling for him to 'stay out of her house with that Bull.'

I chuckled softly under my breath before I noticed Johnny standing extremely close to me, not paying attention to the match at all.

"Umm, blow your whistle!" I whispered to him without even looking in his direction.

That snapped him out of it, but it was too late. Jess was on him. "What are you staring at her like she's a lollipop for? Blow the damn whistle; tell everyone I won the match and BACK AWAY FROM MY BEST FRIEND!!" She was up pushing him back now. I grabbed her before she could do any serious damage and pushed her back with a victorious cheer.

"Let's go! I have to get me back to class," was all I could say as I yanked her into the hallway, throwing back an apologizing glance at Johnny as we went.

He was stunned. This was a part of Jess' new phase that I hoped would end soon. She was becoming less of my best friend and more of a territorial teenage boy, and I didn't like it one bit. *Was she taking steroids or testosterone or something?* I thought to myself as we moved into the hallway. I was having a hard time explaining these mini bursts of insecurity to pops, so he could help me explain myself to Jess, but at this point, it didn't matter. I was going to address it. *Was I not supposed to be able to talk to anyone else ever?*

"What's your problem?" I said in a slightly angrier tone than I meant to. "You can't go pushing around every boy that looks at me. You don't even know what was going on. And then, the outburst with Ken this morning. I mean yes, we all know and love that fire Jess keeps right under the surface, but I haven't seen it this much since 2nd grade. So, you can either tell me what's going on now, or I can ask you later; but you WILL tell me."

She spun around so fast, eyes on me, looking like she might suffocate. Now it was her turn to remind me of the lurking eyes and ears.

"Not here, not now. I'm sorry, I thought I had a handle on things. I was just excited from the win," she whispered.

Did she just try to lie to me? Or was this a show for the lurkers? I rolled my eyes so she knew I could tell she was lying and played along.

"Fine, I gotta get back to Choir. I'm sure she's sent out a search party by now. I have to practice my duet. Congrats on the win," and I turned on my heels and walked away briskly without another look. That'd teach her not to lie to my face. By the time I got back to class, I was seething, and I didn't care who saw.

Not So Popular

There were mean girls everywhere in this school. Some because they felt entitled. Some just unconsciously mean. Some the 'you just don't understand because you're still a kid' kind of mean, and some just plain old 'this is who I am, deal with it' mean. No matter the reason, they were all mean. They all wanted to exploit your flaws and get in your business. They ALL loved to gossip. So, when word got around that Jess and I were having a rift, I wasn't surprised. Irritated that now I had to act like everything was okay between us to cover up the actual fight we were about to have, yes. Upset that she tried to hide something from me, absolutely—but not surprised at all.

News traveled faster than any email service I had ever used around here, and it seemed that if it ended up on the gossip train, then it must be true. No doubt, some stuff was, in fact, true, like the argument that was now being reported to anyone who would listen by God-knows-who—but the real kicker to me was that I wasn't the popular one. I was just a regular freshman who had a couple of friends from Middle School who happened to be attending Jonesy with me.

Jonesy was a Charter school, so not everyone from our middle school came over with us. Not everyone probably had the grades or ambitions or parents who thought they were destined for greatness. Some kids just wanted regular old public-school learning. But Jess, Jess was the star athlete at our last school, and she was kicking the Varsity Squad's butt in practice so far this year. Football, basketball, track, you name it. She was winning it. The Football coach hated it, something about pretty girls and how they shouldn't be on his field and *NEVER* in his locker room, but he couldn't resist the large donation he had heard her father made every year she played. His remark about her dark ruby red and blonde highlighted hair being too long for a helmet just fueled her fire to play harder. She had decided really early that she wanted to be on the Football team, and her dad forced the school to let her. *Turns out, when your dad is an all-American alumnus, and you can afford to get new equipment for the whole team almost every year, you can probably be a fish and still get to play.* It helped a lot that she was their best player, though. What they didn't know was how she opted for the football team to please her father instead of being home to watch her mother be his punching bag.

He wanted a boy so bad, so he tried to turn her into one, and she didn't mind it. She liked sports and intimidating people. She loved spending time with her dad fishing, hiking, and shooting hoops as a kid; but that one time she tried to play with a doll, or once when she wanted to paint her nails, or when she had wanted a pleated dress instead of slacks, the outcome really made the decision for her. Sure, he obliged, but then he turned around and took his frustration out on her mother for not being able to produce a son for him. How could he not see that she was sick, dying even? Sure, her mother hid it from the world well, but not from Jess and not from me.

As good as Mrs. Mathews was at putting on a brave face and getting it done, she couldn't hide her sickness and worry from Jess, nor her sadness. I like to think that while she is a lot like her dad, she gets her bravery and strength from Mrs. Mathews. Since nothing had changed in the last eight years, Jess had opted to go with the flow and act out at school like any other 14-year-old boy would do when they rebelled. She never said as much, but I think she wanted to be a boy just as much as her father wanted her to. Either way, her quick moves and her daddy's fat wallet made her as good as in for the Varsity football team and the girls' basketball team, who hadn't won a game in 5 years. That part was a no-brainer.

I thought about trying out this year for varsity. My dad was anxious to see what sport I'd pick, and Jess and I had always hooped together. It just seemed like an easy choice, but something held me back this year when I saw the signup sheet for tryouts. Of course, Jess signed both of our names, so I was trying out whether I wanted to or not, but I pondered that first hesitation for a long time after it was there and gone. *Was that what this was about? Did Jess sense the hesitation also? Was she scared that I didn't want to spend that time with her anymore?*

I was wondering all these things and a whole lot more by the time she finally made it to the table at lunch. Growling at the other guys, who had obviously been on her team in kickball and lost, as she sat down, she looked me square in my face and said, "I knew this would come back to bite us in the butt."

I cocked my head to the side and tried as hard as I could to hide my rising agitation. "What?" I demanded sarcastically.

"I knew it would get out if you started yelling in the hallway," she said pointedly.

Although it took everything in me not to start yelling now, I replied to her in a fake calm falsetto that I knew would get under her skin. "Speaking of that, we're still not done with that conversation." I then relaxed a little as I saw the tension come back to her face.

Ahh. She was trying to get me so mad that I would forget about what I said and what she did that started me yelling in the first place. Interesting. So, she was definitely hiding something from me. I was wondering what it was, when the Varsity QB, Brody, came over to chat about the upcoming tryouts. Grateful for the distraction, I slowed my breathing to help me relax and turned to the rest of the cafeteria to see if any of our friends had made it in yet. Nothing out of the ordinary until I noticed it out of the corner of my eye. Clarynda, sitting alone at the window, watching me. Unsure if she was looking at me or Brody, or Jess, or anyone else, I brushed it off and looked away. What could she possibly want with the not-so-popular girl in Jess' shadow? It made me uncomfortable, though. I immediately got up and left.

"Going to the bathroom," I said I rushed out of the cafeteria. Feeling a little dizzy, I ran to the bathroom to splash some water over my face and think things through. Jess is keeping secrets, Clarynda staring at me, Trey being nice to people. What has this day become?

Just when I thought it couldn't get any worse, Susan busted into the restroom, trying to catch anything that she could report back to the gossip mill. Sorry Susan, better luck next time! I smirked as I shoved past her with a little too much might, and she fell into the stall door. I caught myself by surprise with my strength.

"Oh, my goodness! Are you okay? Let me help you. I'm so clumsy sometimes," I stuttered.

She turned to look at me and rolled her eyes. As I was walking out, I heard her muttering to her friend, "I came in here to get dirt for gossip, and here she is still apologizing and being so freaking nice! She couldn't even shove me properly. It's so annoying!"

I guess I didn't think about it like that, Susan. Thanks for the compliment. I smiled to myself and kept walking straight past the lunchroom. Oh well, maybe another day I'll stand up for myself.

There was a small park close to the school. Now that we were in high school, there were no monkey bars, no playgrounds—just open space to think, trees to curl up under with a book and study, and parking lots to sit in and jam out to the radio. Being 14 without as much as a learner's permit, I wasn't headed there. I figured I could take a stroll through and listen to the latest hits on my way to the park, though. I didn't really know when I decided I was going to go there and get some space, but that was where I was headed.

This high-school thing was much different than I expected, and even though I knew things with me and Jess were the same, I was also noticing how they were becoming different. I didn't know if I liked it at all. Sure, it had only been a couple of days, and we hadn't really had a fight like everyone said, but it felt like we did. Did we? The simple fact that she was not with me at the moment telling me that going to the park off-campus in the middle of the day was a bad idea, even if we did have a study period, told me a lot about how Jess was managing high school and even more about how I wasn't and that what we just had was, in fact, our first high school fall out.

I wasn't extremely popular in Middle School, but I got by. I'd known almost everyone by name or face, I was on the welcoming committee for the incoming 6th graders, and my teachers loved me. Now, my history teacher couldn't even pronounce my name. I couldn't describe the emotions that I was feeling, and that made me feel awkward. "Awkward with yourself?" I asked out loud to no one in particular as I finally passed the parking lot and turned the corner to the park. "How can you ever master social acceptance if you aren't even comfortable with yourself?" I stopped. What am I talking about? I am extremely comfortable with myself. I am happy not to have the anxieties of popularity, I am content with my true friends, I am free to make whatever decision I want, and I know they will love me regardless. I am, most of all, NOT awkward with myself. I'm having this conversation with myself just to prove that! I giggled.

As I stepped up to the swing, I tried to sort through my thoughts and the day that I had been having, along with whatever was happening between me and Jess, with a little more decisiveness. She was the most complicated part of this whole thing. I would need to sort the thoughts with her involved last. Those always brought me back to reality anyway.

I swung slowly, looking off at the clouds in the distance while rubbing the new charm Gran had gifted me this year for Christmas. I missed my Gran a lot more these days. She was sick, and no one was surprised. A stout 82-year-old woman, still driving herself to the grocery store and smoking like a chimney was my Gran Jin. She took no sass and held no punches; she didn't care one bit about how you felt about her actions unless she loved you. That was me, her favorite grandchild. She would tell you her favorite was the one she was talking to at the time, but I knew better. I was the apple of her eye; some even called me her twin. I didn't see it, with my eclectic background of various cultures from the mixture of Daddy's brown skin and Momma's Korean heritage, but she loved when people said it. I missed her more the more I thought about her and our talks about everything and nothing at all in front of the fireplace with a large mug of hot cocoa with a hit of warm vanilla.

We didn't get those luxuries here in San Diego, it was too hot, but when we were visiting her for the holidays in Minnesota, she always put the fireplace on for me. I asked her one time why she had to live so far away from us, and why she had to pick someplace that was so cold. She told me that the cold froze her wrinkles and kept her young and that it was just too hot out in California for her liking. Mom was home with us, but because Gran wasn't doing well, she should have been up with Gran. I kicked the dirt at that thought. She was so selfish. I would have gone to be with Gran if Pops would have let me. In fact, I was hoping to convince him that we needed to take a weekend trip to see her before school got serious and that we missed something important, just this morning.

I was hoping my candid smile and tactful argument, mixed with the huge curls, dimples, and eyes that look like his would win him over. He always loved a good debate. Pondering the tactics needed to engage him, I continued to rub the pendant on my charm bracelet harder and harder, too deep in thought to notice the sparks I was somehow creating, I burnt myself. "OUCH!" I yelped, looking down at my wrist to see a burn was forming there. Confusion left me vulnerable to Jess's approach.

"I thought I would find you here, pouting."

I spun around, trying to hide the shock to see Jess, a ball in her hand dribbling in circles like she was about to go full-blown practice drills on me.

"How'd you find me?" I asked, irritated.

Jess shrugged. "I know you, and since there are no monkey bars to hang from until you're blue in the face, and there's a class in the gym playing kickball, I figured a swing would be the next best thing."

She was right. I liked to shoot free throws until my arms were soggy when I couldn't figure something out, and the monkey bars thing came into play when I first met the smallest King, Trey.

When he was born, his face was blue and purple. Daddy said it was from all the blood rushing to it during delivery, so naturally, I wanted to find out what that was like. I never wanted anything to hurt my baby brother, or my mother, for that matter. So, anytime there was a suspicion of pain, I tested the waters to see what it felt like. Come to find out, blue in the face wasn't so bad, but anything worse than that and someone would have a serious problem on their hands.

"So, what are you pouting about today?" Jess asked, seeing that I was in no mood to offer up information.

So, I played along, finally putting the pieces together and guessing at where some of these hidden emotions I thought were my own had surfaced from.

"Have you ever felt awkward with yourself?" I asked as if I was directing the question to myself but turning to see her reaction.

Right on cue, she blushed and turned away, pretending to lose control of the ball. Not slick at all.

"Hmm. That must mean yes. That MUST be what you think you are hiding from me." I turned, feeling the heat rising to my plump cheeks. The heat quickly soothed. I was feeling just a little bit better about myself for figuring out the plot until I saw her face. Anger laced it with white specs of confusion and sadness. I wasn't ready for another 'come to Jesus' talk just yet, and judging from the look on her face, neither was she. So, I abruptly interrupted her stammer of what she was going to try to get out and lied.

"It's just..." I rubbed the charm again, this time with much softer hands, "ever since they gave my Gran only a timeline on her life, I have felt extremely awkward. Like confused as to how I should feel about it. You know?"

It worked. Jess dropped the ball and took up the swing next to mine. I tried to apply my question to something I could relate to myself, so I didn't sound attacking, and the topic was right there for me!

"Like, I mean, Gran's 82. She lived a long, good, fascinating life. She has traveled to plenty of places and done even more things. No one is surprised that she is finally getting to this point. So, I should be happy, right?" I stopped to angle my head on the swing where I could see her out of my peripheral, but she couldn't tell.

Pain. There was actual pain coating her features as I talked about Gran. Like it was her grandmother that was going to the 'pearly gates.' Like it was her own flesh and blood that would no longer be here with us. Seeing how this affected her, too, any notion of a fight I had left in me dissipated.

I continued, "But I'm sad. I feel... guilty, I think. I feel like she has been here for 82 years, and I didn't spend nearly enough time with her. I didn't learn half of the things she knows; I wasn't even interested when she wanted to show me those old things she got on her travels. I should have listened more, asked more questions, and enjoyed her company so much more than what I did." Real tears were sliding down my face now. I knew this was affecting me, but I did not weigh just how much until I put it into words. I shocked myself.

"And now I don't even know if I will get the chance to say goodbye." The reality of what I was trying to use as a cover story being real hit me, and I started to sob. An all-out swing shaking, snot running, emotions open, and raw sob, right there on the swing when Jess grabbed my wrist and yanked.

"What the hell are you doing? Are you trying to go with her or what?" she shrieked. I looked down. The friction of me rubbing my charm had started to form a low purple fire right there on my wrist. I blinked, and it was gone.

"I don't understand. I don't know, what in the world was that!?" I stammered to Jess. She Just looked at me wide-eyed.

Finally, after a long silence between us, she asked, "You're saying you didn't mean to do that?" I searched her face for the joke, was this her way of trying to cheer me up?

"UMM, no, I did not mean to start a fire ON MY WRIST, with MY BRACELET; that would have burned me alive and left YOU and TREY with no one. If that was a joke, it wasn't funny." I was halfway out of the swing when she grabbed my arm and spun me around so fast I thought I was about to get whiplash.

"Calm Down! It wasn't me, Starla King. I didn't do anything but watch in horror when you just about went up in flames!" She gave me the most serious look she could muster. "Why would I joke about that?"

I hated it when she used my full name, and she knew it, but it also meant she wasn't lying. Before we could discuss anything further, I spotted the high school student security. If he caught us here, we were getting that ISS for sure. "Run," I whispered just loud enough for her ears only.

Seeing the intensity in my face, she knew what I just spotted and ducked behind the slide to grab her ball and run for the school. I followed close behind, trying not to make a sound, and praying that he didn't see us. When we got to the sidewalk, we took off in a dead run. I couldn't get ISS on my 3rd day of High school, and neither could she. We made it back to school just in time to hear the bell ring. Last period of the day, and I was already ready to go home.

3   *Nothing Like A Present*

Home Economics was our last period of the day, and even though I loathe cooking without Pops or Gran, there was always something sweet to eat afterward. So, I guess that made it okay for me up until now. Today, I wasn't so sure. Jess and I were kitchen mates, obviously. Even though things seemed okay between us at this point, I couldn't shake the question in her eyes. There were definitely some in mine too. Not to mention the fact that I had no clue what in the world had happened with the charm bracelet that my Gran had gifted me.

It was not like this was a surprise to receive a new charm. My Gran had been gifting me charms twice a year since I first got my bracelet in 2nd grade. It was just after Jess had come clean, and I was feeling a little defeated that I couldn't do more for my friend. Gran had stopped in to say hello during her layover from some island that she had visited—Tahiki, I think she had said. I remember being a little confused because after she left, Pops helped me google the island to see where she went, but the computer said it didn't exist. We just chucked it up to her getting the name wrong and never thought anything more about it. She brought me a present back from her trip but could see something was troubling me when she came to give it to me.

Knowing I could confide in her without hesitation, I told her of Jess and her arm and the terrors that lived within the walls of her home. I told her how angry I had gotten and how unfair it was for someone who would never hurt anyone on purpose to be treated in that way. I was on the brink of tears when she cupped my hands in hers, stopping my banter, to tell me how proud of me she was. She explained that many people felt something was wrong with the world, but not many looked for ways to fix it. And that the action of wanting things to change was good, but to still be concerned and looking for something to help with that change made me a conqueror. I listened intently and clung to every word. Drank it in, hoping it would fill the empty parts of me. I was feeling all tingly in my gut for letting Jess go home, and her words mostly calmed the storm below. There was something there in those words that still drove me now, to not only change things, but to understand. That part in my gut just seemed to be getting bigger and bigger these days.

So Gran, uncommonly excited about the sad story I had just given her, gave me a piece of advice and a gift to keep me company in 'times of uncertainty.' Her advice was, "If you are unsure about the actions of others, put yourself in their shoes. See from their point of view, but never pass judgment. Offer as much self-encouragement as possible, but never take their burdens as your own." And with her advice, she gave me a charm bracelet with my first charm. She said it was a replica of the mountains on the island that she went to visit. She told me to wear it to help me remember to be strong like the mountain and stand fast to the winds and transitions of others.

I had worn this bracelet ever since that day. I had 14 charms now, and everyone meant something so special to me. If I lost even one, my whole world would come tumbling down around me. I had, in fact, lost a few at this point, but Gran found them for me. As we walked into the kitchens and turned on our stoves, I looked at the newest charm that Gran had given me. It was a thermostat, filled with purple measuring liquid instead of red. Gran knew my favorite color was purple. She said she had gotten me this charm to remind me in high school that sometimes I might need to check the temperature of a situation before adding my 2 cents. I laughed then, but I was grateful for it now. I had used it to get out of several hot situations. These high school girls could be so catty, and Gran knew it too. She was so smart that way.

When she met Jess, she smiled at her so big with a knowing look and said, "2 peas in a pod." Then she just turned and walked away like nothing happened. I did appreciate that I could be calm when Jess was not, and when I was not, Jess somehow found an inner calm that was only meant for me. Like the Ying to my

Yang. Give and Take, a real friendship that was based on trust for one another and a knowing that we were always there for each other.

While I was lost in thought and Ms. Sternbough explained to the class what we were going to cook today—an open-face egg sandwich which Pops makes for a late-night snack as often as there are late nights—I noticed something happening with the same purple charm as before in the park. I studied it for a second, completely confused as to how the temp could keep rising to the point of combustion when we were just standing in one place. My thoughts were suddenly interrupted when Jess ushered me out of the classroom, telling the class I had a bloody nose that she needed to assist me with. When we made it to the hall, she dragged me as fast as she could towards the football locker rooms. There was a locker room area set aside just for her, being that she was the only girl on the team. When we finally made it in, she closed the door softly and locked it behind us. I sagged in reply as I realized I had been holding my breath this entire time.

"What is that thing!?" She asked me, head cocked to the side, trying to get a better view.

"It's my charm bracelet, same one I have always had," I said to her with a look in my eyes daring her to reach for it.

She huffed and sat on the bench behind us. "Oh, it's more than a bracelet, my friend. Have you not been paying attention? It has almost caught you on fire twice in a matter of an hour!"

I had noticed that, but I wasn't about to admit it to Jess. She would insist I take it off. I had worn this bracelet for 7 years, and now as my Gran was slipping away, I was not about to take it off. It was out of the question. We would have to get to the bottom of this—and fast.

I turned to look Jess square in the eye. "I'm not taking it off. So, what are the other options?" I crossed my arms in response and covered the bracelet to make sure she didn't reach for it anyway.

She took one look at my serious face and my tight stance and laughed uncontrollably. I just stared. After she caught her breath and laughed some more, she finally decided to explain what she thought was so damn funny.

"I'm sorry, it's just…" a long pause for the Jess theatrics, "boy, have we had a crazy day. Arm-wrestling challenge before 9 am, word around school is we're fighting… or dating, no one is sure, and then Susan told everyone she saw you crying in the bathroom. We almost get caught by campus security, and then your bracelet tries to kill you. And yet here you are holding strong to that calm tough girl act even when you know there is something seriously wrong with that damn thing being about to blow up!" She pointed to my wrist, where I currently had burn marks.

I blushed. I thought about the crazy day I had been having, then I added the foolishness that Jess had also been subjected to. I was probably as mad at her as she was at me, and neither one of us said anything. I turned to say something, and I saw her staring at me, face turned slightly like a panther watching its prey. She had one leg up on the bench in the Captain Morgan stance, and her hair was blowing in the wind. Her blue eyes were glistening from her laughter in the dimly lit locker room. At this, I finally laughed.

I laughed until I was blue in the face, and after her anger subsided and she realized what I was looking at, she slid down onto the floor next to me, and we laughed together. We just sat there and laughed until we couldn't laugh anymore. Then we laughed some more.

"We will get the hang of this high school thing if it kills us," I whispered to my friend.

"So, we shall," she said with a nod, and we stood up to make our way back to the Kitchens as if nothing had transpired.

We missed the entire class, and to make matters worse, when Ms. Sternbough called the nurse's office to check on us, we weren't even there. Standing in the doorway, tapping her foot, waiting for us to come back and get our stuff, she said, "Your parents would have a fit if they knew you girls were skipping class on the third day."

I winced at the thought. My dad would have my hide if he knew, and Jess would be in a worse state than me. There went my plans of going to see Gran, right out the window. I looked at her with real tears in my eyes, and before I knew what was happening, I was sobbing and lying. Again.

Bonnie Baraka

"I'm sorry. We went to the nurse's office, but there was a line," I said between sobs because there was always a line at the nurse's door.

"But the blood wouldn't stop, so we went to the bathroom to get tissue and try to clot it. Jess finally managed to stuff enough tissue up my nose that it finally did, but then I was a mess because..." Think fast, girl. "Well, because my Gran is sick and she used to make me those open-face sandwiches when I was sick, and I just couldn't sit in class and look at everyone without crying and being a mess." I sobbed.

I had struck gold. Ms. Sternbough knew my grandmother. Information I had conveniently forgotten until I needed it. I turned to Jess, who finally understood what was happening.

"I was only trying to comfort her since she hasn't been able to see her Gran in a while, and I remembered her telling me the stories about the funny-faced sandies that she used to make," Jess said, trying to seal the deal.

Good job, Jess! We were so close to our goal that I couldn't even smile at her and throw the whole thing off.

"Your..." Ms. Sternbough started in bewilderment. "Your grandmother is ill?" she finished a little flushed and confused looking.

It even seemed like she was upset herself. She looked down at my burnt wrist and right at the new charm that had made the scorch and then at Jess.

Initially stiffening about the news of Gran, she seemed to take inventory, then relax and make a split decision at that moment.

"Well, I won't call your parents, but the cooking today was for your first real grade. You ladies will have to stay late and finish the assignment before you go," she said in a tone built to take no sass.

Jess squealed in protest. "But I have Football tryouts tonight! I can NOT miss them!" She said, knowing an F in Home Ec would mean nothing to her dad compared to if she missed those tryouts and didn't make the team.

Ms. Sternbough looked at Jess with confusion on her face. "Relax, Miss Mathews, you could show up to tryouts and sit in the stands, and you would still make the football team." She rolled her eyes. Her confusion was probably how Jess could not be aware of this factor. "But I guess that IS important as well, so you will have two choices. A, you can stay and complete your assignment as a team the way the rest of the class did. Or B, you can go to Tryouts today and cook by yourself on Thursday when they are over."

Jess looked mortified at the choices in front of her. Stay and get a good grade but miss the first day of football or come Thursday and show Ms. Sternbough that she had no actual skills in the kitchen. I was stunned that Ms. S even gave her options, but the decision that Jess made caught me off guard to the point I stumbled back a bit.

"Are you sure coach won't be upset?" Jess asked as if she was considering the latter.

"I'm sure he can't penalize you for having to participate in class. Will he be upset? That I cannot say," our teacher said lazily. Ms. S was clearly getting bored with this back and forth banter, and Jess sensed it too.

"Okay, then. I guess I will be out there early tomorrow to get the details on all the stuff I missed," she said with a forced smile. With the decision being made, we all walked into the Home Economics room to get cooking. I followed Jess; a bit dazed that she would pick cooking with me over her love for sports.

I wasn't sure where to go once we got inside. Looking to Jess for some sort of direction and seeing only her blank face, we walked quietly behind Ms. S until she noticed us. When she caught my reflection behind her, she turned around to finally give the directions.

"It is not necessary for me to watch you ladies. I evaluated your kitchen skills last week on the first and second days, and I know you are capable. If you are in need of directions, you should refer to your books. It will give you all the information you need." And with that, she strutted around her desk to collect her purse. As we turned to take up our places in our kitchen unit, she stopped me.

Grabbing my wrist atop of that burn where it was now throbbing under her touch, she said with true sadness in her eyes, "I am truly sorry to hear about your grandmother, Starla. If you should need ANYTHING in the future, please do not hesitate to find me." I sucked in a breath at the pain seeping from my wrist, hoping she didn't hear, but she continued, saying, "You will be a wonderful woman when you grow up. She instilled in you many great qualities and attributes. Hold on to them, and she will always be with you."

Before I could respond, she had gone. No tears came at her words, only a little confusion, as I strode back to meet Jess' also confused expression chiding me to tell her what Ms. S had said. And so, I told her.

4

"**S**he was just expressing her condolences for the situation with Gran, nothing major," I said as I walked over to grab the Home Ec book.

Jess looked at me curiously, sensing what I wasn't saying. "But I mean, what exactly did she saayyy?" She asked. "Her and your Gran, they were like, really good friends, right?"

"Yea," I said, remembering the first time I met Ms. S. "They went to college together, and I think they were in the same sorority," I added, scratching my head. "I actually forgot about it until just now. I haven't seen her since I was 5 or 6 maybe. She used to come and check on us a lot before Kiki—my mom—pulled her Houdini trick. Then it seemed like we didn't see any of Gran's friends, and we only got to see Gran every once in a while." I pulled the items we needed out of the fridge and brought them over to the counter, remembering the time before Kiki came and changed our family of 2 to a family of 4. "Book says to set the oven to 325 degrees." I nodded to the cookbook on the counter.

"Why do we need the oven for a fried egg sandwich?" She asked, more irritated than confused, going over to the oven to set the preheat. "Shouldn't we be making it on the top part?"

I laughed at her. This was my chance to show miss know-it-all that I was smarter than her in at least one thing, and I was going to take it. "Well, yea, you have to fry the egg on the eye, but then you have to butter the bread and melt the cheese on top. So, to get the cheese melteee...." There it was again; my bracelet was glowing as bright as the sun.

"SHUT IT OFF!! SHUT IT OFF!!" I yelled; alarmed and confused.

A little nervous that she had done something wrong, Jess didn't even notice the glowing as she sprang into action at the pure alarm in my voice. I was shaking.

"What the hell happened?" She screamed at me as she was going over every inch of the oven to make sure she didn't set a fire, then spinning in a circle to check the rest of the classroom. Finally, she turned to look at me and saw it. The same purple thermostat charm was glowing and humming like it was going to rip right off of my arm. She grabbed me by the shoulders, pinning my arms to my sides.

"Calm down," she breathed, "it's probably just a magnet or something."

"Okay, but what about at the park? There were no magnets there, and it sparked a whole damn fire!" I was panicking now. Something was not right.

Jess looked me in the eye. "Your Gran would not give you anything that would actually harm you," she said. She shrugged her shoulders as to say, 'on purpose.'

She was solid, where I was putty. I sucked in air, calming at her steadfast answer, and hoping she was right.

"Here., I remember something in our science books like this, let's look it up," she said, grabbing her book and flipping furiously through the pages. "Magnetic Energy, often confused with Kinetic Energy, is the study of two magnetically charged items either pulling together or pushing each other apart," she read aloud.

I looked at her with both curiosity and disbelief. "Soo... what does that have to do with my wrist starting to randomly combust?" I said with a little annoyance.

"Okay, okay, okay; calm down, pissy pants. Maybe I read the wrong passage." She continued to skim the page as fast as possible. "Here, Kinetic Energy is the energy an object possesses due to its motion of frequency or vibration. It can also be defined as the needed acceleration an object exerts during takeoff. Having a certain frequency, the object then maintains the frequency and holds the energy until its speed is physically changed."

I looked her up and down once, not understanding anything she had said, and she read every bit of confusion on my face.

"Look, my teacher was saying sometimes things that vibrate with the same art of kinetic energy vibrate at the same frequency, and if you get a lot of them together, they start to shake and try to pull towards each other. It's normal." She released a breath as she finished, clearly trying to convince herself just as much as she was trying to convince me. "The heat could just be from the friction of the other charms. This charm in particular could be reacting to other things in the room because it was made at a higher altitude and frequency. Didn't you say she got it for you when she was somewhere in the Alps?"

I nodded shakily.

"Well, there you go! The Alps are at a much higher frequency than here. No big mystery, it's all here in the science book. Now, how about we cover it with a scrunchie, and let's get this over with before our parents figure out we're missing," she said, putting the book down. She positioned herself on a stool between me and the oven and then handed over her extra scrunchie.

I did as she said. The charm sizzled a little at the impact of the scrunchie, but it soon calmed and dulled. There, I thought. Back to normal. I took a deep breath. I hope.

"Okay," I said, trying to calm myself. "Well, let's just get everything together and fry the eggs before we turn the oven on to be safe."

She nodded in agreement.

In about 5 minutes, we had everything set, and the egg all fried and ready to go into the oven.

"Alright, last step. I'm turning on the oven," Jess whispered so I could barely hear her from the refrigerator where I was standing. I knew this was on purpose so I wouldn't freak out, but I didn't need to hear her to know. I knew the oven was on as soon as the dial clicked into place and my wrist began to get warm.

Bonnie Baraka

"JUSTINA!" I yelled to her, spinning around swiftly, and grabbing her arm, but it was too late.

With the oven on full blast to preheat for cooking, the charm went crazy. Her eyes widened at the sight before her. I looked down to see what was happening and noticed her eyes weren't the only thing getting bigger. The thermostat charm had begun to shake and stretch, leaving the purple liquid inside turning brighter and thicker as it went. I had a sudden feeling of being swallowed by lava and began to panic. Jess yanked at my wrist with both hands, trying to pull the bracelet off. I pulled against it as well. At least if I can get it off, I won't lose my arm, I thought. Then I could figure out what to do with the charm and whatever it burned a hole in after that, but it wouldn't budge. The light just kept getting bigger and brighter until it felt like we were actually inside of it. I reached out to touch the thick purple jelly slopping in the vile. It was cool to the touch. This had me turning back to Jess in shock. I abandoned my struggle to release my arm and clung as tight as I could to Jess, looking around the room for anything that could help us before we died. Death. Is this what death felt like? That's it, the ovens must have exploded, and we were going into the light to meet our Maker.

Then I saw her. She rushed in without a moment to lose, or so I thought. I took a sigh of relief when I thought Clarynda reached it in time, but she didn't come over to us to help at all. Nor did she look confused about what was happening as Jess and I did. She went straight for the oven and turned it off. Then walked back to Ms. Sternbough's desk as if nothing was happening.

"Oh, thank you!" I shouted in my head because the words wouldn't come out. As Clarynda walked to the back of the classroom, I couldn't help but think, no wonder she's been staring all day, she was planning her murder series. Nothing I had experienced in my 14 years of life had prepared me for what was about to happen, though.

It was either the flash of light so bright I felt it pierce my chest or the thud of wind that I felt brush through me that shot me back onto the floor. When I finally looked up, both Clarynda and Jess were gone, and there in front of me asking me if I was okay was Ms. Sternbough and a girl I had never seen before.

"Are you okay?" The girl said, panic and something else I couldn't pinpoint clear in her voice. "You were running so fast we didn't even see you come in, and

I... I didn't mean to hit you with the door. Oh, man! I'm sorry!" Breathing as if I had been running, I tried to sit up.

"Ugh, I um." Before I could say anything else, Ms. Sternbough scooped me up and sat me in a nearby chair. The same chair Jess was sitting in only seconds ago. I was dazed for sure. I looked around in search of her but saw a classroom full of students instead.

"Well, looks like your nose is bleeding and you hit the floor pretty hard. I think we should get you to the nurse's office," Ms. Sternbough said with all sorts of matter-of-factness that I had never heard her use before. I reached up to touch my nose. It didn't feel like it was bleeding at all, but there it was on my fingers— blood.

"Okay!" I said slowly, trying to get my bearings.

"Don't worry. I've got you," she said and carried me off to the nurse's office without another word to the rest of the class.

5

A Whole New World

In the nurse's office settled in a back room on a cot, I finally got a chance to breathe and gather my thoughts. *Where had Jess gone that fast? And where did all those kids in the class come from? I didn't get a good look to see who was there, but who was that girl that hit me with the door?* I looked around the room, trying to remember the last time I was back here or saw anything that looked familiar. I jumped as I heard Ms. Sternbough talking to the nurse outside of my small room.

"She needs to rest. I'd say at least this period; she should be okay for the next couple. Hopefully, she doesn't have a concussion, but she will be drained from her trip. She ran into that refrigerator door pretty hard. I'll come back and check on her after class. No sense in calling her father, he won't answer." She said the last part with a hint of sorrow in her voice. My internal warning bells were on full alert and blasting at this point.

"Yes, of course," I heard the nurse reply in kind. "I will check her head and vision here in a bit after she gets some rest." And with that, they walked away from the door.

There were several things that had just happened in a matter of minutes that didn't sit well with me. All the normal pictures about asthma and sports were on the walls in the room, but as I lay on the cot, I began to notice things out of the ordinary. What was A-rom-a-tology or Herbletics? I had never seen these posters before at all. Nor had I heard of these things. Then there was the uneasiness the nurse had given me when she was talking. Since when did the nurse take orders from Ms. Sternbough? Or let anyone 'rest' in her office? Our nurse was plump, sweet, and hell-bent on making sure students were mended and sent back to class or sent home if they were contagious. Am I dreaming? I must have fallen and hit my head in the kitchens, and now, I'm dreaming.

I closed my eyes and took a couple deep breaths to calm the throbbing in my nose and the fuzziness in my head. I played with my bracelet as I did so, tracing the areas of my wrist that still felt hot from earlier, probably a nice burn there now. I glanced down. Nothing. I pulled my wrist as close to my face as I could get it. There was no trace of a burn mark, a bruise, or even a scratch, but I could feel the places where the burns had been just below the surface of my skin.

"I know I am dreaming now," I whispered as the door opened. It scared me so badly I jumped from the cot and landed face down on the floor. "Oaf!" I moaned from the surprisingly warm floor.

"You are awfully clumsy today," someone said and giggled from the doorway. I looked up to see the same girl from the kitchen staring back at me with curious grey eyes.

"Oh, umm, just a little tired today... I guess," I said to her, trying to keep my voice level.

She cocked her head to the side and peered at me through a squinted view. "You've been Dem hopping without me, haven't you?"

Confused and alarmed at the question, I said, "No, it's just my brother has been keeping me up at night concerned about school, and I'm exhausted." I sighed and put my shoulders down. When did I get so good at this lying thing?

"OMG! He's home?" She squealed and, in one swooping motion, sat down on the floor next to me in a meditation pose. I must have looked totally lost because she said, "Oh, you mean like, figuratively. Sorry." She looked me over again. I wasn't sure what she was looking at. "You must have hit your head pretty hard then if you're as confused as your face says you are." She elbowed me with a smile. When I didn't get the joke, she stood up and offered me her hand. "Alright, Starla King, I think you need more rest than you are letting on, and I am determined to make sure you get that rest for my name isn't Katiyah Strauss."

Bonnie Baraka

She held up her right hand with something that looked like scouts honor sign and helped me back down onto the cot with her left.

At this, I giggled and stood, facing the girl in front of me eye to eye. There didn't seem to be anything off about the slender girl with long wafting hair standing in front of me, so I replied, "Alright, Kat. Thanks for the help." I beamed and closed my eyes. Something about calling her Kat felt right, but I couldn't put my finger on it. She gave me an encouraging smile that fit her round face but didn't meet her eyes and left.

With the door closed behind her and me finally alone again, I did some serious thinking back. Why did it feel like I knew this girl, Katiyah, so well? I mean not just that our conversation was for some reason personal, but like, my mind and body kept alerting me that we really knew each other. Almost as well as I knew Jess. Speaking of Jess, where was she? I would have to figure out the answer to one question at a time. I couldn't much figure out where she was if I didn't know where I was myself. I pinched myself to make sure for a final time that I wasn't dreaming. Ouch! Too hard. I looked again at my bracelet.

The Alps, or were they some other mountain? I couldn't remember. I just remembered Gran saying, "always take the high road," and if I thought of it like being in the Alps, I would remember to say only what was necessary, because the air up there was thin. No time to waste precious breaths on bickering.

A picture of me and Gran that was from our day at the beach. She said she chose this picture because it looked like we were lifetimes away and not in San Diego anymore. That day we were on the beach, she told me the story of Dorothy and the wizard of oz. It still stuck in my head like it was yesterday. When I asked her if the story was real, she took a long pause and said, "This version is only a half telling of the actual story; but if you sift through the parts that are meant to make you believe it's a children's fantasy, you will see the true meaning behind it."

The purple Thermostat that didn't seem capable of exploding any more than the toaster, with just the normal amount of liquid this time.

The golden heart that Gran had given me shortly after my mother left us again. "Things will be different now, my little star," she told me while she was brushing my hair. "That little boy is innocent. He will not understand that this is not his fault. He will look to you for guidance and comfort, and he will be difficult to bear at times. But take this golden heart and remember to always be you on the inside, even when it seems easier to be the you on the surface."

I never understood that sentiment, but I sometimes saw what she meant when I grabbed for the gold heart and reeled in my patience for Trey's weird behaviors. It wasn't his fault. Kiki put us all in this situation, and then she got up and left us to deal with it.

I clutched the heart now, feeling my anger boiling. Even though I hated her for what she had made Trey into, I still loved her. The old her, though—the one that was there with me and Pops before that weird shift. I still couldn't explain it, but I felt it for sure. There were three charms left.

The empty caged heart that Gran told me was to remind me that if I allowed others to change me, that was what my heart and soul would become.

The blue tear drop that were to remind me to be careful with my words. "Once they are said, they can only be forgiven," she told me. "They will never be forgotten." I looked to it for encouragement the most to remind me to speak life into others and to keep my smart comments to myself.

Then there was the prayer box. The Prayer box was given to me on my 12th birthday. I started my 'womanly change' for the first time just the week before, and I was grumpy. Gran took one look at me and said, "Alright, get up! We're going to get chocolate and ice cream!" Then whisked us away to this amazing ice cream parlor I had never been to before. It was at that ice cream parlor that she gave me my present and a day early too. I was so excited when I ripped into it that I nearly broke it. When I finally got it out of the wrapping, I must have had a very confused and upset it-wasn't-a-new-toy-or-the-cell-phone-that-I-wanted look on my face, because she took my hands in hers and asked me so softly that I had to lean in to hear her, "Do you know what this is?"

"Yea Gran, it's another charm for my bracelet," I said, rolling my eyes at her to make sure she knew I was over these little charms.

"Yes, but do you know what it is?" She chided at me.

Bonnie Baraka

Deciding I didn't have anything better to do than to entertain her at the moment, I looked the charm over, examining it in both hands, careful not to break the latch. It looked like an ordinary box. "It's just a regular old box, Gran," I said, truly frustrated at this point.

"No, sweet girl. It's a prayer box. See?" She unhooked the latch on the box to show me the pages inside. "Well, you're gonna need a rather small paper, but you take the paper and write your prayers and dreams down, and then you give your worries to your Maker. This is to remind you that there are many things you can control and change in your life, but there are some things you just can't. Put them here, pray about them and let them go, or they will consume you." Seeing I was cautious about the box, she added, "I have one too!" She lifted her wrist to show me her prayer box. "It helps to come back and read your prayers from time to time to show your growth, and help you to remember that things may seem impossible, problems may seem large at the time, but you can get through anything if you take your time and put your mind to it."

I was such a jerk that day. Gran didn't let it bother her one bit. She came and snuggled me in that booth and held me tight until I felt better. Then she gave me the cell phone I had been wanting. Boy, I missed her. Once I figured out what was going on here, I would convince Pops to let me go stay with her until the inevitable.

Tears filling my eyes, I dug into the prayer box to see my last note. It wasn't from me at all, but Gran. I sat up straight and looked at the note she had written.

"If your reading this, you're in danger. Things are different here, trust no one. Get home and find our letters. Love you to the moon, my little Star. -Gran."

My breath caught. I didn't understand. What does she mean? The nurse knocked on the door, giving me another startle. "Come in," I said in a very shaky voice as I stuffed the note back into the box and laid down before the door swung open.

The nurse came in and was just as I remembered her; only she wasn't. She was much shorter than I remember, and she had rosy red cheeks, unlike the nurse I knew her to be. Her voice was much higher, and she was overly polite.

"Is everything okay? You look like you've seen a ghost?" she asked, deep concern crossing her face.

"I'm, uh... I'm okay," I stammered, taking all of the changes in at once. What was this place? If it's true what Gran said, I better play it cool. Danger was the last thing I wanted to be in when I didn't even know where I was! And what about Jess, was she in danger too? Is she here, in another room? I had to get out of the nurse's office and fast.

"I was just sleeping, and the knock startled me a bit." I thought I was doing a good job at keeping up my lie, but the nurse looked at me just as confused as I was. Bad move. There must be too much uneasiness in my voice, try a little more directly.

"I'm okay, really. I should get back to class now." Making my statement firm and to the point, I hopped up and strode past the nurse in one swift motion.

"Wait, don't you want your bag?" She said, turning to me with a half-curious, half-knowing look that said it was better to get out now.

"Thanks," I said as I snatched it and dashed for the door.

"SLOW DOWN! That's what got you here in the first place!" She called after me, hands on her hips, but I kept going until I was alone in the halls of what I thought was Jonsey High.

Boy, was I wrong. There were banners and trophies that said we were still right at home at school, but the school colors were different. The floors were glass, and the doors were thrown open to let in a wonderful summer breeze. As a huge fan of a good sea breeze, I was enthusiastic about it, but I knew the campus security would never allow the doors to be open the way they were. They would site some sort of hazard that no one had ever heard of and close them promptly. I knew this because I had tried it just this morning in fact. Heading my Gran's warning, I walked as fast as I could, turning the corner swiftly, heading to the doors that were closest to my house.

CRASH! I ran smack dab into Ms. Sternbough.

Bonnie Baraka

"I'm sorry, I'm so sorry," I was stammering before I realized who I ran into. I turned to see who I had clobbered. When I noticed who it was, I was mortified. I was supposed to be in her class.

"I was just coming back to check on you. Headed home? Not feeling the best after your icebox blunder?" She coaxed the words into me, and I ate the excuse up without hesitation.

"Oh, yes. I was just feeling like I needed to lay down some more," I whined.

She looked me over once, and then at my bracelet. That's the same look the other Ms. S gave it in before she stormed out of Home Ec. Why does she keep looking at it? Was she who I was in danger of? As I stepped back anxiously, the more unknown Ms. S looked up to meet my confused scowl with understanding and sighed.

"Very well, but before you go, you may want to retrieve the rest of your belongings from the gym locker room. Your father will need to wash them," she said, turning her nose up as if I was currently wearing the stinky clothes.

"Of course!" I said and turned and walked off in the direction of the gym. Once I hit the corner of the locker room, I slid down the lockers to where mine was. Only in the place where my empty locker should have been, were streamers and banners and articles spilling out with congratulatory words. I reviewed the stuff on the locker slowly until I heard a thud. I spun around to see who was there.

THUD! There it was again, only louder this time. I noticed the vibration coming from the equipment closet, so I went over to listen at the door.

THUD THUD THUD! BOOM!

The latch on the closet broke open, and out came Jess, sprawled on the floor in a heap of volleyball nets and soccer balls. My heart stopped.

"JESS!" I yelled. Before I realized what was happening, I was grabbing her and pulling strings to get her out. Wrong move. Once she had one free arm, she pounced, pinning me up against the wall.

"Where am I?" She said with those predator eyes.

"Justina Mathews! If you don't get off of me right this second and act like you have some sense about you!" I yelled, making the best impression of her mom as I could muster. She didn't like it.

"I SAID..." She stopped dead and looked me up and down. She looked at my clothes and the cheese still stuck to my knee. She looked at my necklace that read Best Friends Forever, to which she herself was wearing the other half, and finally, she looked at my wrist.

"Take it off, Star! Take it off right now!" She lunged for my wrist.

"No!" I snatched away. "Jess calm down. It's okay!" I used all the strength I could muster to go low and tackle her to the ground. If I let her get the upper hand, she would stomp the last heirloom I had from my Gran before I could explain what the note said. We tussled for a while. Finally, I managed to pin her. "STOP!" I said. Nope, she was just taking a break. Remembering the technique she made me help her study to fend off predators, I slid out of the fight completely and let her continue to tumble until she realized she was on her own. Then she stopped. I took the volleyball net and ran in a circle around her, tying her in place. She was like a bull, kicking and screaming and trying to get free.

"Would you stop it already!?" I asked her.

She looked at me, "The Starla that I know, my best friend, would never tie me up and leave me helpless!" She yelled.

I cut my eyes at her. "First of all, I haven't left you anywhere. And second of all, you are much stronger than me, and I don't have time to wait for you to calm down. You are a far cry from helpless girl. We need to talk. NOW." I got close enough to reach her and stuck out my pinky.

"Pinky swear you won't attack me, and I will let you out." I said it in good nature, but I knew without a shadow of a doubt that if I let her out, she would attack me. "Ugh, okay, just listen then. I woke up in the kitchen with Ms. S and some girl I don't know, but I feel like I know, standing over me. They said I knocked myself out when I ran into the refrigerator door. My nose was bleeding and everything. Then Ms. S carried, I mean literally carried me to the nurse's office. I've been in there since then, trying to figure out where the hell I was. At first, I thought I was dreaming, and then that girl came in and was talking to me like I was supposed to be here... and the nurse is the nurse, but she's different, and I found this note from Gran." Completely out of breath, I showed her Gran's note.

She looked at me in pure horror. Taking the note in her three loose fingers and getting it as close to her face as possible, she read the note from Gran three times over before looking up at me with her gears clearly turning.

"What letters is she talking about?" She asked, a little confused.

The fact that she was talking to me about what was happening and not who I was or taking off my bracelet gave me a false hope that it was okay to let her out of her cocoon. I slowly crept back around her, trying to give her extra time to think. She sprung from her binds and wrapped me in the tightest hug we have ever shared. I stopped to wonder what had happened to her when she woke up.

"I'm so glad to see you. Never do that to me again," she said, sounding like she was on the brink of tears. I gave her a squeeze just as tight.

"I'm just glad you're here with me. I know I can trust you," I said, and I meant every word. "I think she means our family letters between her and my papa. They are home in the attack. We should probably go there now anyway." I released her and wiped my forehead in relief.

"Have you noticed that it's only 4th period?" She said to me, clearly upset. I hadn't. Fourth period, right before she found me in the park, when I burnt my wrist.

"Explains a couple things," I said, hoping my Gran's letters would explain the rest and suggest a superb psychologist after all of this was said and done.

"And park on the way to my house." I held up my wrist, showing her that I had no burns to speak of.

Eyes wide and searching, she grabbed her bag out of the closet, and we walked out of the locker room, headed for home.

6

Take Me Home

The locker room we were in had a direct door to the practice fields. They happened to be in the furthest corner of the grounds, which meant the farthest point from my house, but we needed to get out of the school as fast as we could, so we didn't run into anymore prying eyes. I turned to the direction of the door with no hesitation.

"Where are we going?" Jess said, scrunching her face.

"As far away from this school as we can get," I replied and started for the door.

"You don't think Campus Security will stop us if we go that way?" Jess asked with anxiety in her voice. She still thought we were back at our school, maybe. I didn't blame her; this looked like our locker room.

"I think campus security is the least of our worries right now," I pointed out. "This is not our school. I don't know if we're dreaming, if we died and this is Heaven, or Hell maybe." I looked around, realizing it could very well be the latter, "but things are much different here, and I'm not quite ready to see exactly how different yet." I turned and half-dragged her out the door. She was in mid protest when she unwillingly stepped out of the side door and stopped in shock. There were the soccer fields just like we remembered them, but only half of them were still intact. The other half had been replaced with gorgeous Gardens. Huge flowers of red, yellow, pink, and white with streams running through them and a low steady sway that made them look as if they were dancing slowly in the breeze. Dancing flowers, how lovely.

Jess didn't seem to share my sentiments about this view at all.

She scowled hard, "What is THIS? Where are the Softball practice fields? The football fields? How can we practice with no practice field?" She was on her way to tell someone what she thought about the change when I noticed campus security.

"Stop." I grabbed her and threw her up against the door we had just come out of. She snatched away with a strong, stiff arm.

"Campus Security, fool," I whispered. At the realization we were somewhere else entirely and there was still campus security to worry about, she went stark still as I shoved her down behind the closest bush. Seeing campus security enough to know them by name back home, alerted us that this was not the security we knew when they passed. They were even grumpier and even more on the lookout for anything that was not where it should be. We held our breath as they passed us, not even looking in our direction.

Jess finally had time to take it all in. "So, is this even our school at all?" She asked as I could see the fight in her eyes begin to dull with clarity.

"I told you, I don't think so," I answered honestly. "We just gotta get out of here and find out what's going on," I said as I stood up and looked to see where our best chance to get away without being noticed was.

"Let's go!" I grabbed her hand, and we ran for the gardens, taking in as many sights and smells as I could on the way. When we finally made it to the street and off campus, I chanced a sigh of relief. "Finally, I thought we'd never make it."

"YOU!" Jess turned to me with conviction in her voice. "That was the SCARIEST, most horrifying, most..."

I could see her judgment wasn't set towards me as she trailed off, and her whole body started to shake as she tried to get whatever had happened to her out of her head.

"It's okay, we're here together now," I said, giving her hand a squeeze of encouragement. "What happened, though?" I whispered so as not to scare her. "How'd you end up tangled in the equipment closet?" Curiosity had gotten the best of me, and I kicked myself for even asking about something that had traumatized my strong friend.

She cocked her head as if to sift through her memories to pull the correct answer out. "I'm not really sure of everything. Some things I won't relive to tell you of them, but in the end... someone pushed me into that closet. Someone I knew, I couldn't put my finger on who it was, though. They smelled like cotton candy, though, with a hit of cinnamon. I would remember that smell anywhere. When I fell into the closet, they closed the door behind me. It was crazy dark, and it felt like I was falling for hours. Like I was everywhere and nowhere at the same time. My mind kept going weird places, and I saw people there that I too felt like I knew or should know but that I have no recollection of meeting ever before. I saw my life literally flash before my eyes, repeatedly. I just kept thinking, 'I hope Starla is okay' and 'How could she leave me like this?' at the same time."

"I didn't leave you!" I shouted, feeling defeated. "I didn't even know where I was! I didn't know where you were! I was scared and confused, and I had no clue where you were either! I came to the locker room, by chance."

She gave me a nod of understanding and continued to explain.

"I finally got up the courage to reach out and see if I was actually falling and how much space there was around me to catch myself from the end when I felt the door handle. Desperate for some kind of light and hoping I wasn't falling at all, I felt the cracks until I realized I was suspended in the air, probably by all the gym equipment, so I found the jams and removed the bolts, then I felt for the latch. Once I found it, I just kept hitting it until it opened." She took a deep breath as if blowing out the breath would release the memory. She looked exhausted.

I reached out and grabbed her, and we walked arm in arm until we got to the intersection. We looked at each other knowingly. There was something almost apologetic in Jess' eyes. As if she was remembering our morning and the chain of events that eventually brought us to this point.

"Well, we have to pass it on our way to your house, no sense in trying to avoid it." Jess nodded in the direction we were walking. The park was just up ahead. We slowed our stroll to a crawl as the gravel and plastic figures came into view.

"Yea, I guess we do," I said with as much confidence as I could muster as we crossed the street. Once across, Jess grabbed me.

"Let me go first," she said firmly, and I nodded in agreement. We continued to walk past what we thought was our park when Jess turned to me with a look of pure uneasiness. I looked past her and immediately got upset. Where is the park? My park? The park Trey and I went to every Saturday morning to fly kites in the summer. My thinking space. Where is it!?

In the space where I had sat on the swing just this morning was a camera, or was it a statue of a camera, I couldn't be sure from behind Jess. There was not even a hint of a park to be seen, only what looked like a TV Studio in its place. The sign on the outside of the building read 'Studios of Tomorrow. Your Energy is our Specialty.' This made no sense to me. I ran over to the camera, thinking it must be just a prop to draw in the crowds, and touched it. There it was again, on me faster than I could understand what was happening. Wrist burning, bracelet vibrating, energy soaring in a state of alarm on my tippy toes at this point. My panic was so strong that I was vibrating right along with the little bracelet.

"What is happening!?" I sobbed over the fear in my chest and the hum of the vibrations in my ears. I started to see the bright purple light in the lens of the camera this time, as the jelly in my bracelet sloshed loudly. I looked at my thermostat to find no color change or anything out of the ordinary. When did the color shift to the camera? It is getting brighter now; it's really happening again!

"Oh no, oh no, oh no, not without Jess," I thought aloud as I turned to find her face.

Just as she came into my view, I felt her slam into me like a mac truck, flinging me far in the opposite direction of the clearly activating camera. She landed right on top of me with her knee in my thigh. That's gonna leave a bruise. She was breathing heavily as if she had gotten a running start to knock the wind out of me.

"Sorry!" She sighed through deep breaths. "Didn't mean to." She looked me over to make sure I wasn't injured. "I just didn't know what else to do." Finding that I wasn't missing any limbs, she rolled over on to her back and tried to catch her breath. With the extra weight off my chest, I took in as many large gulps of air as I could before sitting up.

"Thanks!" I swiped the curls out of my face trying to come to terms with what was about to happen to me again. "I froze and..." I heard my voice trail off. I couldn't finish the sentence. I rolled over onto my side to look at Jess, trying to decide the best way to say what I was thinking, but Jess was staring at the bushes. "What is it?" I asked, alarm rising in my throat.

Noticing the high octave of panic in my voice, Jess looked away from the bush.

"Nothing," she said quickly and got up to help me off the ground. I wasn't sure if she lied to keep me in the dark or to calm my nerves, but for either reason, it worked, and I let it go. We had far too much more to be concerned about than what animal was watching us act like fools. "We should probably go," she said, pulling me up and half-dragging me back to the street.

We broke out into a run when we saw my house. Finally, I thought, sanctuary. As we got closer, my feelings changed. There were too many differences in this place not to notice that this wasn't the house I remembered at all. The grass was brown and unkempt, the shutters were closed and looked as if this was their permanent stance. Then there was the missing pet. Where was Snikkers to greet us when we stepped onto the porch?

I fumbled with the keys at the door. Of course, Jess noticed. She grabbed my free hand to steady me.

"It's going to be different than you remembered," she said calmly. "It's okay."

I sighed. I weighed her words in my head and slowly decided she was probably right, and with that reassurance, I turned the key, and we walked into a version of my sanctuary that I was not even remotely familiar with. I opened the door to Snikkers yelping loudly in a tone I knew meant she was hungry. My reflexes kicked in automatically, and I went straight to the kitchen to get her food before I took in my surroundings. Filthy. Dishes in the sink, a litter box that hadn't been emptied in some time, trash overflowing, Pops would have literally passed out at the sight of this house.

"Oh my gosh!" I breathed and looked at Jess, who was doing her own intake of what was wrong with the room we stood in.

"We gotta get this cleaned up before he gets home," she said, eyes wide, thinking of his reaction, no doubt. Without another word to each other, we started rushing around the kitchen like two dancers in a well-practiced performance, cleaning the dishes, feeding Snikkers, taking out the trash, and even starting some dinner for good measure. We were halfway through the kitchen when I heard a rustle from the other room.

At the sounds I heard, I immediately grabbed Jess and put my finger to my lips. She stilled. I motioned for her to stay in the kitchen as I crept closer to the living room. There on the couch this whole time was an unmemorable half version of my father. Buried under a mountain of blankets, and unbothered by the noises that were coming out of the kitchen. I motioned for Jess to look at what I had found; she looked back to me with a blank stare of concern. This situation was getting more and more confusing by the minute. To think Pops had been here in this mess this whole time and had not lifted a finger or protested one bit made me anxious.

She shrugged off her concern, going back to busying herself in the cleaning and whispered, "Maybe he is sick today." It sounded like the only option we had to go with now, so I walked in and made my presence known.

"Hi, Dad," I said as I kissed him on the cheek, which for whatever reason clearly caught him off guard. He nearly fell off the couch. His massive biceps reaching out to balance him in place and right himself on the couch. He turned to see who I was as if he was not used to people being in his space.

Pops and I had been inseparable since I was born. Football player turned banker, his running back build told you he was not to be tested, and his demeanor let you in on the fact that he was extremely protective of the daughter that had him wrapped around her finger effortlessly. My heart broke a little as I took in the sight of my hero on the couch, wrapped in a Jonsey High blanket, with large bags under his olive-toned eyes. He needed a haircut and a shave bad, which told me he had been in this same place for more than one afternoon. It was at that moment realization kicked in. This was not my father. The similarities to my own pops were uncanny, but I could tell the difference in the man before me and the father I knew and loved who raised me to be strong and independent.

I played it cool like I didn't notice the slight downward turn of his head or the moistness in the corner of his eyes that continued to come and go as if he was holding back a downpour and continued with my conversation, however one-sided it was going to be.

"Nurse sent me home early. I'm not feeling the best," I said with a half-smile.

He looked up at me like he was seeing me for the first time. Grabbing me by my shoulders, he pushed me back to have a better look, and then pulled me in close. I stiffened at the strength in his hug that was not shown before. Immediately accepting the embrace and deciding that a hug from a Dad to his little girl in any place was worth it, I hugged him back as tight as I could, remembering the hugs my own daddy would give when I was having a bad day and filling my arms with that warmth and love as I did. I smiled into the hug for good measure. Gran always said to be a light!

"In the attic," was all he said as he released me. Pushing me towards the stairs with the tiniest smile, I saw his eyes glaze over, as tears started to stream down his face. Although I could tell he was feeling a little lighter, I felt for him as I saw the gates of emotions he had been holding back begin to open.

Confused at what was happening, I said, "Okay, Daddy. I love you!" I gave his arm a squeeze and turned to leave, but something shifted, and I rocked back on my heels. I could almost feel the air in the house thin out. The tension cutting. A thought instantly crossed my mind. Can he tell that I am not the Star that he raised? I was hoping I was doing an okay job with the charade, but more questions flooded my brain. Why isn't he the Pops that I know, the one who could get through anything? What is wrong with him? Is he really sick? Something was happening here that I did not like but could not put my finger on. I had so many questions buzzing through my head when I walked away from that encounter. I picked up the trash that littered the floor in the living room and opened the blinds to let in some warmth and sunshine and walked back into the kitchen to meet Jess' prying eyes filled with just as many questions. She looked more concerned than I felt. I pointed upstairs to alert her that we shouldn't talk where we were. She agreed, and we took the stairs by twos up to what I thought was my room.

"Well, that was interesting," Jess said, trying to sound unsurprised as she sauntered over to her normal spot on the bed. After she sat down, she took in the rest of the room. Nothing about this room was the Star she knew, and Jess had no problem saying so.

"Where are we?" She asked, picking up some sort of pouch that smelled of mint & honey. "Is this like, the twilight zone, or what? And where is Trey?" Lights went off in her eyes at this question, but I paid her no mind.

"At school, I would assume. Since it's only 4th period, remember?" I said, shaking her off and looking around the room for anything that would be something I could relate to, something that I would actually choose for myself. I wasn't sure that this was my room at all after that evaluation.

Jess stood up abruptly, seeing the conviction in my eyes.

"Let's go check then," she said, changing the subject back and sliding past me before I could grab her and tell her she was being ridiculous.

"Jess, how can we check and see if he is at school, if he is AT SCHOOL!?" I yelled after her, praying Pops didn't hear all the commotion we were making.

"Something just doesn't feel right," she said. "Let's just check it out. If everything is normal, no harm, no foul." She pushed past me again in the doorway and swung Trey's bedroom door open.

I turned to yell at her about personal space, when I saw what lay behind the open door. This was not the bedroom of a 7-year-old boy. Before me sat a teenage boy's room, only not. Cartoon characters, toys, and dinosaurs everywhere, but the bed was for an older boy. There was no personality in the covers, and it looked as if it hadn't been slept in for a long while. There were books on the shelf boasting 4th grade English and History, but the shelves were covered with plastic as if this room were not used at all. This was confusing to me because the Trey I knew was interested in books about Math, not History. At 7, he had not played with dinosaurs in at least a year, and the only toys you would find in his room were the ones he built or created himself. There was a mobile that looked identical to the one that I made for him in art class right before he was born stuffed in the corner on a shelf; only this mobile was slightly different in ways I could not explain.

Looking around at this room and seeing all the things I remember from the first steps to the first words of my favorite little boy covered in plastic and not his at all set me on ease. I flew past Jess and ran through the hall, not caring if Pops heard me. I opened every door I could get to. Maybe Trey wanted a different room, or maybe an exchange student or something? Whatever the reason, I was determined to find Trey's space in this big house. I searched the first 4 of 5 rooms on this floor with no luck. When I finally got to the door of the 5th room, where my parents' room should be, Jess stopped me.

"I have a strong feeling that you do not want to go in there." I tried to push past her, but she held on tighter. "Judging by the rooms we have just seen, the state of the rest of the house, and even the things in your own room, you DO NOT want to go in there." She hugged me with both arms at this last proclamation.

"We need answers before we start to jump to conclusions," she said, pushing me away from the final straw that she knew would leave me broken.

As I got myself together, she continued to guide me further away from Trey's memories and down the hall to the last doorway. The Attic. Being so consumed in what I had just found, I had forgotten that the point of coming here was to find out why we were even here in the first place. I tightened in her grasp; at this, I felt her soften against me.

"It's gonna be okay, Star. We will figure it out for sure," she said with confidence, and we turned around and headed for the final door. Behind that door laid the only staircase in this house that had always scared me to my core. Only now, it seemed more like a stairway to freedom.

I opened the door, and the lights snapped on, inviting us in.

"After you," I said, extending my hand for her to take the first steps. She started up the stairs with a slight hesitation, back straight and shaky hands, but she went straight up those stairs like a warrior with her head held high. We were in deep, no doubt, but with Jess by my side, I believed we could take on anything.

Bonnie Baraka

I started up after her, praying we found something good instead of what my gut was dreading at the top of this staircase.

7

"This used to be where Gran would stay when she came to visit," I remembered with a smile, which was immediately wiped off my face remembering that she hadn't stayed up here in quite some time. "She stopped staying up here the last time she came. Kiki told her it wasn't safe for her to try and maneuver all these stairs. Gran was pissed." I felt my fists clench at this. "I'm pretty sure I hate her," I said out loud to no one in particular.

"No, you don't," Jess said. "You hate some things she's done, and you hate that she can get away with those things; but let's be honest, as much as you are like Pops, you and Kiki are almost twins." She turned and looked to see my scowl and the fighting stance that I had just taken.

"You, being the smarter twin, obviously," she said with a playful batt to my raised hand.

I rolled my eyes and strode further into the room. I rubbed the charm at my side on the way in. I kissed my teardrop charm to calm the thunder that was on the brink of rolling out of my mouth.

"Let's just find what we need and get out of here. I'm starting to miss Gran more and more." Looking around the room to see all of Gran's things carefully placed just where I remembered them made me shiver.

"Maybe it's not a bad thing for you to remember Gran right now," Jess coaxed. "I mean, Gran is the one who got us this far. Maybe we may need to rely on your memory of her a little more to make it back home."

I sighed, she was right, and I didn't like it one bit.

"This is true. I guess I better dig in," I said, looking around and noticing things I remember Gran telling me about. Jess started her search on the other side of the room.

"What's this?" She asked, pointing to what looked like an incredibly old and quite small suitcase. "Do you think it might have something we can use in it?"

I came over to help her put it on the nightstand where Gran used to have it.

"No, it's not what you think." We opened the lid, and I showed her. "See, it's like really old. I mean, I don't even think they make actual vinyl records anymore, but before MP3s and CDs, they used these to play music for parties and stuff," I explained. "Here, see you wind this part right here. Then you put the record on, and the needle goes on top."

She turned to pick up the record that was originally on the record player and dusted it off. She put it on, but no sound came out of the megaphone—just static.

"It's probably on the wrong side," I told her. "You have to make sure you use the side that is words up."

Before Jess could change the record, I heard Gran's voice start to sing a melody I knew like the back of my hand. "Wait, Wait!" I yelled at Jess, scaring her back from the record player.

"It's Gran!" I said, sounding just as shocked as I felt about this whole day.

Gran's voice was lovely, but she was not a professional singer by any means. For her to have recorded on a vinyl record, I had to listen. I took a seat on the bed and listened to Gran's voice. I closed my eyes and imagined that she was singing it to me for the first time.

"Some may say I'm crazy, but I don't careee. I know my happiness is out there somewheeerrreee. Out thereeeeee. I wish, and I hope for things to be complete. But life changes ten times with every soul you meeeett," came Gran's voice from the megaphone. She sang so beautifully.

Then the song stopped abruptly, and I sat straight up and looked around with a new pair of eyes... with Gran's eyes. "Notice the things hiding in plain sight. Pay attention to all the details," I said aloud in an impression of Gran. She had prepared me for this moment my entire life. I looked to Jess, who was watching me intently.

"She knew," was all I could manage without changing the trajectory of my thoughts.

The feedback started again on the record player, and I knew something different would play this time. Jess reached to turn off the record player, and I stopped her again. Gran began singing again, but this time I heard the talking in the background.

"Gran told me about record players when I was young. She said if you play them forward, there is one song, and sometimes if you play them backward, there is a completely different message. She said in the times of prohibition, people used records like this to get the location of the Speakeasy's out." I cocked my head to the side to hear the talking in the background closer with no luck. "Maybe, let's try it backward and see what happens."

So, we took the crank from the record player and turned it backward. We started the needle in the middle of the record, then sat intently listening for anything out of place. There was the dead air, then the singing that was backward, and then in the middle of the song. There it was... Gran had left another message. Jess ran for a pen and pad to write it down.

"For any Stars who dare to listen. Things are moving fast, and I'm sure you are a little scared. Use that to fuel your journey on this day. You were born for this love. Get the letters and the books hidden in plain sight and get out of here before they discover you. Things have changed many times since this recording. I cannot tell you who is an ally. So, you must trust no one on your journey, unless you have a Yang with you and if I know you, you do. Keep Yin safe, my darling Yang. She is your only hope! Take what you need and get out!"

Bonnie Baraka

There was a loud 'thunk' outside that told me we might have less time than I first thought. Jess' eyes were wide.

"She knew I would be here, but how?" She said, reading back her note.

"Did I close the door behind us?" I asked her, rushing to the stairs. I could make out two people talking. Sprinting and sliding, I just made it to close the attic door as I heard footsteps on the stairs.

"Is Starla home from school? I went to the nurse's office to check on her, and she said she went back to class. Obviously, she didn't come back to class. So, I thought I would check and see if she was here," Katiyah asked on her way up the stairs. "Wow, who actually cleaned your kitchen?" she added. Talking a mile, a minute, and obviously taking inventory of what was out of place.

Pops didn't say a word to her in response. Odd. I couldn't tell if we were friends or not. On one hand, my heart said, I knew this girl. On the other, Pops and Jess hung out without me all the time. He would, for sure, have answered every question Jess asked. If Kat were my friend, he would have answered.

"Ugh, I guess I'll just go check for myself." Kat snidely threw in on the top stair as if she wasn't already doing just that. I heard her stomp down the hall to where I was standing on the other side of the door. How dare she talk to Pops like that.

From behind me, I heard Jess say, "What is plain slight?"

"SHHHHH!" I told her and locked the door just in time for Katiyah not to discover us hiding in the attic. I turned the lock slowly enough that the click was almost inaudible and leaned hard on the door. If she thought to check in the attic for some weird reason, she wasn't getting in.

"Where did that girl go now?" I heard Kat say from the other side of the door through clenched teeth and chanced a deep breath. "Maybe the gardens. She's always hiding in the gardens, even if she does try to convince me that she hates them." Shaking her head, she walked back down the stairs and out the door. I slid down the door and came face to face with Jess, who had crept down the stairs and was right behind me, waiting to see what was about to happen.

"She left," I said, reading the question in her eyes. Her shoulders slacked a bit at the news.

"Was that the girl that hit you in the nose?" She asked, looking like she was ready to open the door and punch her.

"Yea, but she didn't do it on purpose. Hell, I don't know if she actually did anything at all," I said, trying to remember which version of my afternoon nosebleed was actually the correct story. That was less than important right now. I sprinted past Jess to find the things my grandmother had hidden. "I remember when I was little, and Gran would stay with us. I would come up here and keep her company until she fell asleep listening to old records." I laid on the bed now, remembering the game we would play.

"Eye spy with my slightly, good eye," I whispered to myself and looked around the room for clues.

It took me years to catch on to Gran's strategy in spying things. She would spy something that was barely there until you turned away from it. Abstract is what Pops told me the things she was looking at were called.

"Abstract," I said aloud to myself.

"What is Ab... Um, what is that word you keep mumbling?" Jess said from across the room. I almost jumped out of my skin at her question. I had completely forgotten that Jess was here. I sat up and looked at her.

"Sorry, I was... well, I don't know exactly where I was, but it wasn't here," I said, being honest. "Come here, and let's look together," I patted the bed next to me for her to sit on.

"So, she never told you where the letters were? We have to FIND them?" She sounded irritated with her last question. I looked at Jess with all the seriousness I could muster.

"She knew, Jess. She knew this would happen. She even knew that you would be here with me. Whatever she has hidden is for me—well, us alone—to find and must be important and would obviously be harmful to our family in the wrong hands. My Gran has been training me for this moment my entire life. Little games to get me to notice the abstract things around me, things she knows that only I will notice. Like the note in my prayer box. Or the SLIGHT differences in the people around me, like Pops or the nurse. All the play dates and games and stories; they were all to prepare me for whatever is happening to us." I let it out like word vomit. I finally understood the quirkiness about the things my grandmother had taught me. Did this mean I would never see her again?

At this, I hung my head. No matter what she taught me, no matter what I went through here, I had to make it home to her before she left us for good. Determination in my eyes and finally noticing the awkward silence, I looked up to see Jess, who had figured out what had changed my excitement to pain. She looked at me in silence with a stained face that said, I promised myself I wouldn't cry about it.

I sat up a little straighter and started the instructions of the game, brushing off our sadness like nothing had happened.

"Okay, have you ever been to a restaurant and gotten a kids menu with the brain teasers on it? Like, find all the hidden items or something?" I asked, trying to find anything that might help her with the task ahead. She nodded slowly. "Well, Gran and I used to play a game fairly similar to that. I think that's why the record said slight instead of sight. To clue me in on what we should do now to find the rest of the pieces," I said confidently.

"Annndddd, what if we didn't play the record first?" She said, uncertain of my findings.

"Well, I wouldn't have gone there first I don't think, but chances are if she knew you were here, she was probably betting that you would ask what it was," I said, giving her the side eye.

"And you would never pass up a chance to show me that you know something I don't." Jess said, a little annoyance in her voice.

I smiled. "Exactly. But I'm sure she took other precautions as well. Like..." I looked around the room to see if there were any more clues and immediately noticed Gran's prayer box on the nightstand. The one that she kept all of her previous prayers in after she took them out of her bracelet. I had seen her do this a thousand times. "I bet there is a note in here just like on the record player," I said, confident I would find something. I opened the box, but it was plum empty.

I sat back down on the bed as Jess peered over the edge of the box. Her face changed as she knocked on the top and the bottom of the box several times. I watched as she continued to knock until. Thunk. I looked at her with wide eyes as she tapped again. Thunk, Thunk, Thunk. There it was, in plain sight if you knew what you were looking for, a trap bottom in the prayer box that could be removed to hold secret messages. I stepped in closer as Jess pulled the fake bottom out of the box and turned it over. Letters on top of letters and prayers on top of prayers.

"How can so much fit into something so little?" Jess asked, amazed as the letters kept coming.

I looked over at her in total disbelief.

"You're the science wiz, anything in that crazy book about something like this happening?" I asked jokingly until I saw her face light up with recollection. There had apparently been a lesson on folded matter in her science book as well that she had skimmed over the summer. No matter how much she tried to hide her smarts from the rest of herself, she couldn't shake her interest in science.

"Let's talk about it later," I said, and I picked up the first colorful letter on top of the pile and began to read. Shock filled my toes as I learned it was, in fact, addressed to me.

"My darling, Star. It seems you have taken the first step into a new dimension, whether you wanted to or not. I think you will find that your somewhat unconventional training over the years should serve you well in this situation. I don't know all that will come from this trip; I just want you to be safe and smart. Keep Yang close to you and remember to keep your head about you. Life is about balance, so make sure you remember to balance each other out. Trust none of what you hear and only half of what you see. Use your memories to sift through your journey until you can make it back to me. Sleight of hand Sleight of eye, I'll see you soon, my cherry pie! Love you to the moon, little Star. Gran."

Looking down at the words on the page, I wanted to curl up in Gran's bed and cry. I read the letter three times before handing it to Jess and lying on my back on the bed. With Gran's help and guidance over the years, I knew to check the rafters before we left, to check the closet for trap doors, and to check the tv for something that could have been recorded to tell us where to go from here. I couldn't do any of those things right now. All I could do was sit and cry. Yin to Yang, how could she have known that Jess would be here with me? I haven't seen Gran in months now, how could she know that Jess and I are still friends? I guess it didn't matter now, did it?

I sat up, expecting to meet Jess' steadfast eyes on me, but she wasn't there. I spun around to see her lying next to me on the bed—no contact with me, just lying next to me for support. At this, I cried again. Not a long sob like last time, though, just one small tear that rolled down my face as I looked over to see her being there for me regardless of whether there was a reason for my tears or not. I knew this was hard for Jess, the crying and emotional stuff. Not because it was "girly" because I knew as hard as she tried to be a boy, a girl was what she would always be; but because neither one of her parents had taught her how to accept her emotions. How to accept love or how to appreciate those who love her unconditionally. I knew this was hard for Jess, and yet there I was, whimpering and blubbering like I had no control. I brushed her hand with mine when I laid back down on my back next to her, staring at the ceiling. "Sorry!" I said into the silence as we laid there for the next couple minutes while I tried to wrap my mind around what exactly was happening. I figured we had wasted enough time at some point, and I started to explain the things around us.

"So. Another dimension. That's fun right?" I joked awkwardly, knowing there was nothing fun about our circumstances.

When no response came from Jess other than a shift of her head to look at me, I decided it would probably be best to dive in and get out of there like Gran had told us.

"Okay, look at the vaults in the ceiling," I started to tell her as we laid on our backs, looking up at nothing. "Now, look for anything that looks like it could be something else." Gran was so good at this that I knew I would need some help. "Name everything you see. Some things are just like that, and some could be planted there by Gran."

She pointed. "Car, on the side of one of the rafters?"

"That was Trey, trying to make decorations for her when she came last time." I giggled, remembering Pops trying to put those up.

"What about the light? I feel like there is something we should be looking at right there." She said cocking her head to the side to get a better view.

I looked at the light. It had been up here for a long time, and the regular wear and tear was evident, but there was something to say about how it wove into the ceiling when the fan was on, and all you could see were these pretty stones. They looked just like the ones Gran wore on her bracelet. Her bracelet. Duh! I sprang up from my resting place, jarring Jess and scaring her half to death. After confirming she was okay, I started to jump up on the bed to get good leverage as I reached up as high as I could to grab them.

"That's because we are! Good Job!" I said, trying to keep jumping to reach the other ones. "Those are the charms from Gran's bracelet. If they are anything like my charms, I think we may need them." At the word bracelet, Jess grabbed my leg and pulled me back down to the bed.

"Don't you have enough things pulling you to other places already!" she shouted at me, startled.

I looked at her and thought about her question before I stood on the bed and began to grab the charms again.

"You see those ones over there that twinkle without light?" I pointed to the charm I was currently trying to pull down. "These are stones from the Secausian Sea, from a lost civilization that claimed to have magical and healing powers. They were forged in the underwater volcanos there. The different shades of blue and purple represent the depth of where they were made. The deeper the volcano, the deeper the color," I said, trying to get a good bounce in to grab the charms, but Jess wasn't yet satisfied. She bumped against me softly, trying to throw me off the case. I glanced over, showing my teeth, "They are often known as 'Stefilia's Stones.' "

At this, her eyes widened, having heard the story of these stones in our history class just the other day.

"It is said that the stones like to be lost and are only found by those deserving of them. People pay large amounts of money for them and for no reason, in my opinion, because you can buy them and if you are not worthy, you will lose them before you get them home. But people will always continue to search for them because of their healing powers and their ability to ground you," I finished, and she moved out of the way, so I could bounce higher.

"Ground you to what?" She asked curiously.

"To the earth, to your purpose, to your loved ones. It really just depends on what you are needing at the time, I guess. We didn't really get into that part too much, but Gran told me all about them. She probably left that part out because it had something to do with an alternate dimension. She gifted me one, but it wasn't the right time yet, I guess, because I lost it," I said, bouncing higher still. I remembered the charm that now hung before me on the string. I finally stopped bouncing completely and took a good look at it.

"Okay, get up," I said to Jess, grabbing her arm and hauling her up onto her feet. Her eyes were bright in anticipation. "Bounce up, and snatch as many as you can. I'll jump to offset your weight, then you jump, okay?"

She nodded and focused on the twinkling, colorful stones above her head. I bent my knees and bounced as hard as I could, but I missed them all. Before I could land, Jess shot past me into the air and connected.

CRUNCH!

As she caught the first two stones, the fan shook like a wounded animal. It sounded like the whole ceiling was about to come down on top of us. There were three left.

"Three more! I need you to get them all in one swoop! GO!" I yelled as I bent into the bed as hard as I could so as to give Jess a good boost.

She didn't even need it. She sprung up and grabbed all three with ease. Then she dropped her shoulder and rolled right off the bed and ran to the switch to turn the fan and light off so it wouldn't drop on my head from the beating it just took. I sprang off the bed to meet her in the middle of the room. She opened her hand to show me two blue stones, one swirled with black and one swirled with white. Two deep purple stones also swirled in the same manner and one pinkish-red stone that wasn't one of Stefilia's stone at all.

"Well, these are mates, but I'm not sure what this is at all." She held up the blood-red stone. It looked like a melted heart dropping into blood.

"Maybe there will be something in the letters that says what these are for." I opened the drawer on the nightstand and pulled out a little pouch to put the charms in. I turned the pouch over to make sure there was nothing hiding there first. Out fell a silver corded bracelet with a small note attached. I read the note to myself and then turned to Jess.

"For Yang, the blood diamond will suit you well," she read aloud, shaking her head. "No, not for me, why would it be for me?" She backed away, slightly confused.

I opened my hand where the charms were to show her what was happening.

"Oh, yes, they are," I shouted unintentionally. "Open your hand," I said to her, and she tried to step away further.

She looked at me, confused, but opened her hand. In her hand laid the red stone charm as well as the blue and purple charms swirled with black. Like the Yang side of the coin. She looked from them to me and then threw them on the floor. I rolled my eyes.

"You can't be scared NOW. After all that has happened in a matter of hours, NOW you're scared?" I said, exasperated. "These are yours; you obviously need some help being grounded, and maybe a little healing. So, they were called to you, whether you want them or not on the outside, inside your soul is reaching for them." I slid them onto the chain and shoved the chain into her hand. "Wear them, don't wear them, that's up to you, but they are yours now. You found them. You caught them. They belong to you."

At my final statement, I turned and walked in the opposite direction, fixing the other two found charms to my bracelet. Like the Stefilia's Stones, there were many times I remembered being drawn to one of Gran's items. I tried to remember them all now. I walked over to the closet and threw the doors wide. Where was her beautiful jacket that looked like it would never fit me? I tried it on every time she came to town. I just knew it was in this room somewhere.

"Where are you, little treasure?" I questioned to myself. I scanned the closet for things we would need while I searched. I took the items I found out and laid them on the bed; a scarf, a gifted sparkling backpack, an extra jacket for Jess, my favorite no-tie joggers that Gran bought me, and an umbrella, all in a row. I reached the back of the closet, and I still felt like there were things we were missing.

While I investigated the rest of the closet, Jess came to terms with her new bracelet by pushing it as far down as she could into her pocket and shaking out the thought of how it made her feel. To get her mind off of the weight in her pocket, she clicked on the TV to see what Gran was watching when she was last here.

"Pack that bag with the prayer box that the letters are in, the items on the bed, and whatever you want to keep, so we consolidate our stuff and figure out how to get out of here," I said from the closet. She wasn't listening. I leaned on the wall to look out and give her a piece of my mind, but I slipped. "WHHHOOOAAAA!" I yelled at the top of my lungs. Jess raced over to see what was wrong. Too late.

"Where are you!? Are you okay? I don't see you!" She yelled into the empty closet.

I banged on the back of the closet until she pushed right through, and we were both in the back of the closet stuffed somewhere other than in the attic.

"The letters!" I screamed to her. She immediately turned around to catch the sweeping closet before it could latch and pull us in.

"I got it," she said coolly, but I noticed she was having trouble holding the door open, so I slid around her and through the door before it could close again.

"Umph!" I fell face-first onto the closet floor back in the attic just as the back swung into place.

"Hey!" Jess said from the other side.

"Hold on, I have an idea," I said, and I gathered all the stuff we had laid out on the bed to bring with us and stuffed it into the bag. Everything folded and fit into the bag with no problem. A trick I was going to make Gran show me for sure when I got back home. I reached for the battery-powered candle on the nightstand and noticed a picture of Kiki and Gran. I took it too for good measure. Then I opened the closet, ready to run through, giving it a once moreover to ensure I hadn't forgotten anything important and took a running start toward the back of the closet.

As I pushed through, I heard Jess yell. "What are you doing? It's getting dark in here!" But it was too late; I was already powering through the door and falling into the darkness. Once through, I clicked the candle on and spun around to come to a stop next to Jess. Panicked as I came through, she reached out for the door, nearly slicing her fingers right off.

"What are you doing!? Now we're stuck in here," she said, anger piping at the edge of her words.

I sat still for a second, taking in my surroundings. Old, dirty, dry wall. "I wonder if there is a place like this in my house?" I said out loud with a chuckle, even though I could tell from Jess' face that she did not think that was funny at all. "I mean, back in our own dimension." She blinked. "It's alright, Jess," I said as I gave her arm a small squeeze. "I have known that our house has had secret compartments and passageways since we got it, that was the biggest seller for Pops. We just couldn't ever find any of them. Not that we were ever really looking," I said and glanced around us. Hanging on a nail right inside of the wall was Gran's jacket. The one I had hoped was somewhere in this mess waiting for me. I reached for the jacket before turning to take in the rest of our surroundings.

8

I slid the silky fabric over my fingertips for a second, remembering the scent she carried—English toffee and rose petals. Not all at once, though, it was like a wave of crunchy to get your attention and then a pillow of petals to soothe you. I breathed her in, hoping it would bring me closer to her as this journey went on. Pulling the jacket off the nail, I felt the weight of it against my skin to see if there were any parts that I didn't know about. Of course, there were. Out of the corner of my eye, I saw Jess slide down the back of the trap closet door and look out into the darkness.

"When will the madness end!" She said, frustrated.

My friend was losing her grip, and I couldn't even blame her. I had been so hell-bent on finding my Gran's clues and getting out of here that I didn't think to stop and check on her. I slowly reached for her pocket that held her protested charm bracelet.

"No," she said as I was mid-reach. I stopped and looked at her, surprised that she had even seen my hand in the dark. I waved at her just to see if she was actually looking. She wasn't. Finally, tearing my thoughts away from Gran to focus on the girl in front of me, I sighed. It was probably on me to get her out of this rut then.

"How about this, maybe none of this is real. Maybe we are somewhere asleep at school, dreaming. Or hell, maybe the kitchens really did explode, and we are in a coma somewhere trying to find our way to the out of our own brains."

I stopped to look over at her to see if she was still with me. "But if we're dreaming, we're doing it together! We still have each other, and we're still in one piece. The only way I see us getting back to normal is getting out of here and finding something to help us get back home. We still have to reach our goal in the end and wake ourselves up or find the light at the end of the tunnel or something to get home. Like you said, things will be different here. I'm not quite sure where here is exactly, but... it's okay. One thing at a time, one foot in front of the other," I finished and noticed that she breathed a little easier with the realization that we couldn't sit here in this dark hallway to get home. I went back to investigating my new jacket.

"Things will be different, regardless." She sighed. "You don't get it."

I looked up to see her studying me now. Her eyes swept over me from the tips of my toes all the way up to the widow's peak of my forehead, then back down to my bracelet. She paused there for a while searching for what I had no clue. I probably really didn't get it.

"I have known you for most of your life, Starla. I have watched you grow and learn new things and change. Watched you go from Daddy's only baby girl to big sister of the year. You are truly your brother's keeper. I've watched you struggle and fight, and, in the end, you always manage to make it through whatever comes your way. Always. Whether someone is there to help you or not, you will find a way. I have always known that there was something special about you, with or without me. So, I know whether this is actually real or not, you will figure it out. You will be okay with or without me but the fact of the matter is, I do believe that this is real. I do believe you are special. But am I? Am I here because I'm supposed to be, or was it by accident? Can I make it through what is to come? Can I produce enough of myself to get through whatever this is?" She tugged at her ripped jeans to distract herself from the pain in her voice as she bared her truth. "I am not upset or in disbelief because of what is happening, but it's already hard to gage whether I even deserve you in our normal lives, let alone what we just walked into. A secret this big, a burden this heavy, who said I was good enough to trust with it? Who decided this was what I wanted?" She put her head in her arms, and for the first time since first grade, I saw real tears drop down her face.

Seeing those tears sparked something deep inside me. I pushed past her protests and snatched the bracelet from her pocket. Jess yelped unexpectedly in dismay, only protesting silently for the rest of the process. I pressed Stefilia's stones into her palm with so much force that I could have sworn I saw blue sparks fly from them. She jumped at my unusual fierceness.

"You are most certainly deserving of anything you think you want out of life, Justina Mathews. You are solid and kind. You are quick on your feet. You encourage others to stand up for themselves. You give all you have to anyone who needs it. How dare you speak that way about yourself!"

I turned to the side to try and catch a breath and not blow smoke out of my nose at how hurtful she was being, especially to herself.

"My Gran told me you were my Yang the day she met you all those years ago," I continued on, remembering that day during Christmas break when Jess came over all bruised up from 'family traditions' and acting as if she was unbothered by the ferocity of the wounds she sported. "She literally called you Yang. She had not spoken to you; she did not get to know you before she chose this title for you. She simply took one look at the friend I presented, fierce face, playing checkers, bruises, and all and said that you and I would be Yin and Yang. I brushed it off because, I mean I was 7 and I didn't even really know what Yin & Yang were. But even then, she saw the big heart you have, the talent you show, and the intellect you hide. She saw those things when you were 7 years old! This is us, Jess. I've been here this whole time, if no one else knows you, I know you. We are in this together, we always have been. PLUS, it's too late to second-guess it now! We're here, and no matter how much you don't want to be, or you would like not to be, you are. Nothing this important could have happened by chance. I mean, yes, you had a choice to be here or not, didn't you? What if you would have chosen to go to football tryouts instead? But you didn't, did you? Why is that Jess? Because you didn't want to cook alone? Or because you didn't want me to?" I sat down next to her on the little stoop and took a deep breath. The more I thought about it, the less I understood why she was so quick to second-guess herself so much. "If this hasn't shown you that you are capable of anything, I don't know that anything I have just said will either." I tried my best not to scold her with my tone as I laid into her doubts with my steam roller of facts.

"Do you need an example?" I asked, changing my angle to put myself in Jess' shoes and try to understand this tough situation. She nodded slowly with her head still down. "I didn't even get a choice in the matter, why didn't I get to choose whether I wanted to be here? If I did, I don't know that I would be. I would probably have been too scared that the choice was wrong. You got an out today, and you didn't take it. Why, I'm not sure, but regardless of the reasoning that helped you justify it in your mind, you didn't. That means something about YOU. Not me, I wasn't given that choice, I didn't make the choice to stand by anything or anyone; you did. That was all you." I finished with a 'humph' and sat back against the door.

Jess sat quietly, mauling over what we both had said. Without a word, she handed me the bracelet still in the palm of her hand and held her wrist out for me to clasp it. I said nothing, hoping that this would be a step in the right direction for Jess' own confidence. Now was not the time to get all excited and sway her decision to be nicer to herself. The new phase she was going through made a little more sense to me when I thought about how hard she was on herself. Easier to be someone else than to think about how you were letting yourself down, right?

We both sat quietly as I clasped the chain, and when I finished, we shared a long-overdue deep breath.

"Here goes nothing," she said, still looking at something fixed in the darkness.

I turned to see what she was staring at but couldn't see anything outside of the little candlelight that was holding fast to a small area.

"So, where do we go from here?" Jess said, pointing to the nothingness ahead.

"Well..." I said, suddenly feeling ornery. "We're in the attic, so I would assume we will need to go down." I cheesed at Jess as she rolled her eyes at my joke.

"Okay, Captain Obvious. You've lived in this house most of your life. Do you remember anything that stood out, or didn't seem to fit?" Having made a decision with the bracelet, I could tell she was in no mood for joking.

I reigned in my laugh and thought about her question. "Hmmmm..." I thought for a minute longer. "Well, there is that weird angle in the dining room, and I never really understood why it seemed so much smaller than the other rooms." I remembered like it was yesterday, Trey slamming into that oddly shaped wall trying to duck from a bath. Wait, that was yesterday. I sunk a little further into the darkness. Yesterday seemed like so long ago. I shook my head to get the memory out of my mind's eye.

Jess interrupted. "Okay, makes sense. Let's go straight until you think you are close to the kitchen, then we can take a left," Jess directed, suddenly back to normal and taking charge.

I nodded, and we set off down the hidden passage to a possibly hidden room in my house, in a possibly hidden dimension. Light Bulb.

"Something that girl Kat said to me that might help us figure out where we are? She asked me If I had been 'dem hopping.' Do you think we're in a hidden dimension?" Jess stopped in her tracks and turned to me with far too much excitement on her face.

"Maybe not a hidden one but judging by the fact that so many things are the same, but weird, I think it may be a PARALLEL ONE!" She clapped her hands to hold in her excitement. "Another dimension," she mumbled to herself. "Chip would never believe this." She started down the hallway again. "Makes the most sense, with the Kinetic Energies and all," she finished her thought as giddy as a toddler in a candy store.

"Great, thanks," I said flatly as she half-skipped through the passageway.

I hated science class. True, I understood the basics; but I was no Astrophysicist in the making for sure. Jess, on the other hand, formed ideas and understood calculations like science was putty. There for her molding. I probably needed Jess more than she realized if this was going to turn out to be one big science project. I let that thought go, trying to focus on where in the house we now were

"Here," I said confidently. I could hear the dishwasher still going. We made a sharp left, and I immediately felt my heart fly into my throat. Shooting down a slide of all things, right there where the dining room angled off. I had to bite down on the scream that was gathering with my newly placed heart as I grabbed for Jess on the way down to who-knew-where.

THUNK. We hit the bottom to find some fairly old pillows waiting for us there. Clouds of dust and debris flew up all around us, sending me into a coughing fit.

"When we get back, I'm going to have a little chat with Gran about her sour since of humor," Jess said, pulling feathers from an old pillow out of her hair.

I stood up to take a look around. The scene was immediately astounding. Aside from the old pillows, the room was immaculate. Everything in its place. I looked over at Jess to see we shared the same wide-eyed look.

"Wooow" was all she could say.

I couldn't even say that. I was caught in seeing and unseeing the room around us. If I turned to the left, it looked like just one old room. Insulation getting old and floorboards creaking. If I turned to the right, a completely different place. "I don't think we are still in one of those hidden rooms in the house," I said, looking at her sideways.

"What do you mean?" She finally turned to look at me, and her face slacked. "Ewwww!" She said, turning her nose up at the mold gathering on the walls on my side of the tiny space.

"It could possibly be a loop like, umm..." She stopped in her tracks and reached for her science book again.

"If that SCIENCE book explains what's happening in this room, I will be completely done." I gave her as much side eye as I could muster while continuing my assessment of our surroundings.

She opened her science book to the middle and slid her comic book out of it. Of course, she was hiding cartoons in her schoolbooks. That would explain why she always looked so interested when we were told to read paragraphs alone, and why she snorted when nothing was funny. Why didn't I think of that?

"So, what are we looking at?" I asked, now irritated that I wasn't let in on her brilliant way to pass the time in class.

Bonnie Baraka

"So, you mean you've never seen Guardians of the Galaxy?" she asked, not looking up from the comic.

I looked over at the tree on the cover that often reminded me of my own little Groot brother I had at home. "Yes," I said with a loud sigh.

Jess looked up, also remembering his nickname, and in an effort to redirect my now-declining state of emotions, she pulled my attention to the page she was reading and began to explain.

"Pocket dimensions are used a lot in Guardian of the Galaxy comic books; they use them as dimensional storages. I think they use them in that Poke' thing too, but I don't watch those." She pointedly turned her nose up at the series. "Anyway, they are portions of other dimensions that are ripped out and fitted into other places. I'm trying to remember if there is something special we must do to get in or out of one. I'm almost certain that this is a pocket space. I mean, look at the outlines of the room, and then the other side is obviously the actual house. I don't think this room would fit in the space between the living room and kitchen, so it must be a pocket dimension." She looked up at the mold again, scrunching her nose. Then stooped down to get a better look at the place where antique met modern. She reached out to touch the seemingly floating room, and her hand slipped right through to the splintery floorboard. "That's weird; maybe it's the different vibrations?" She said, taking off all her jewelry and things she felt could alter the energies. She then stuck her free hand directly into the see-through wall. Her hand slammed into thin air with ferocity this time, and she drew her hand back with a hiss. "Welp, there must be something that we have to do special to get into it," she said, irritation gnawing at the back of her throat.

I stuck my hand out to lean against the invisible wall, assuming I would get the same outcome, and nearly fell on my face. There was no wall in front of me, invisible or otherwise. I stood up and looked at my palm. It was red, and my bracelet was again on the hum.

"Put on your bracelet and try it again. Bracelet arm first," I directed Jess without even looking up from my palms. They looked like they belonged to me, but they felt like something different, something foreign completely.

Just for good measure, I grabbed Jess' hand and pushed her towards the invisible barrier. I saw her falter at the threshold as if it seemed to push back against her. I thrust our linked braceleted hands towards the newly located pocket dimension and wished for it to bend at Jess' touch, but I probably pushed too hard. Jess was flung through the invisible barrier that was previously holding her back and sprawled across the floor, dazed and unmoving. I turned around to grab our belongings and follow, but when I reached for the bag, it felt like it was miles away. I rushed over to the bag and grabbed everything on the floor in my arms. As I looked up, I saw that our pocket dimension was shifting, and my window for entrance was about to close.

Jess looked up, feeling the vibrations of the now-moving pocket dimension. "Starla, GET IN HERE NOW!" She screamed huskily. Is that fear in her voice?

I jumped bracelet arm first over the threshold with ease and landed in a sitting position next to Jess.

"Keep your panties on girl. I was coming," I said, flashing a smile to mask, trying to catch my breath.

"This is no time to take chances like that, crazy," she replied through clenched teeth.

"Okay, well, what kind of time is it then?" I asked, trying to get her to calm down. "I had to get the pack, not to mention your precious science book you just left lying around." I rolled my eyes at her as I stood up and looked around. Now, getting a chance to fully take in the sight before my eyes, this was worth all the crazy stuff from the rest of the day. This I could get used to. "Video games, basketball courts, snacks, computers. We are definitely not still in my house," I said, giving a twirling glance around the room.

"If it is, you have seriously been holding out on me," Jess said, finally getting up to have a better look around. She walked over to the computer and took a seat in the comfiest-looking oversized computer chair I had ever seen. "How do you turn this thing on, I wonder?" She said, picking up what looked like a TV remote. Her eyes widened as she looked at all the buttons. "This is no regular remote," she said, pointing it at me. "I wonder if I can turn down your hair with this thing?"

I looked up at my hair. Curls were now busting out all over the place. Exhausted with taming my not-so-manageable curls, I took the scrunchy that Jess originally gave to me to cover my now-exposed bracelet and used it to lock my curls on the top of my head in a generally messy bun.

"Whatever!" I said through my struggle. I walked over to the computer systems. "Isn't this kind of what the pilot's dash of an airplane looks like?" I asked, seeing the weird nobs and not understanding one bit.

"That's a weird conclusion you've drawn there, but I guess I could see where you're going with it," Jess said, cocking her head to the side to make the comparison make sense. "It looks more like a music producer's office to me," she continued, pointing to the parts that made her feel differently.

"Either way, it's not a regular old computer, and it doesn't look like it has a regular old on switch either," I said, plopping into a beanbag kind of seat and immediately forgetting all about the computer. "AAhhhh, what is this? It is soo comfy," I said from inside the chair. "It's like a very soft hug that you can sit in." I giggled.

Jess was paying me no attention, still focused on finding the power button.

"Check the back; the power buttons are always on the back!" I drawled lazily from under the pillows that accompanied my new favorite chair.

She looked over at me, giving me all the stink-eye she could as she walked around to the side of the control board to peer into the back. Clearly humoring me. Her face quickly changed when she looked down and saw that it was, in fact, unplugged, and the cord was lying next to the wall.

"Even in a pocket dimension, we have to plug it in?" She said, more to herself than to me, as she bent over and found the right direction to fit the plug into the socket.

The minute the plug touched the socket, there was a steady hum that filled the room. Then a loud sputtering noise; this room had clearly not been used in quite some time. Neon lights lining the floor kicked into play, and the monitors blinked into action all at once.

"Hello, traveling descendant, welcome to the Heir's Hideaway." All the monitors spewed out at the same time, sounding like a chorus.

On the monitor was a young lady that looked like my Gran, only it had to be a much further distant relative because my Gran's hair had never been that shade of red.

"Please verify your identity," the computer requested.

The monitor to the center changed, and the lady moved to the side to show an encrypted key that needed to be input. I looked up from my comfy chair with alarm and over to Jess, who was already inching away from the screens.

"She didn't give me a code!" I yelled to her, panic rushing in.

"That's because she hardwired everything in your brain, Star... but YOUR BRAIN not mine. Get up and figure it out!" She half-whispered half-yelled at me from the back of the room where she had taken up a watching position.

I rose out of my comfy chair to approach the monitors. At my presence, the screen changed again, and the woman moved back into view.

"Please speak your name," she prompted.

"Starla Supreme King," I said with all the confidence I could muster.

"Please tell us your mother's name."

At this, I grimaced. I didn't know my mother's maiden name or her middle name, for that matter.

"Um, Kiyoshi King?" I pushed out.

"Thank you. Welcome Starla King of Dimension C. We have been patiently awaiting your arrival. Who have you brought with you today?"

Sometime, during the course of my questioning, Jess had inched her way back into the line of sight. She was standing at my side, slightly out of reach. "Justina Mathews of Dimension C," she said to the computer, following suit with where the computer said I was from.

"Ah, Justina Mathews. Yang to the Yin, apple to the orange. Hot to the cold. Yes, we were expecting you as well, but could not be certain." The computer spewed a review of the things I had heard Gran call Jess.

Bonnie Baraka

"Please place your finger on the scanner for confirmation."

And with the request, a cover slid back to show a finger reader. Jess placed her finger on the scanner cautiously, uncertain what would happen.

"Confirmed! Thank you, Miss Mathews. You, however, are not from Dimension C. I believe the two of you traveled here from the greatest secret in the solar system. Dimension X is very new in comparison to the dying Dimension of C. That is where you were created. Justina Mathews of Dimension X—that is who you are." The computer seemed to even turn to Jess when making this proclamation.

"Wait, how am I from C and she's from... X, but we grew up together. I have known her all my life." I was half talking to the room, half talking to myself as I stepped up to the computer. Not expecting a response, I jumped when that nice lady gave me one anyway.

"You were created in a dimension that was made in love. A dimension that was believed to never falter, much different than others. Dimension C, just the third made, was much different from the others; because of this, it was kept hidden for an exceptionally long time. When it was discovered, instead of fighting to keep the dimension intact and possibly causing a rift in the cosmic equilibrium that would have affected all of the other dimensions, everyone from that dimension fled to others. Your family chose Dimension X, where you met Miss Mathews." The computer paused as if it was actually looking to see what we were feeling. "I can see from your face that you don't believe my words.

Haven't you ever dreamed of a time when your family was happy, when your family was whole? Don't you often wake up in cold sweats, reaching for something you feel you have never felt before? Well, that is your home." She stopped and looked at me for a long moment, reading the uncertainty in my face. "Now is not the time for a proper history lesson. I have been told of the confidence in Miss Mathew's ability to keep you safe, so we will get into something far more important."

I looked from her to Jess and back again before I saw she was about to continue and interrupted.

"Wait a damn minute! You spring all of this information on me and expect me to just move on like you didn't just say I am not who I think I am? I need a minute to process this crap. You force me into a completely left field situation with NO WARNING. You put me here with no guidance. Tell me nothing and make me find clues to get to this point. Then you say, that's not what is important right now? What could be more important than figuring out what the hell is going on?" I stormed back to the comfy oversized bag and plopped down. I was done. I had made it to my wits' end. I felt stupid for yelling at a computer screen and even angrier that Gran let this happen to me. Gran knew all of this was going to happen, and she never said a word. How could I justify this to myself? How could I have expected Jess to just accept this? How could I put her in a situation where we were just winging it?

"Calm down!" I heard Jess say from where she was still standing next to the computer. At that moment, the woman in the screen stepped out of the screen and sat on the keyboard. Just slid down, as if that was what all computer people did.

"Jess, move!" I yelled hysterically as I ran to the computer to defend my friend. Jess swung around to see our new computer friend perched on top of the keyboard. Her face lost all color, and she immediately fell back into the computer chair.

"What. Is. Happening?" she mumbled from her chair.

The computer lady that was now sitting next to Jess finally realized what had set us off and explained.

"Apologies for startling you. I am your A.I., you know, like Artificial Intelligence? I exist only in this space with this computer or software when it is on." She paused, as if she were weighing what information to give us just now. "Well, I can exist in a few other places, but mostly this is it." She beamed at herself, swinging her virtual legs from the desk. This seemed like the watered-down version, and I had every intention of asking more questions later, but she continued. "My name is Suzie Roi. I am only a virtual replica of my former self. I gave my life to create this sanctuary for the Roi- King heirs. I am, unfortunately, not all-seeing or all-knowing. I am knowledgeable about many things, but there are plenty of things I still do not know." Then she was silent as if to give us a minute to decide if we wanted to believe her. I didn't, but Jess' mood seemed to shift to an enjoyable comfort. She was eating up every bit of having an actual A.I. at our disposal.

"Well, Star, what do you want to do?" she smirked at me.

"I don't want to do anything! I want to go take a nap! I want to see my Gran!" I said brashly as I sat back down again in my chair.

"Think about how important this must be if your own family put you through this without warning. There must be something seriously important going on if she's telling you she doesn't have time to fully explain." There was a sense of urgency in her eyes I recognized immediately. So, I stopped to think about what was happening around me. What could be so important to pull me into this mess? Gran would never allow me in something that she knew would hurt me unless she had no choice. Yet there she was leading the voyage up to this point.

I looked back at the lady on the screen. She looked so happy, so fun, so much like my Gran.

"Is my Gran going to die?" I asked her with as straight of a face as possible.

Our computer host looked mortified. "Your Gran. Your grandmother is Jin? My darling, Jinny?" Her face was taught, and I realized, she didn't know.

"Yes," I said slower than intended. From her reaction, she knew Gran well. "She is sick."

"I have not seen the future and cannot answer that question. I can tell you that we are not immortal and can only hide from the griever for so long. I hoped and thought that I would see my darling Jinny again before she made her great decent, but this question I cannot answer for you now." I could see tears of realization forming in her eyes, and I felt terrible.

"Wow, intelligence so grand that emotions are understood! That hasn't even been made yet!" Jess whispered to me, but I was too busy seeing those tears and feeling that pain for myself. I felt the tears I saw in her eyes stream down my own cheeks as I thought about life without my grandmother's guidance.

"I'm sorry," I said as just loud enough for her to hear. Straightening my borrowed jacket, I wiped my face and gathered myself up. "Okay, let's hear it. What is the current danger? And it better be the world is going to end danger, for us to have been dragged away from her and all that we know right now," I said with the most attitude I could muster.

"Unfortunately, it is," Suzie said with sorrow in her voice. "In fact, your very existence depends on it."

9

Debunked

I looked at Jess. "How can our existence in another dimension depend on what is happening here?" I asked angrily, knowing she was wondering the same thing.

"Hey, I'm here listening with you, remember?" She crossed her arms firmly. "Why don't you cut out some of the attitude, focus on what's going on and let her tell us."

I shot her a surprised and hurt look. No doubt, she was right; I still had a serious thorn in my side, and everything was coming at me fast, but she didn't have to call me out about it. On the other hand, if our whole existence really depended on whatever was or wasn't happening here and now, then we definitely needed to stop it before it was too late. So, without another word and mostly to hide the angry face I was giving Jess, I turned to rearrange the pillows behind me. I pulled my seat closer to the screens, fluffed the pillows again dramatically, and plopped back into its squishy warmth, finally getting comfortable again. "Fine," I said from my newly placed chair with a hint of annoyance, "tell us then." Seeing that I was not going to say anything else, Jess turned her seat towards Suzie and, after giving me one last check, waved her on.

"Well, isn't it lucky that you brought your cosmic guide with you on this trip?" Suzie said, giving Jess a warm smile before she began again. "Jess, did you happen to study relativity and its cause and effect rule yet in school?" At this point, I felt like Suzie was ignoring me completely. Fine by me.

"Ummm..." Jess cocked her head to the side, straining to remember. "I think I read about it over the summer in our new science book," Jess said, blushing and looking at me out of the corner of her eye to assess my reaction. She reads science books over the summer? I trained my face on Suzie so Jess wouldn't notice that I caught her assessment. There seemed to be more and more things about Jess that I didn't know, and I wasn't sure I liked that. "Something about how if something happens somewhere far off, gauging the relativity can tell you how likely it is to affect something else closer to you by calculating its size, type, and frequency. Like white noise. It is constantly happening, but if you get the right type and frequency, it could shatter a crystal glass."

It felt like she read the answer directly from her textbook. Something in my brain finally clicked into place. I looked her over once, twice, and then once more for good measure. Jess had grown over the summer. Sitting straight in her swivel chair, not slouching like she was ready to go through game tape, or on the bench ready for the whistle at a football game. Her hair was still pulled back, but I had to look away in surprise because, was that a bang poking out? It must have fallen out of her ponytail when she gave me her extra scrunchie, and I hadn't even bothered to notice. All this time, I thought she wanted to be one thing. Now I was noticing something different completely. I thought she was engaging these gossiping, giggling girls at school to keep her popularity status, but was that the real reason? Or did she enjoy the girlish aspect more than she let on? I knew she liked science, and I knew she paid attention in that class, but reading over the summer? There was definitely a change happening, and I was too wrapped up wanting things to stay the same to realize I had forgotten to be there for her. I looked at my shoes.

"So, is that what's happening here?" Jess asked, not even realizing I wasn't paying attention anymore.

"Things are always happening here," Suzie shrugged. "It is just like the white noise, though, you are correct." She slid off the desktop and turned around to look at the screen.

"If something hits the same vibration far away, something else will happen here that will mess everything up?" Jess said, a mixture of pride and curiosity started to swirl over her features. She had fit the pieces together nicely, I had to admit.

"Not quite," Suzie said, beaming at her prized student. "It's actually the other way around. The cause will be here, and the effect will take place in every other dimension as if it were happening in real-time right there in front of them." She looked over at me to see if I was understanding what was about to happen.

Every OTHER dimension? I was so completely lost in thought that I just let her continue to explain.

"It's kind of like when there is a freak accident in nature. Chances are, there was something that happened in another dimension that created a ripple in the relativity, and the effect was a rockslide or an avalanche or a dormant volcano erupting. Those things do just happen, but it is more common for there to be a cause in somewhere else completely." Suzie ended her explanation and stepped back from the monitor to show us what she was looking at, a diagram of cause and effect in nature. She paused there to allow the evidence of what she was trying to tell us sink in.

"Great," I said, sarcasm heavy on the tip of my tongue. "And just how many of these 'other dimensions' are there that we should be worried about?" I said to Jess directly, hoping she was thinking the same thing.

"Well," Suzie started to try to explain, looking shocked. "I guess I don't really know the answer to that question." She blinked. "Time and Space are also relative. There could just be the ones I know of, A through Z, or there could be an infinite amount. Like A (1 to infinity) through Z (1 through infinity). There could be solar systems that name their dimensions after colors or animals, or who don't speak or who are extremely intelligent. I can't really answer how many we need to be worried about." Suzie's face grew grimmer with every word she spoke, as though she had never thought about this question and its severity before. "Well, do you know what this big event we're chasing is going to be?" I was too far lost in my emotions and confused to focus on her reaction for any more than a second.

"Unfortunately, I don't," Suzie said, throwing her hands in the air. "I can give you history, and I can tell you what the final blow will hypothetically be, but I am not an oracle. I do not have any information on what is to come. Merely speculation." She looked away to investigate her virtual nail polish.

Something gnawed at the edges of my memory. I was starting to think she almost looked like she was happy with herself for this answer, until she noticed how confused we actually were.

"Ugh, I see you two have no clue what I'm talking about. So, let me just start from the beginning." She put her hands in the air like she was doing some sort of yoga move, and the rest of the screens behind her began to change and sort itself. "When I was a young girl, there were many things that were different. We as a people hadn't evolved into who we are quite yet. Because of this, there was an organization forming to keep the balance in places where balance was a second thought. There is a specific group of humans that can travel through dimensions effortlessly or Slide for a better terminology. Now, Sliding is reserved for those of us with a specific blood type. Type O or the Original, as I like to call it. I should clarify that even some O blood type individuals are not able to Slide. It is an extremely specific formula that goes into whether you are able to use this gift. It's in the positives and negatives and the balance between the two in your bloodstream and other factors that we can go through another time if you're still interested later." Suzie looked over at Jess with a wink, noticing how intrigued she was with this information. "Anyway, Sliding happens when subject matter vibrates at a frequency higher than the dimensional barriers that separate the realities around them. When this happens, they are able to Slide through those walls and enter a new dimension all together."

I stopped her before she could continue. "Wait, new dimension. Okay, so we can get to any of them? On any system?" I asked her a little overwhelmed.

"Yes, the possibilities are infinite; once one ends, another begins. I don't think anyone has actually seen them all. However, I can say there are about 28 that I am aware of in our system as of now, all with different names and meanings. Like the dimension we are in right now. V, also known as the Various Dimension, was created to house various kinds of gifted individuals. This dimension has a high awareness for the gifts from the Creator, and they use them often. This is drastically different from X or the Xyloid Dimension. It was named as such because it is the dimension that is furthest away from being aware of its Creator and the gifts given. People have tried to awaken this dimension in the past, but it always ends in bloodshed and the restart of the same old beliefs that there is no one or nothing out there in the universe, except for them and the Creator. Because of that, the Creator named them something that was close to the cycle of nature or wood. Killing itself off and being reborn in the same space with the same mindset." She looked at Jess as she was saying this to see her reaction to this news.

Jess seeming impartial, spoke up anyway.

"I think we have made great strides over time, but we still have much more to go. Just because we don't move as fast as the rest of you doesn't mean we are wood," she said, dully rolling her eyes.

"Well, none of that will matter if we don't figure out what's going on here before everything goes wrong. So, I guess you may be right." Suzie nodded in agreement.

Jess made no motion to show she was happy to hear this, but I thought I saw her light shine a little brighter.

"Moving on," Suzie said, turning back to the monitors again to continue her show.

Why are all my relatives so dramatic? I thought to myself as I leaned in to get a better look at what was popping up behind her.

"Sliding wasn't always a known gift from the Creator, but it was always there. For many generations, people in our cultures could only go and never return, and thus Sliding was considered a gift to those who were outcasts or evil. That is until someone's Great-Great-Great ancestor..." Suzie turned and stretched her hand out to me, "figured out the science and confusion behind what was actually happening and why these people were unable to make it home. He then added some key components, like Seraphina's stones to keep you grounded, charms to help you remember home, and things or people that can help give you direction back to where you started."

As she spoke of the different items that were added to the process, a timeline began to pop up behind her head. I studied it to see if there was anything that I remembered hearing as a young child from Gran.

"Once our people were able to master the direction portion of the travel, the rest was history. It sparked like wildfire, no longer being the dark omen, but more of a light in the dark. See, people didn't understand that when your energy spikes or your adrenalin gets high, which could be for a good reason or a bad reason, you can create higher vibrations, or lower ones. Now they may be different in color and feeling, but they are like sisters happy and mad. They are not identical, but they give out extremely high frequencies in their own right. One may very well be a vibrant and playful purple," Suzie pointed to the thermostat at my wrist, "and one may be red or blue, but both belong in the rainbow, high above us." Suzie reached for Jess' healing stone and then threw her hands up to the monitors again where the stones on the screen arranged themselves in a beautiful rainbow. "So, when we are intensely anxious or mad or happy, we are creating a vibration so high that we can disappear from where we are completely. With the right tools, of course." Suzie waved her hand, and the rainbow behind her cleared and shaped back into the previous timeline. "Once it was put in a new light, everyone wanted to do it. It was like a trap door, an escape from reality, or a new start when you messed up your old life. Those who could but didn't know how wanted to learn, and those who couldn't wanted to be taught or taken with. That meant more to study and more to learn. Would this type of travel kill those who weren't created to do so? We didn't know then. How would this affect the system? The worlds? The way the Creator intended it to be? Again, we didn't know. What was the effect on other things around the act?

"All questions that needed to be answered before we could move forward, but they weren't. Many people mastered the art of Sliding from dimension to dimension, some going places and becoming a part of civilization and never leaving. Some taking the easy way out and being greedy, and others who exposed our culture for good and bad in dimensions who didn't know any better." As she spoke, new things kept popping up on the screens behind her; wars, bombings, volcanos overrunning entire cities, Tyrants, and even some beautiful creations were shown and then put neatly into the timeline above. "What we soon found out was that a person who is not of the Original blood type could not and should not slide through the barriers. They were created in their home dimension, and that is where they should stay. There were those that yearned to leave anyway. Some survived the slide; most didn't. We also found that humans with O negative blood type had a harder time creating vibrations necessary to evoke the act. However, with practice and patience and a couple other variables, it is possible for them to do so as well. Though, it is extremely draining to their life force, and their lives are normally plagued with sickness and disorientation after. On the other hand, there have been O negatives that have been able to master their Slide technique thus far.

"We have also learned some especially important facts that no one knew so long ago about the song and dance that ties all these factors together. When a human who is created to Slide does so, it is a normal feat and nothing changes, but when a person who is not of O blood and was not created specifically for this gift, such as a human with AB or O Negative blood types use it, there are consequences. Every time a person who is of no original blood is taken from one dimension to another where they do not belong, a microscopic tare is created in the barrier where they crossed through. This can have several effects. A, nothing happens because the tare is microscopic and so small that they are not effective enough alone. B, a group of tares form, but they can be found and repaired if the right person finds them and has the gift from the Creator to do so until they are naturally filled over time. Or C, there can be so many tares in one place in one barrier that they can bring down the entire system. Thus, collapsing all the dimensions on each other and creating a cosmic black hole that will suck in this entire universe." Suzie paused, for dramatic climax, no doubt.

Kiki used to do this often—have you hanging on the edge of your seat in anticipation. I growled. Suzie looked over, noticing my dislike for her silence, and continued promptly.

"I am not sure what effect that will have on other systems. Good question, though," she chided sarcastically at me. "In most dimensions, this poses no problem at all because the tares are small and far apart. There was a large opening found in a barrier once from a war that also could have decimated the universe, but we were able to stabilize it until nature repaired it herself. We were also able to study it and make the conclusions I just shared with you and the people who are gifted to physically see these barriers. If the previous tare was not stabilized and monitored, the dimensions would have felt it over time, slowly sucking in dimensions one by one until they were all swallowed into the darkness of that whole. Luckily, the Organization was there, but this time, it will not be." This time Suzie paused, visibly deep in thought and not for speculation. "No, I think this time will be vastly different than that one was. This time, we do not know the location of where this rip may happen. We just know that it is coming. Like our Organization was to keep people safe and balanced with their gifts, there is a group of people that believe our gifts should be shared and that we are selfish not to. They believe that the Creator gave us these gifts to see how we would use them. This group teaches O-'s to use their vibrations, sometimes killing them in the process. They assist in the transport of others who are unable to Slide—for a fee, of course—and they have a strong disposition for anything they think the government is doing that is 'muting the voice of the people.'" Suzie put up her air quotes at the last part and rolled her eyes. "We call them Slicers. Slicers are those of Original blood that make money from the transport of people and things through the dimensional barriers. Each time they Slide with something or someone that should not do so, they slice the barrier into pieces, and yet they continue to do so knowing the consequences. Most are harmless; they continue to help the sick or homeless by taking them somewhere that they will fit in better, or even sometimes taking them back to their home dimension. Others, like the ones your Gran was tracking, are not so harmless. They take large groups for money and artifacts. They have a routine and use the same area of the barrier each time thinking, if it is weakened here, I should be able to Slide through without creating a new slice, but they do not know the science. Once a tare is made, anytime anything encounters it, it begins to rip open like a broken piece of paper. It does not matter that you are not physically touching it because it is already ripped, your aura has passed through, and it continues to rip further. Fortunately, Slicers are not common in many dimensions. Unfortunately, it only takes one to put down this entire system."

Suzie turned to Jess, who was raising her hand so hard I thought she might fall out of the chair. "Yes?" Suzie answered her raised hand with a smile and a posture of excitement like a teacher calling on her favorite student.

"So, how many sliders... or no, Slicers, no. How many people in our home dimension, wait, I mean my home dimension... are there that can Slide through to other places?" Jess asked the question, still working this information through in her head as she spoke.

"Let's say about 25% of all people in X are Type O. Of that number, 15% are posy, and 10% are negs," Suzie said, her eyes distant as if she was calculating or actually finding this information from somewhere for us. "Of that 15%, there are probably 2% that actually know that it's even a possibility, and maybe less than 1% have the actual training and tools to try it." Suzie finished finding the information from wherever her cyber self had gone to retrieve it and came back to us with a smile.

Although it was creepy, at least I knew if I needed some info from the world wide web, she could find it for me. My mind exploded as I thought about the actual information that she had just given me. "Wait, that's just X, though, right? That means at least 1 percent of every dimension? That's like..." I pulled out my fingers to help with my crappy math skills, "26 percent?" I replied unconfidently.

"Not quite," Suzie whispered, trying not to burst my recently inflated ego. "That is just in X. Some dimensions don't have any O types at all, and others have as many as 30 percent of their population. Like the one you are in right now. This is the Slicers last known headquarters, and most people here know of them and their gifts. The organization that was keeping a handle on them disbanded after what happened to you." Suzie's eyes glazed over, and she looked away from me quickly, with disgust. I couldn't tell if it was something I had done or something she was remembering of herself.

"Happened to who?" I said, not understanding why she hadn't finished her sentence. Suzie looked at Jess, who showed understanding in her eyes and changed the subject. Was that for my benefit? I was trying to wrap my brain around who they could be talking about when she changed the topic entirely.

"My dear Jinny and I had been tracking some large kinetic energy and movement here, and we think we have it narrowed down as close as possible to here and now. This dimension was made to be a safe harbor for the gifted. Not all of its inhabitants are gifted, but all are aware of the gifts around them. Humans that are not of O Type do not generally want to leave this dimension because it is so excepting and free. All here believe, and because of that, there are many more trained Sliders and Slicers alike. Schools teach meditation and techniques to control your gifts instead of suppressing them. There are many children here who are not completely ready to make decisions in an adult world but are in possession of gifts that can end life and alter realities. They are in need of teaching and encouragement. This is what makes it difficult to figure out exactly what is going to happen and who to focus on the most.

"Unfortunately, neither you nor Jin has been in this dimension long enough for me to gather new intel, so it will be extremely hard to tell you where to start. I can tell you that your grandmother was investigating much of your father's work, or so it seemed, but he has since given it up. I would keep digging there, though, maybe check the new outlets or anyone who could be considered a friend. I have a list, not all of your friends are friends of the King family." Suzie put in a side note to remind me of Gran's don't trust anyone warning.

"If Charlie will talk to you, that is probably your best starting place. Your Gran and Charlie of V spent quite a bit of time together in years past. He may know more than he lets on. Whatever path you choose, move quickly. Do not falter on your mission, and make sure you are on the lookout for any distractions. Once they figure out that you are on to their trail, they will do everything in their power to stop you." The fire that was dancing in her eyes with her final declarations scared me and made me feel something else, another emotion I hadn't used in a while. What was it?

I looked away from Suzie to regain my strength and gather my thoughts. Scanning the rest of our new pocket base, I concluded. "Why couldn't Jess get in? Is she allowed into this place without me?" I asked Suzie to confirm before sharing my next thought with the room.

"If you will it, so it will be." It was all Suzie said in response.

I looked over to Jess. "For the time being, this seems to be our new home. Our safe zone—the place we know we can come if one of us is ever lost or in need. Do you agree?" I asked, nervous that Jess wouldn't feel about our new hideout as I did.

"As long as you don't call it something stupid like honeycomb hideout or HQ, then I'm in," she said with a smug grin.

I released a breath of appreciation and retorted, "Aww, man! Those were my first two choices!" I smiled to show her I was joking, and I went back to scouting the rest of the space.

"I guess we better start looking," Jess said, standing up to reach for what looked to me like a gaming controller. Pointing it at the monitor behind Suzie, the closest to her, she said under her breath, "I wonder if they still have ABC and TBS." The monitor clicked to a TV guide, and Jess began to scroll the channels like she was at home looking for her favorite show. She clicked a channel and sat back down to tune in.

"So how do you know this is the real news from this dimension? I mean, like from today?" I asked her, curiosity getting the best of me.

She leaned over to the monitor to point to the bottom corner. "Time and date stamp," she said without turning around. "I guess it could be a different day, too," she mumbled mostly to herself. "Plus, if we were home, it would be much later than 4:45," she finished her calculations.

"4:45 pm, just in time for the 5 o'clock news," I said, turning to investigate some papers I saw spread across a nearby table. The news anchor came on just as the clock hit 5 and to tell about the stories they would cover tonight. I heard something about a royal concert, a new drink that helps you remember important forgotten dates, and something about the kickoff of a new project that could affect us all. I was beginning to wonder what station Jess had turned to when I heard an extremely loud squeal and dropped all the papers I was now rifling through. I abandoned the papers and rushed over to where the squeal originated to find Jess frozen in place. I was dumbfounded as to what could make her make such a girly noise like the one that just escaped her throat, but when I glanced up, I knew exactly what it was.

There on the monitor, I saw the scene of a TV anchor interviewing a young lady. A princess, judging from the captions. I read the caption aloud to make sure I was understanding this correctly. "Princess Tina to announce the winners of the 'Help feed the world' campaign Monday here on CRS." I took a step closer to the TV. "CRS? What is CRS?" I turned to ask Suzie.

"Celebrated Royalty Station," Suzie said, a look of disgust on her face.

"Interesting! Princess Tina, is it? Well, hello there, Princess!" I said, unable to hold in my laughter as I looked from Jess to the screen and back again. Identical. Understanding rushed in, and I laughed even harder. There was a reason I couldn't find any trace of Jess in our school this morning. She did not live here. In the Various Dimension, Justina Mathews was Royalty. I laughed harder until I turned to see Jess' look of half-terror half-wonder. I reached over to make sure she was, in fact, still breathing. "You okay?" I asked, knowing the answer.

Jess didn't say anything; she didn't even flinch. I knew seeing someone with her face would come into play eventually, but I didn't think it would hit her quite this hard. She was too busy tracing every curl in that princess' hair. Jess wore hers bone straight and tied back in a low pony. Her eyes took in the rest of the scene, and she noticed every curve of the Princess' body that was accentuated by her form-fitting blouse and A-line skirt and every shade of makeup that covered her face. I could see this being a sight to Jess since her normal attire consisted of basketball shorts, possibly jeans or sweats, and a muscle shirt. A Tshirt if she was absolutely made to. Once her mom made her wear a dress to Church, back before she got too sick to go, and Jess had ripped the whole thing before they even made it inside. With her mouth gaping in confusion, you could tell that she didn't believe that she could be so beautiful, and I read it right there in her reaction.

"I'm, I mean... She's gorgeous," she finally said after realizing we were watching her instead of the TV. I turned to study the monitor again. The princess was, in fact, stunning in her royal garb.

Turning back to Jess, I mocked, "She literally looks just like you. Every day of every year of your whole existence. Why does it surprise you so much that she is pretty?" I felt her tension rise in every word I said. I guess she didn't remember the church dress she demolished then. Judging by the escalated tension in the room and the amount of locked emotions I could sense rising to the surface, I chose to slowly back away and let her continue to marvel at herself in peace. I could still hear the TV as I went back to rifling through pages and looking for anything that could help in our search.

"Princess Tina, can you give us a look inside your project and what it is for?" The newscaster's voice came through the speaker like honey. She had definitely done this before. Princess Tina seemed to have some skill in this area also, but nothing like the newscaster.

"Well, Shirley, this project is to help feed not just our world, but other worlds as well. We want to have an impact on life outside of the normal and juvenile ways of old. We want sustainability for our future generations. We are trying to nurture the nature around us and leave only an imprint, not only for ourselves but for the many, many youths to come after us."

I had to hand it to her; she was very well-spoken and firm. I believed every word of what she was uttering, and I had never even met her or had any idea what she was talking about. As she finished telling us about her project, I realized that Jess wasn't the only one who was in a trance being drawn to listen intently to her every word. Jess was still unmoving and focused on... well, on herself as if nothing else we just spoke about mattered.

Bonnie Baraka

As Shirley continued her questioning, I finally snapped out of the warp I was in.

"Wait, did she just say OTHER worlds?" The alarm in my voice both scared me and snapped Jess out of her immobile state. "How can she possibly feed other worlds without GOING to them? There can't be that many employable Sliders." I was still trying to wrap my mind around the lingo. Trying to do something good, only to kill everyone instead. I looked first at Jess, who was still dazed and trying to get her bearings on what was happening before her eyes, then to Suzie, who was picking her virtual nails again.

Suzie didn't look the least bit interested in what was going on with any person who might have been in royalty, but she answered anyway.

"Your father has been working on something for that project for years now. The rules say it must be something that won't affect any barriers in any way that will bring harm to anyone else. However, if the risk would only affect this dimension and is small enough, she may allow it. Her mother started this campaign when she was with us, but she fell ill, and we haven't seen her get out of bed in many years." She looked at Jess to see if she had heard the news. She did, but I knew as well as Jess that her own mother was in bed just as well; this was no surprise. She didn't want me to know, but I was well aware that it was only a matter of time before her own mother was bedridden for good and gone from their lives. I saw it chip away at Jess every day.

"Another requirement is that it is self-sustaining, it can't be something that will use up all of V's resources and leave them empty-handed in the end. So, it should have nothing to do with your search, but we all know when good ideas are given, bad ones are around the corner. I'm not really sure what the connection is, but I know Jin did feel it was important enough to investigate through your father's research. The royal family was a part of her search, but I'm not sure how that fits in."

I looked over the pages I was sorting to see if there was any further information about Pop's project and the unveiling of it.

"Says here, presentation of the working models will be on display at the 'World of World's Fair' four days from today, in jolly old London." I looked at

Jess and smiled, shaking my head to alert her that I was aware of our next destination. It wasn't going to be an easy ride either.

"There are a few things that I should mention that you may not find in your research, Star." Suzie pulled me to the side while Jess began to pack up our stuff and work on devising a plan. "First, I know you haven't had any actual training, but Jin showed you the way without telling you what you were learning. That means stay true to yourself, go with your gut. If something feels off, it is probably something you learned and didn't know it. Remember what your Gran taught you; it will come in handy on your journey the most. There are things that can change you here, so make sure you are smart and safe, but most of all, make sure you stay away from those..." BOOM BOOM BOOM. Suzie was cut off before she could finish. The room went black, and I jumped as I heard all the electronics die.

"The power?" I said, trying to decipher what happened. "But how?" CREAAKKK. I looked over to Jess to see if she was as scared as I was; she wasn't. Jess had continued her gathering in a steady motion and was in the process of gathering the last things we needed to accompany our journey and some things I think she just wanted to keep. I spun around, trying to compose myself and noticed a book laying where Suzie had originally sat on the edge of the computer console. I grabbed it and bolted for the entrance. Jess was on my heels. We peered out into the rest of the house through the cracks in the drywall.

"I think that was a door," Jess whispered into my ear. "Think where we could be in the odd places in your house that we used to ignore." She was so close to me now that I could feel her breath on my ear. I thought about where we could have landed after our slide down from the attic.

"The pantry," I said a tad louder than I had meant to. I could hear a commotion coming from the other side of the wall.

We exited our pocket base hand in hand and immediately spun around to see where it would go. It hadn't disappeared completely, but it was so small now

I couldn't help but wonder if we would ever find it again. I heard a clank on the floor as if something had fallen from the sky and walked to where the entrance previously stood. Three charms. They looked like small mirrors. Like a pocket mirror or a locket almost. Picking them up, I felt the hum of the Heirs

Bonnie Baraka

Hideaway under my fingers. Unsuspecting unless you knew what lay inside waiting for you. I handed one over to Jess and fixed another onto my bracelet, placing the third one in the small front pocket of our travel bag.

"We can't just leave this one here, can we? I mean, what if someone finds it?" I asked Jess as if she had all the answers. She shrugged in response and continued clasping her charm onto her own bracelet. Hearing more noises on the other side of the wall, we booked it to where the pantry should have been and out the door, closing it behind us.

I ran out of the pantry full speed and ended up in the kitchen next to the still running dishwasher, just in time to see Katiyah walk through the entry. Before I could say anything, I turned around and pushed Jess and the pack back into the pantry, coughing loudly to cover her protests.

"Fancy meeting you here, in my house, Katiyah," I said so Jess could hear me.

At Kat's name, Jess' movements stiffened. I wasn't sure whether I should smile or growl, but I was sure of one thing—the uneasiness in my tummy at these random encounters with the girl who stood across from me in my kitchen was growing.

Katiyah was so consumed with the anger coming out of her ears that she completely missed the noises coming from the pantry. "I have been looking all over for you! Where have you been?" Kat said through clenched teeth.

"What do you mean?" I responded, forcing my heart rate to calm to keep my voice level and dry.

"I came here to check on you after 4th period, and you were NOT here. I even asked Pops, not that asking him anything will actually change the outcome, but still, I ASKED HIM." Kat was exploding with anger at my nonchalant response to her apparently eventful day.

Feeling as though her head might actually explode, I moved around the kitchen island to take a seat in one of the bar stools. I would not give her the satisfaction of bending to her anger, and I could tell that was all she wanted.

"I checked the gardens, the nurse's office, the gym. Hell, I even checked that creepy camera studio you are so intrigued by. You were in none of those places. I mean, what is your deal?" Kat finished with exasperation on her face.

I looked her in the eye and saw something I wasn't prepared to see. Oceans of anger rippling through her. She was angry about something far bigger than not being able to find me. As she noticed my gaze, she relaxed, and her eyes changed.

The tides within those seemingly hardened eyes soothed and calmed under my stare.

Focused on what I had just seen and not the conversation at hand, I said, "What is it that is so important that you felt so adamantly about stalking my life today?" There was venom dripping from every word. I held her gaze as she realized that I was not about to bend to her anger.

She looked at the floor. "Sorry, I was... I was concerned that's all. I mean, you did hit your head pretty hard on that door and I felt a little guilty about it."

Lie. I could spot a lie a mile away. Even Jess knew not to lie to me, no matter how small. I felt my cheeks warm at the realization that there was something that she was trying to hide from me, or as she thought from her best friend. Remembering Jess in the pantry, I made a quick decision to lock that information away for another time. I chose a calmer tone and sweeter answer when I responded to her blatant lie.

"We must have just missed each other. I didn't even know you were looking for me until I got here. I did stop in the gardens, and I took a stroll around the studio, did you know they have a park over there? I wasn't in a rush to be bored in this house with nothing but my thoughts." I raised my hands and let them fall slowly, encompassing the vision of the place I once called home and hoping she got the full emotion of being stuck in a house that reminded you of anything but what it should be. I wasn't sure Star of V felt this way, but it was a bet I was willing to take judging by how gloomy the whole house felt. I felt like this was a relatable statement. I was uncomfortable with the state of things, and I had only been here for a couple hours.

Kat took the bait, and I saw her shoulder slack slightly. Either she was happy I didn't press her on the lie, or she felt like I was telling the truth. Either way, we changed the subject, and she sat down in the stool next to me to catch up on the drama at school like nothing had just happened between us.

"So, Susan is up to her antics again," Kat started telling me about her day. I was assuming she meant that Susan started a rumor about my trip to the nurse. "Oh, right. What did she say now?"

Kat leaned in to give the details. "She asked coach if she could challenge for your spot. Said since you might have a concussion that the team is gonna need someone to keep the morale up while you're out. I looked over and asked, who said she was even gonna be out? She's just at home for the day; you want to be captain for the day? Sheesh! Coach didn't fall for it, though. So desperate! That girl is always scheming for your spot. It's crazy!" She finished with a smug smile, I guessed at the fact that she still couldn't get my spot.

My spot? I trained my face not to look surprised. I'm captain here? I just expected Susan to be a rumor starter here too; I didn't realize she might be something completely different. Although it would be hilarious to see 'little miss perfect—smarter than the rest—rumor mill' Susan on a basketball court. I would have to save that for another time.

"That's what she gets. Coach sees her backstabbing ways. It's not a secret." I smiled back, enjoying the conversation far more than I should have. I was getting lost in this place and forgetting why I was here.

As we talked, Snikkers jumped up onto my lap and began to purr and yowl for more food. "You're hungry again?" I said to her cocking my head to the side in curiosity.

Kat stood and made her way to the pantry. "Oh, she's always hungry, I'll grab the food."

Finally remembering what, or rather who, was in the closet, I stood up and ran to the pantry. "Oh no, it's okay. I think we're out anyway." I made it to the pantry door at the same time as Kat, but Snikkers beat us both there, batting the door open and exposing my guest that was crouched in the shadows hiding until it was time to go.

"OMG, WHAT? Who? Star, run!" Katiyah turned to grab me and head for the door, but I stopped her.

"No, it's okay. I know her," I said to Kat, looking her in the eyes and holding her gaze until she calmed down.

Kat was on her toes in a stance I had only seen one other person dawn so comfortably. Jess, noticing it too, was drawn out of the pantry to peer into the eyes of her opponent falling into her own fighting stance. Seeing Jess in the light took the edge off the situation, only slightly. Recognition flooded Kat, and her expression changed from one of pure venom and hatred to awe and discomfort.

Kat had clearly met the person standing in front of her before, great problem number 2.

"You're hiding a princess in your kitchen pantry?" Kat said, letting her fighting stance fall away. "Is that why you are being so jumpy?" She said with a smirk and too much tranquility for it to be believable.

Something happened here, and neither Jess nor I had a clue what it was. We did not have the upper hand on this one. My stomach sunk with the clarity.

"I, um, I'm actually not sure," I said, squinting as if trying to remember what was happening and taking in the body language Kat was giving off. What did she know? I wondered. We had to get her out of this house and off the trail so we could get to the real journey that would soon follow. "I mean, she was here waiting for me when I got here. I couldn't remember anything about yesterday or the last couple actually, but she seems to be okay. I mean, I don't think she's here to hurt me," I said, touching my forehead as if I had just had a shooting pain and needed some attention. I turned to face Jess to make sure we were on the same page. She picked up on what I was putting down without hesitation. I wondered if she felt the connection between her and Kat as well.

"I believe your friend here should be able to answer any questions you have." Jess raised one eyebrow like she had seen the princess do one tv just minutes ago. Even her voice was smooth and demanding like the princess' when she spoke. I was shocked. I looked to Kat to see if she was buying it. Judging by the now straight back and the surprise that came across her face, she was. Jess was drawing her out, and she didn't even know it. "I am in a hurry. I don't have time to doddle or for you to lie to me." Jess stepped in closely, calling Kat's Bluff.

"I don't know what you are talking about," Kat said in a shaky voice, so small I would not have imagined it could come from the snooty, aggressive girl that stood before me just a minute ago. So, she did know something about us being here then, didn't she? Judging by the way her first expression changed so quickly, she thought no one else knew.

"Oh, yes, you do, and you are going to share it with us. On our way back to London," Jess said, thinking quick on her feet and looking to me for confirmation.

Slicers

I tried to give a short nod of encouragement. That tiny movement gave us away completely. That or trying to get her back to London did. Either way, Kat saw through our makeshift plan and headed for the door.

Backing away towards the door slowly, she said, "I don't know anything about what you're talking about, I'm not going anywhere with you, and you can't make me. Star, why are you so calm?" She looked from me to Jess and then at our bracelets. She stopped mid-step as realization flowed over her. She looked up at me again and then turned to run, almost escaping through the door when Jess swooped in and grabbed her. I came in close and looked at her own wrist to see a bracelet that was identical to the one Jess now wore. Dead giveaway that she was not the Princess of V.

I looked from my best friend to the best friend of my doppelganger. The tension between them was suffocating. I couldn't help myself, and before I knew it, I was pushing between them. "Okay, stop it," I said, grabbing Kat by the arm and pulling her back into the kitchen. Kat let me pull her in and looked me in my eyes—like really looked at me for the first time since she walked into the kitchen.

"You are not the Star that I know and love. You are not my Best Friend at all. So, who are you? Where is she?" Kat said in shock and backed away as far into the corner of the kitchen as possible. She leaned in from where she now stood to investigate further, not believing her own proclamation. "Are you?" She looked at me with disgust that ran so deep and strong it rocked me back on my heels.

Confidence. I urged myself forward, trying to think of something to clean up the mess we just made. I had to be sure to proceed with confidence. Otherwise, this could go very badly. What did that book we were reading in class with the laws say? That's right say less than necessary. Choosing to give her just enough information to be believable and hope she thought I was telling her the truth but not too much that she would see through it and poke holes.

"No, I am not the Star you know, and she is not royalty. However, we are on our way to help clear up some unanswered questions and gather some information. This trip is also to help with some things your friend may have already gotten herself into. My guess is she is already well on her way to search for herself. We are losing time sitting here arguing about who is who and what is what. We have to go. I tried to keep you out of this, but since you were so adamant about finding me, here you are in the thick of it all." I spoke as fluently and as even as I could muster while putting all my energy into Kat understanding how important this was about to be without actually telling her all the details. As I finished, I felt Jess spring into action behind me, grabbing our pack and making sure she was in a good place to grab Kat if she tried to run again.

"Wait. What?" Kat grabbed my arm. I was happy to see that my efforts of emotions were not lost upon her. "What is she mixed up in? I told that girl not to go looking. Why does it have to be at the worlds fest! I told her to stay away from there specifically! Charlie told her too! OMG!" Kat was hyperventilating as she continued her rant. The hard trained ready-for-action girl who stepped into this kitchen was a mess of mixed emotions flowing through her without a second thought—anger, sadness, nervousness, fear, joy, and back to sadness. I wasn't sure whether to push her down or give her a hug. Maybe my initial observation was wrong about Katiyah. Maybe she really did care about Star. Maybe I was just nervous about confiding important information in someone other than Jess. It was then that I heard what she actually said. It was a delayed reaction for sure. What made her so far on edge and so cool in our earlier convo. Jess had already stopped moving behind me and was making a beeline to Kat to get on with the interrogation.

"What did you just say?" Jess rushed in for the up close and personal examination of what Kat was trying to hide in her emotions. Kat had already understood her mistake, and her face was showing how upset she was about it.

"I, um, it's nothing really. I mean, we have had conversations about the worlds fest, of course. Everyone is talking about it." She looked to see if we were buying it. Not a chance. "I mean Charlie was working on something to enter. He told us it was dangerous, so many projects that are untested and hypothetical, so many different backgrounds entering it. He said it was gonna be trouble. He told us not to be anywhere near there." She looked at me pleadingly. Now, that I believed, but that wasn't what was keeping Kat from the Worlds fest.

"I don't believe for one minute that you would not go to something that you were interested in because Charlie told you not to," Jess chimed in before I could confirm my thoughts. She couldn't tell her we listened as she yelled at Charlie hours ago when she came looking for me the first time. I knew she must be used to people believing her lie because her face was flushed with anger and surprise.

"Not to mention, no one said we were going to the world's fest," I added.

"I knew if she kept digging and looking for answers, she would find herself mixed up with some bad stuff or on the wrong side of some bad people. I told her it could get us all in trouble, and that sooner than later, someone would start looking at us instead. Now here you are standing in her kitchen, with her nowhere to be found. Every kind of person will be at that festival with all kinds of intentions. I think my feelings to stay away were spot on, regardless of how I feel about Charlie." Kat snarled out the last sentence. Jess cringed.

I could see the steam coming from Kat's ears; she was so upset. I wasn't sure if it was for the loss of her friend, though. The first part was defiantly a lie; but the last part... the distant glaze of her eyes, the downward turn of her lips and the emphasis she put on certain words pertaining to Star of V, showed me that there was more truth in her explanation than she wanted to share. She felt bad about whatever was happening to this family. Something about that gnawed at me. I also found out some new information about what was going on.

"What happened? I mean, what did she go looking for?" I asked slowly, fearful of what the answer would be.

Looking both me and Jess over as if we had several heads each, she said, "So you guys don't know what happened to this family? Who she might be looking for or where she might have gone?"

My confusion deepened.

I reached out to remove her hand from my arm softly, and as I did so, I took her hand in mine. I felt Kat tense under my touch. I once knew someone who shied away from my touch in this way, and as Jess stood next to me now incapable of that previously normal movement, I beamed. Only for a slight second, though, saddened at the realization that my double's best friend had not grown into the same confidence.

"Let's sit so you can tell us what happened," I said, guiding her over to the kitchen Island. Katiyah looked at me, first with confusion, then with a sharp glare of understanding at the pity in my eyes. She allowed me to lead her over to the stool, but her guarded actions were showing me more and more that Kat knew more than she led on and not just about the normal things going on in this dimension, either.

I didn't even realize that Star wasn't here or to ask where she could have been. Charlie thought I was her, the teachers thought I was her, and even her best friend thought I was her. So, she must have been here this morning, right? Was it even possible for us to be in the same dimension at the same time? Was she okay? What happened here? And where was her own Gran to show her the way? I filed the questions in my head away to be sure to ask Suzie later when I had more time, hoping I didn't forget. I'm sure she will know.

"I..." I looked over to Jess for some sort of signal on what we should ask her first. Telling her we didn't know anything might alert her as to how much of the story we were unaware of, yet it seemed almost wrong to lie to her now. With a slow shrug, Jess gave confirmation that she was as lost as I was on where to start.

"So, you don't know," she stated definitively as horror replaced Kat's normally sarcastic face. Poor Kat. I know how I would feel with a lost Jess, especially in a place I told her not to go. At the thought, my Seraphina's stone began to hum and shine bright at my wrist. It drew in everyone's attention, and Kat reached for it. I snatched away before I even thought about it, missing Kat's grasp by less than an inch.

"How did you get Star's stones? And if you have them, how is she traveling?" Kats questions came flooding.

"THESE are Mine!" I said, cradling my wrist into my chest and enclosing my bracelet into a tight hold.

Jess swiftly stepped between Kat and I, her defenses kicking into place with razor-sharp precision.

"Why do you have her stones?" Kat asked again, gritting her teeth.

"I just told you that I don't. These stones are mine. They may look alike, that's normal. We're the same, a lot of things about us are exactly that. The same. Calm down!" I said more to myself than to the room. My skin was starting to boil with being accused of taking someone else's things. This hit me a little harder than necessary since I did take someone else's things. Gran's.

"That's not how it works. Seraphina's stones are different," Kat said with her guard still up, ready to pounce.

"Look!" I pointed first to her wrist then to Jess'. Both sported their own charm bracelets. "Almost identical, two different dimensions, two completely different people, two separate origins. No red flag, no alarm, and no third degree.

So why would you assume that mine are stolen?" I said, defending myself and justifying my thoughts at the same time.

"You have no idea what is going on, do you?" Kat's stance slacked. Bad move. Something in her aura shifted, and I could feel her take the edge that she had the upper hand again. I didn't move, and neither did Jess.

"Depends on which topic we are considering at the moment. I have plenty of ideas. I know plenty of things. I just don't know what exactly you are implying at this current moment, and it's pretty annoying," I noted, fury in my eyes and growing by the second. I turned and sat back on my stool again, focusing on the action to calm myself enough to throw her off my trail. I was actually angry with this game and annoyed that she continued to play it as though both the world and her best friend weren't at stake.

Kat felt it. She looked up to see I was as serious as a heart attack and backed off just enough to let the hot air out of the room.

"Anyone who is from a dimension where the ways of a Slider are known and studied is fluent in the history of the King Heritage. What you just tried to justify is nowhere close to how Seraphina's stones work. There are only a few places in any dimension that these stones can be found. Well, true stones of Seraphina's blessing that is. Some were born massive and then broken into smaller pieces to share like the identical ones your friend and I now wear..." As she said this, she walked over and fitted her stone in perfectly with the one dangling from Jess' bracelet. "...and others were microscopic in comparison, receiving the full blessing and being of great power. Those stones were only large enough to create one jewel." She looked at me with anger in her eyes as her rage was swiftly returning. "Now, I will ask you one more time. WHY do you have Star's stones?"

I pushed Jess out of the way and looked Kat in the eyes.

"I have said it already, but maybe you didn't hear me. These Do Not belong to the Star of the Various Dimension. I can promise you that." The confidence in my declaration radiated off me like a hot pocket. I was not going to give this girl any reason to think that I would even participate in an activity that would leave someone I cared for, someone that was essentially me, in distress. I also would not give her the inkling that she would be able to force me to back down. I remembered the first time my Grandmother showed me her charms and the stories she told. At the thought of Gran and my emphasis of them not being stolen, my Seraphina's stones shone brighter still. In spite of herself, Kat looked down at the stones now illuminating the Kitchen with a pale Gold light. Although she didn't want to, Kat believed the stones. She let off just a little more.

"If those aren't Star's, then the only other person..." she stopped short of finishing her sentence, realization draining the color from her face. Katiyah's entire attitude shifted. "This can't be good!" She said with exasperation, throwing her hands in the air. Whatever clarification she got from putting two and two together made her a true believer of our story. I looked over to Jess, who was checking her watch.

"We have to go," she said to me, plucking me from my attack mode to coax me towards the door and grabbing her pack once more.

"Well, we can't just leave her here now! She knows too much to be blubbering to anyone around here of what's happening." I skidded to a halt in her hold and turned to face her so she could see the conflict in my eyes. "Let's not forget she just found out that her Best friend is missing. How do you think she feels?" I asked the question, but I already knew the answer.

Jess looked me square in the face, setting a large dose of goosebumps down my spine. "I would be enraged, and not that hot rage that everyone can see, but the white rage that is the calm before the destruction that people don't notice coming. I would look for you. I would hunt down anyone who thought to harm you and if you ran away from me by yourself without so much as a note to tell me you were okay, if you ran of your own free will without me. Well, when I found you, after I cried all the tears I could muster and hugged the breath out of you with all my might, I would try to break your legs so you can never leave me again." As her lip quivered with intensity, she raised her eyebrows and looked over to Kat to make sure she understood the message she was trying to provide to anyone who was thinking of laying a finger on her best friend. Kat had no problem believing that Jess meant every word of it and set on her way backing toward the exit. Jess caught her by the elbow.

"Now, where do you think you're running off to in such a hurry?" Jess chided and turned to me. "Does this seem like someone who is having trouble gripping her emotions because her friend is missing, and whatever else she just discovered with her 'can't be good' aha moment?" Jess looked disgusted.

"I was just... I mean, you guys don't really need me getting in your way. I can keep quiet; I'll just go home and watch the Worlds on TV like the rest of the population. No need to make a big deal." Kat was squirming under Jess' force with no luck. "You guys seem much better prepared to handle this than me. I'm sure you will bring her back without a hair on her head out of place!" She tried to coax Jess, with obviously no clue who she was dealing with, and judging by the look on Jess' face at her efforts, she had no chance.

As the girls in front of me began to struggle on, well, as Kat struggled on, I tried to think of our next move. She sure was in a hurry to get out of here for something—that I agreed with Jess on. She also knew far more than we did about several things, although she tried to convince us otherwise. I had a sure feeling in my gut that she knew how to get to where we needed to go, with far more uncommon information than she was sharing, and I knew for certain she had no intention of watching 'The Worlds' on TV.

"So, you DON'T want to find your best friend then? You DON'T want to figure out what's happening and make sure she is okay? You aren't concerned at all?" I asked, getting close enough to Kat that I could feel her breath on my face as I shoved her against the island. "Or, do you mean to tell me that you know something about what's going on, and you're rushing off without us to confirm what you just figured out so you can find her before we do?" I poked Kat in the chest. That poke sent her roaring like a hornet stuck in a coke can. It also gave away her position; she knew something, and she wasn't telling. "Welp, you should thank your lucky knee jerk reactions, 'cause now you have no choice, you're going with us, sweetie pie." I smiled sweetly and put on my best southern bell accent.

Jess snorted. "Trying too hard," she chided in a low grumble over her shoulder, dropping her grip on Kat. "You don't sound anything like a cowgirl. Just give up the act, and let's go." Leave it to Jess to be more concerned with my fake accent than the issue at hand. I looked over at Jess with a grin.

"That was my southern belle, not cowgirl. Anyway, what would make you think now is a fine time to critique my accents? I've been working on them for months, and you haven't said anything, NOW you choose to tell me I don't sound authentic?" I crossed my arms with a huff of internal laughter and turned back to Kat, who was completely freaked out by our side conversation and weighing her options on whether she would make it to the door and out of the house before we caught her. That had to be Jess' plan all along. I was glad she came to her senses with a hard no. I wasn't the basketball champ back home, but I did have one with me, and all those track practices would come in handy if she tried to bolt now.

Jess locked her hand around Kat's forearm again and grabbed her pack with the other hand. "Okay, so, what's our best option for getting all the way to this festival from San Diego? Is this still considered San Diego?" Jess turned to Kat to ask her and found her picking her nails. Lips sealed. She would come if she was forced, but she was not about to help us in any way, that was obvious. I knew she was a valuable source of information, and I knew if I tried to pry, it would come with a price. So, I motioned for Jess to set down the pack and went to the refrigerator.

"Water, juice, cookies, snacks?' I offered, looking for all of them but only finding juice and cookies. No healthy snacks had been in this house for a while as I could tell, and the water looked like it was coming out of the faucet if you were drinking it. I wondered briefly if the water here was as compromised as it was back home. With all the 'natural' stuff they had here in this dimension, I doubted it. Giving them both a juice pouch and cookies, I took a seat back at the barstool and motioned for them both to sit back down.

Kat read into my plan to change the tone of this trip immediately and rearranged her previously angry face with a somber bored one, though I could tell it was a fight within herself to keep it that way.

"Look, Kat. You have already figured out that we know less than what we should about a lot of things here in the V. It would be really helpful if we could work together to get to Star before something bad actually does happen. I saw your face when we discussed the World of Worlds festival. I'm not sure what's going on there, but I know you have some idea. If that is where Star is searching, something bad will happen to her, and you know it. We can't let that happen. So, you do have options. You could come with us and be a part of the team that finds her before it's too late and saves the day. Or you can be dragged with us, and with all our unanswered questions and bumbling through this path, we may not reach her in time, and you may get there to see something truly bad happen to your best friend. You already know how we feel about the best friend part of our lives, but how strongly do you feel about it? Is it enough for you to know we are telling the truth and help us save her, or are you okay with leaving it to us and something worse happening?" I finished my sales pitch with pride. I couldn't believe I had come up with such a great speech. Until I looked over and saw that although there was a turmoil spinning within Kat, her face read that she had other things in mind.

"Oh, I will go with you to Worlds. I will find my best friend, and I will save her. I can help you, and I might, but only under my terms and my conditions. One condition specifically," Kat said, crossing her arms and plastering a smirk that was so slimy across her face that I knew we were going to regret this later.

I looked to Jess to see if she was thinking the same. Jess' face was red with outrage; at my speech, at Kat, and mostly at the fact that I was even being nice to her and giving her options. Honestly, what choice did we have? We were nowhere near accustomed to the world around us, and we definitely didn't know about any other ones. I cleared my throat at Jess to alert her that we could see her reactions written on her face. Blushing, she finally calmed down enough to weigh our options beside me, shifting her weight as she did so.

My curiosity got the best of my patience, and I blurted at Kat before Jess could change my mind, "Well, let's have it then? What are the conditions?" The minute the words left my lips, I knew that I had made a mistake. I gave Kat too much power in this fight, and she would use all of it like it was nothing of importance.

"First of all, you will keep your hands to yourself." She turned and looked at Jess to ensure she knew who she was really talking to. "I mean, if you touch me ONE TIME from here on out, the deal is off. Got it?" She sat back a bit to see the rise in Jess she was hoping for be brandished right across her face. "Next, we share information, so I want to know everything you know. Starting with Star's last whereabouts. And finally, this will be a favor for a favor, so I will help you; but eventually, I will need you to help me. I can't tell you when because I don't know, but when I ask, you can't refuse." Her grin deepened and knocked me off my normally steady guard. She knew she would need something, and she knew we would refuse if she didn't make this deal first. My stomach churned. This was becoming more and more of the games I hated and less of the fun factfinding ones I played with Gran. I looked at Jess for confirmation. She always knew what to do in a game; maybe she had something for this? A strategy or something. Jess was shaking her head hard. I couldn't help but feel like Kat knew exactly what favor she would need in the end; I knew what I would need in the end too. Information. I would need information about Sliders culture, about Slicers, about the Various Dimension, about the people around me, about myself.

I would need an awful lot of information. It seemed the only way to get it was to play the game that Katiyah had set in front of us.

"I will not commit a crime to help you. I have morals. I will not be a part of theft, and I will not murder anyone." I paused to think about anything else I wouldn't do before finishing my own terms. "We will share our information with you, as long as we feel like the information you are sharing with us is truthful and valid. I know that's hard for you." I rolled my eyes hard so she could see that I was on to her. "When the time comes, unless there is something much more imperative, like making sure the world doesn't..." I stopped. I wouldn't tell her anything until the deal was made, and I would only be sharing information pertaining to her situation for that matter. She didn't need to know we were trying to save the entire system from combustion. "Something more lifethreatening," I inserted instead. "I will not refuse your request for a favor... but I do have the right to request one alternative if I feel your request will do me some sort of harm. Deal?" I stuck out my hand hard, and Jess smacked it down out of the air.

"I don't think so," Jess said, turning to me with fire in her eyes. I shied away from her to alert her that she was scaring me. "You don't make deals with people we aren't sure have your best interest at hand. Hell, you don't make deals like this with anyone! Don't you see how your stones flare up when you do things like that? When you tell the truth, when you lie, when you are passionate, every time you do something major like this, they flare up, locking you into whatever you're agreeing to, just like right now." She pointed to the dim gold glow at my wrist. I hadn't even noticed. Being so hellbent on gaining her help and information, I neglected the key components around me. I looked at the ground. Jess was always there to make sure I didn't give all of myself away. She would rather bear the burden every time if it meant I didn't have to. I looked up at her now.

"You think I'm going to let you do it?" I said with tears in my eyes. I wasn't even sure why I was crying. Jess grabbed me by both shoulders.

"Now is not the time to be sappy or courageous, now is the time to play to your strengths. If she needs something, chances are, I would be a better person to help unless she wanted someone to cry for her or talk her to death." She rolled her eyes, knowing her words would come back to bite her later. "I will do it, but you aren't made for this kind of thing, Starla. Play to your strengths," she said with total conviction, stepping in front of me with her hand outstretched to seal the deal I was about to make.

Kat, with excitement in her eyes that I was going to bind a deal, missed the movement of Jess' position. Kat tried to pull her hand away so as to make a gesture that she didn't want the deal with Jess, but Jess' movement was too swift, and she caught Kat's outstretched hand before she could pull away. The matching Seraphina's stones sizzled a hot flaming glow of orange under their enclosed hands, and before they were done, there was a matching burn around their wrists sealing the deal.

"That's not..." Kat started in disbelief. "I wasn't making the deal with... No, I need her help!" Kat whined under the pain of the forming burn.

Jess knew that Kat wanted to make the deal with me all along. She had "played to her strengths." She knew Kat was trying to pull a fast one, 'why not do it first?' I beamed at Jess through still watery eyes. She was now slouching in her chair, finishing her juice pouch like she was oblivious to what had just transpired. Pure Selflessness. I loved that about her.

Bonnie Baraka

I tried to hide my excitement over the look of horror now plastered on Kat's face as I pulled the map from our pack and began to find our way to the World of Worlds Festival in London.

"To answer your question, yes, it looks like we are still in San Diego, New Fornia." I winked at Jess and spread the map out in front of us to see where we needed to go. Kat hadn't moved; she was caught in a look of despair mixed with pure terror at what she had just done.

"Well, since you tricked me into helping you, I should tell you two things are clear to me just by meeting you. You are much stronger than my Star, and you have no clue what you are doing with all that power." She laughed right in my face at her own evaluation. It was a wicked and chilling laugh that made the hairs on my forearm stand up and do a little dance. Great, she was a smart ass. I rolled my eyes and turned away so as not to show her that her words could get to me.

Turning back to the map, I asked the room, "So where does that leave us on getting halfway across the world." I looked up to see Kat was confused.

"It's not that far," she said with a look of wonder in her eyes. "How far is London from where you live in your dimension?" She still hadn't figured out where we came from.

"I think it's like a 2- or 3-day trip depending on how you travel," I said, bending over to look at the map in front of me. Nothing was in the place; I remembered studying it in geography class. Go figure. There were small amounts of water that separated the continents, and I was uncomfortable with it.

"We could probably get there in a couple hours if we fly," Kat said to no one in particular. I looked up at Jess. Then back at Kat.

"You think TSA is going to let Princess Tina just walk through with no bodyguards and fly to London. When she's actually already supposed to be there?" I scrunched my nose, pointing out all the flaws in this plan.

"That could actually work in our favor." Kat jumped up in a newfound excitement. Jess jumped up too, in surprise at the change in tone coming from Kat. I giggled.

"Well, this better be good. We don't have all night, and I am now on edge in anticipation," Jess retorted, rolling her eyes with sarcasm.

"It's gonna take some acting skills from you, though. Maybe we should come up with another plan. I don't think you can pull it off," Kat said, her grin of pure joy turning cold as she looked over at Jess. My heart tugged slightly when I looked at Jess, even though I had no clue what the plan was going to be. I knew it was gonna suck for her.

"Just tell us already!" I could see that Jess was at the edge of anger but working hard to keep it in check.

"Well, if we show up dressed accordingly, I'm sure we could trick them into thinking that Jess actually is Princess Tina on a very secret trip to see another project that is from right here in San Diego." Kat shrugged and added, "You fooled me on the first encounter." She looked Jess over with a hint of disgust. "That is, until I took in your hair close and bare face." We must have looked like we were confused about the plan as Kat continued, "Everyone here knows about Charlie's project, and no one knows he stopped working on it. We could just tell them that it was too big to move and that she had to come and see it; so, no one was aware, she couldn't take the royal jet. We could probably get them to lend us one of theirs." Kat's wheels were still spinning with every passing second.

This plan was getting more intricate as she spoke. I was measuring the pitfalls and judging what we would need when I looked over to see what Jess would contribute. Jess was paralyzed in her chair. She was unmoving; it even looked like she was unbreathing. Jess would not only have to pretend to be Princess Tina; she would have to act like Tina. She would have to be a girly girl and a damn good one at that. She would have to speak confidently—that she could do, I knew. The problem was she would have to play the part that she was clearly struggling with—confidence in her womanhood. Being a girl is something far from what she was accustomed to, let alone comfortable with. Now she would have to not only be a girl that was more than comfortable with herself, but that was so comfortable that she unconsciously ushered others into that comfort zone as well. Jess would have to unlearn everything she taught herself over the past ten years about herself in a matter of hours. She would have to figure this out all while convincing others that she was, in fact, a princess. Lord help us.

Bonnie Baraka

I reached out and grabbed her hand. As our fingers locked, our bracelets clanked together, and sparks flew from them.

"Interesting," I heard Kat mumble from behind us. I didn't have time to turn around and ask what she meant. I was too focused on comforting Jess and making sure she was up to the task. This would be a lot for anyone, let alone someone in Jess' situation.

"If you don't think you are up to it, it's okay," I offered, immediately coming to Jess' emotional defense. "We will find another way to get there if we need to, maybe we can rent a car and drive or something. Or sneak onto one of the boats that go that far. There are options. We can try all of them if we need to," I said with confidence, even though I was completely unsure what our other options would be if we didn't take this one. I had to give it to Kat; this was a plan that could work. I just wished it didn't involve breaking my best friend's spirit in the process.

She looked up at me with pleading eyes. "What other choice do we really have? We can't drive to London... and even if we could, we are in a time crunch, remember? No one takes trains anymore; they are almost extinct. Plus, if they think I am her and we do try to travel on a train... think of the field day the press will have when they spot us?" She put her head down in frustration.

I sat back, analyzing the problem ahead. We would need to change clothes, find a ride to the airport, and we would need to convince them that Jess was royalty. I wondered how much interaction she would actually have to make. I turned my head slightly.

"Don't you go to getting any good ideas!" Jess said next to me, seeing my wheels turning.

"Well, I mean. It is very risky, and you can always say no; BUT if we go in before you and we make it seem like you are trying to be very private and that we need to stay under wraps... you may not have to speak to anyone while we are there. The pilot won't be paying attention in the plane; there are like... doors and stuff in between them, so we should be okay." I looked at her palms up and was as open as possible with what I was thinking we should do. She gave me a sideways glare that said this was the worst idea she had heard in years.

I nodded in agreeance and asked, "Do you have a better one?" She shook her head and looked like she might vomit. "Alright, then it's settled." I stood and grabbed the pack from Jess, turning for the stairs to go back to my—or Star's— room. "Kat get the airport on the phone, sound as professional as possible when you explain what is going on. You know the most about the actual project, so you may be able to drop some SMALL hints as to what's going on without giving away the whole thing. Remember, we can't have them running to a news outlet when we leave since there is, in fact, no project here for them to find." I looked at Kat to make sure she understood her job. She nodded in agreeance and went up the stairs without another word. I turned to look at Jess, who had not left her seat. She picked up my half-empty juice pouch and finished it off like this would be her last meal as herself or something. Part of me wanted to laugh at the spectacle she was presenting. The other half felt for her. I chose a mix between the two and used a seductively soft tone to lure her out of her chair.

"Jess, we have to go. We have plenty to do and truly little time. You will do great, just think of it as a game. You watched the tape, now you have to practice, then when we get to the field, it will be game time." I think my analogy made her sicker.

"I'm fine, Starla, just give me a minute to myself. Go on up; I'll be there in a minute," Jess said, looking at the juice pouch instead of me.

I frowned. I knew this was a hard situation, but there wasn't anything that we didn't share. So why was she now requesting time alone? I put my hand on my hip, and I was about to give her a piece of my mind when Kat called me to come up and firm up details. I turned to go with one last look at Jess; she looked miserable.

When I got to the top of the stairs, Kat was cheesing at me. "They bought it!" She said with her hand over the receiver. "I just need you to get on here and pretend to be the Princess. Over the phone, I'm sure they won't be able to tell the difference, and you kind of have a melodic tone, so they probably won't say anyway. Confirm our travel for this evening; let's say 10 p.m., that will give us some time with pouty pants and say that someone will be to check you in and all that jazz." She was so excited that her plan was working that I almost didn't recognize the happy girl standing in front of me. This must be what she was like with her Star. Clearing my throat, I took the phone and gave all the necessary details for our travel. They never even asked who I was. Golden.

Bonnie Baraka

I looked over at Kat and added, "Please, also arrange for a car service to retrieve my party." Without hesitation, I received a time for pick up and a request for any other accommodations I may need. "Where will my location be at the time of service?" I looked over-anxious at Kat, repeating the question the airline receptionist had asked. Kat coached me through some breathing and then mouthed "The TV Studio." Perfect, the place where I had no control over my vibrations. "Are you familiar with 'Studios of Tomorrow'?" I inquired. They were. I finished the call, setting up our travel.

As I hung up, I looked at Kat, who was smiling uncontrollably. Her smile was addictive, vibrant even. The next thing I knew, we were jumping up and down on the bed in between fits of giggles when Jess walked in and caught us by surprise.

"So, everything is set then," Jess remarked with the worst attitude I had ever seen her unleash.

"Yeah, we're set for travel in a couple hours, AND they are going to come and pick us up! How awesome is that!?" I said, feeling both anxious and as calm as I had felt all day. I looked over to see that Jess did not share my delight and paused mid-jump to figure out what the problem was. I plopped down on the bed and stood up to go to Jess. Kat did the same, going over to the closet to find her 'better-suited attire.'

"What's wrong?" I asked, scrunching my face.

"What's wrong?" Jess was not a happy camper. "How can you even ask that? You should know what's wrong. Instead of being supportive and letting me wrap my head around this, you're up here making new best friends and forgetting all about me sitting down in the kitchen by myself." She rolled her eyes at me and went to the closet, snatching the shirt right out of Kat's hands. "I can figure it out on my own, Thanks," she said with a snarl.

I stood planted to my place right there next to the bed. I couldn't believe she would take that tone with me or think I would replace her with someone I didn't trust and barely even knew.

"You TOLD me to leave you down there! You said you needed a minute to yourself! What did you expect me to do?" I said to her, frustration coming out of my ears. Kat slid past us both and sat on the bed watching the show like a soap opera.

"I was down there for longer than a minute, Starla. Hell, longer than 30 minutes! Then I stood in the hall and listened to you two in here having a blast while YOUR SUPPOSED BEST FRIEND was downstairs by herself, going through it." Jess was heaping mad.

I could feel the heat waft from her like an oven. Had it really been that long? Her face was red, and her hands were shaking. I was wondering how she was resisting the urge to punch something when she did just that. She punched the closet door. Kat jumped next up to me, but I didn't dare look over to her. I inched in closer to comfort my friend. Hoping this was just misplaced anxiousness for the next steps in this crazy plan.

"I didn't realize it had been that long. I just got off the phone with the airport, and everything went really well. I was so excited they bought my impression of the princess that we celebrated," I said in a much softer tone, putting my hand on her shoulder. She shrugged it off. I was getting annoyed at her attitude. "Look, I didn't want to leave you down there in the first place, but someone had to confirm the stuff Kat was telling them, someone had to make sure we got to where we were needing to go. Remember? This isn't home, Jess, and the longer we doddle, the longer we wallow and get off course, the larger our chances are of not ever going there again. No Pops, no mom, no Trey; we won't be able to see any of them again." I turned to walk away with a scowl hoping my words hit their mark. Clearly, this was the wrong mark. Jess grabbed my arm and spun me around with deathly force.

"Don't you talk to me like I don't know what is at stake here. Don't you think I haven't thought about them every step of the way. I know I told you to go upstairs, and I would meet you, but at what point in our lives have we EVER taken each other at face value? I expected you to come up, but for you not to come back and check on me! That's low; anything could have happened! Charlie doesn't know me here, remember? And then for me to finally feel stable enough to come up to see what was taking you so long to come back and see you in here treating HER like your best friend? You're lucky that door took the beating." She let me go with a push, and I fell back onto the bed. Kat was there before I could look up, hauling me to my feet and turning on Jess to retaliate. I put my arm out in front of her.

Bonnie Baraka

"Leave her," I said, turning back to face Jess. "She's got a thorn up her ass, and it's not gonna go away anytime soon. Plus, we need her to get all of this out before we get in that car, because one explosion like this and we will be discovered for sure."

Jess stuck her tongue out at us, daring Kat to come closer. Kat was in attack mode, and my words didn't change her mind about it. I knew what would weaken Jess' attitude, and it wasn't a fight. We would have to ignore her completely. So, I sat down on the bed and decided I was ready to hear about something other than the uneasiness of the day.

"Come on, Kat." I patted the bed next to me for her to sit down, turning my back to Jess and daring her to move. She looked from Jess to me swiftly and then back again to see if she had gotten any closer. I shook my head at Kat to alert her not to engage. "So, how did you and Star meet anyway?" I put my head in my hands and waited for her to sit and tell me like a child waiting for a bedtime story. Her eyes glazed over in memory. When she finally came over and sat down on the bed to tell a story, I could see she was happy to remember.

K at sat on the bed with a sigh. "Well, Star and I met in third grade. I was the new girl. I literally had rags, nothing else, but to be honest... I don't think that was why people didn't like me." Kat chuckled more to herself than me. "You see, I was from somewhere different. Somewhere they didn't understand and didn't even care to try. As open and understanding as they are here, as humans, when we can't explain, understand, or categorize something, people either marvel at it, or they fear it. I was the latter, I guess. It wasn't like I smelled, or they were mean to me exactly. I just didn't have any friends.

"When I came around, they would move or finish whatever they were doing quickly. So, I took my lunch at the table in the farthest corner of the cafeteria. Every day, I would seek out my corner and sit by myself. I mean, I did have lunch at least; it wasn't very appetizing, though." She put her head down, trying to keep the pain out of her voice as she told the raw truths of what really happened to bring her together with her BFF. "So, one day, Star came and sat with me. The first day, I was mean, I snapped at her and told her to leave. I mean, I was vicious. She, for whatever reason, somehow decided that wasn't my true nature. I don't know how. I mean, even to this day, people say I'm a jerk." She wiped the corner of her eye, where a tear was waiting to fall. "While I just figured the other kids were finally bored and brave enough to make a spectacle of me... I had been bullied before. I knew how things started; that wasn't it at all with Star, and it caught me off guard, I guess." Kat paused her story to look up and see that Jess had tuned in somewhere in the middle. She was still seething but much less angry.

Realizing that this was the goal for Kat's story the entire time, she looked back to me with a wink. Jess noticed the gesture and turned back to the closet, frantically flipping through blouses and skirts that she would have never herself worn but still listening all the same.

"Do you need some help?" I asked sheepishly, praying her anger with me was stale. Not quite.

"I can dress myself, you know, Starla King. It won't be my first time," Jess said, rolling her eyes and selecting a mauve flowing blouse that had sleeves that bowed at the ends.

I looked from the blouse to Jess; it would look perfect on her with some, "black skinny jeans." Both Kat and I said at the same time. I looked over to Kat in surprise; her face was a mirror of mine. We giggled, which sent Jess over the top again.

"I SAID I CAN DO IT MYSELF!" She screamed, slamming the closet door closed and grabbing the skinny jeans out of the top dresser drawer. She stormed out without a second glance. She went to change, I assumed.

I shrugged and said, "She gets like this sometimes. Better to ignore it completely and let her cool off than to keep her riled up. She will never back down. We would literally be in here all-night fighting." I gave her a nod to alert her to continue her story. Kat, who had forgotten the story, completely looked confused when I urged her to continue.

"Oh, right. Well, the second day she came back and sat with me again. This time, I didn't make her leave; I just got up and left. On the third day, she sat down and pretended I wasn't there at all. She didn't speak or smile at me or anything. When she finally looked in my direction, we made eye contact, and I noticed something different there. Kind of like when we made eye contact earlier today in the kitchen, you and me. And might I add, the two of you, your eyes are not the same, although so similar that they could probably fool most people. There is a difference. They make me feel differently if that makes any sense at all." Kat was deep in thought, trying to explain what she was saying, what she was feeling.

I nodded to comfort her, but I had no clue what she was talking about. I thought back to earlier in the kitchen, noticing something in Kat's eyes, but that didn't mean I had anything in mine. Kat, noticing the conflict on my face, tried to put to words the slight differences.

"It's like umm, they are very similar looks for sure," she began. "Both are very protective, very emotionally driven. But one, my Stars particularly, her looks have a sincerity that says she has seen the hot side of the sun and has no problem returning there." Kat shuddered at the recalling. "When we made eye contact. I felt like I met someone who knew what it was like to have to go through things and survive, you know? Like she could relate to the storm inside me." Kat leaned back on her arms to give me a slow glance over. "Your look is completely different to me. You can see the need for understanding in the look you give. There is a storm raging behind those eyes, but it is not because of the experiences you have had but more because of the people you protect. It is more like you are a momma bear, and the ones you love are the cubs. Your eyes give a sense of compassion and protection, where she has experience and knowing. Two sides of the same coin, not like a yin and yang, more like a head and tail, I guess." She sighed, and I looked at her with total confusion.

"I guess that's what happens when you're from different dimensions. Some things are different." I shrugged off the feeling that this was something important.

"Anyway, the fourth day, she did the same... just came and sat quietly. The next day, she was homesick... I found out later, but at the time, I just knew she was not there, and I couldn't understand why I missed her presence at the table where I ignored her. This girl that I was mean to but didn't let that stop her. I didn't even know her name at that point, but I missed her. I sat and thought about her all weekend. So many questions. Like what was her name? Where had she been before she came to sit with me? Why was she so hell-bent on being my friend? Was she even trying to be my friend? Were we in the same class? I had no clue about any of the answers. So that Monday, when she came back and sat down at my table, I asked them. I asked every question I could think of, even the mean ones. She didn't mind, which made me even more curious. I found out; she was THE Starla King. Captain of the basketball team, talk of the town, 'miss perfect' and in the end, I found out that my mom had asked her mom if she would be my friend."

There was a turn for the worst in her story. I could hear it in her voice. She did not like this part. I started to ask her what was so wrong with that when she told me.

"Why couldn't I just make friends on my own? Why did she need to go and interfere? She was always interfering then when we first got here, I mean. Some crap about wanting me to have a good life and be able to survive without her one day." Her words trailed off, and it was evident that she had just made a connection.

I could see the tears forming in her eyes as she snapped back from whatever place her mind had carried her to finish her story.

"I shunned Starla away from my lunch table after that discovery. I wouldn't even let her sit down with me for the next month. It was miserable, actually. I really wanted to be her friend, and I hadn't even known it." Kat kicked at the bedpost softly to distract her from the tears that were creeping down her face. "It's like, going from everything to nothing at all when you finally know what having something feels like, is worse than always having nothing to me. If you always have nothing, that will be what you're used to, and you won't have to worry about craving things because you won't know how they feel anyway. I craved Starla's presence; at that point, I think I craved the presence of any other human that wasn't going to be mean and put me down." At that moment, Jess forcefully pushed the door back on its hinges. Kat looked up surprised. Snapping herself out of her memory and returning to the present, she turned to wipe her face before Jess could see what was happening.

Jess slinked into the room, clearly trying a hand at Princess Tina's walk and failing miserably.

I choked down a laugh. It was not the time to make fun when she was clearly trying so hard.

Kat, on the other hand, did not share my sentiments or see my look of alarm. Her response started as a giggle and then magnified into a witch's cackle. I looked over at Kat, grabbing her arm for her to stop, but it was too late.

Jess was at her throat, "WHAT are you laughing at!?" She was inches from Kat's nose and staring her dead in the eyes. It was a scary yet entrancing vision.

Kat, mortified at the thought of someone this close to her, yet ready for a fight was sitting straight up on the bed now, in an attempt to get to her feet for good leverage.

Jess, looking like a real woman inches from her face, with the stance of a mother protecting her young, stepped back to make room for her power punch.

I turned my head to the side, glimpsing another scene completely. The two were angry with each other, but it reminded me of a dance almost, as if they were going to give each other a butterfly kiss.

"Princesses don't kiss girls Jess; not even hot ones like me." A wicked smile crept across Kat's face. Jess' eyes widened, and she shot back from where she was positioned ready to pounce.

"Why the hell would I kiss you! I was positioning myself for a good headbutt that wouldn't also knock me out! We don't need you coherent to get on the plane!" Jess spit out in a whiny tone. Her face flushed, and I wondered how much of Kat's statement had hit a true mark.

"Well, you look good," I said, trying to change the subject. "How about we work on that walk, though; that will give us away for sure. Princesses also don't have things stuck up their butt." I snickered at my own joke. "Those are teachers."

Both Jess and Kat, amazed that I would make such a vulgar joke about a teacher, laughed at me, and forgot their fight momentarily. There, lighten the energy a little so we can get through this test and on to the next. I was just wondering if the real test was to make sure these two didn't kill each other when they were back at each other's throats arguing. The noise level was spiraling higher and higher, and I was having a major issue trying to hear myself think. I put my two middle fingers between my lips and blew. Jess' and Kat's heads both snapped in my direction on cue.

"That is ABSOLUTELY enough from you two!" I punched out every word to make sure they understood that I meant business. I gave Jess a stern look. "We have less than an hour to get you prepared for the biggest show in your life and get where we need to go. We don't have time for bickering or arguing or punching each other. You got it?" I looked from one girl to the other with a pointed finger.

"If you don't have anything nice to say, SAY NOTHING AT ALL, I MEAN IT!" I spat the last words out. I hated that saying, and I couldn't believe they made me use it on them. I turned around in disgust to bask in the quiet that I knew was fleeting around these two...giving myself a couple of extra seconds to gather my thoughts. I turned back to Jess, ready to give a lesson on grace.

Good God, what had we gotten ourselves into?

"Okay, here we go then," I said with a twinge of guilt on my lips. This should be scary for Jess; this should be weird, and it should most definitely be overwhelming. I remembered the first time I put on Kiki's shoes and tried to walk around the house. I almost fell down the stairs, and Pops had a fit. He was a ball of nerves for the rest of that week. Probably didn't want me to turn out like her. Didn't want me to put on those high heeled shoes and walk right out of his life like she did. I paused, then I walked out of the room... without them. When I looked up, both Kat and Jess were staring at me from the doorway, a look of concern on one face and confusion on the other. I pushed my emotions down and waved them off. Now was definitely not the time to think of Kiki. "So, you know how in order to be good at ball handling, you have to have a good rhythm, like be in tune with the ball?" I asked Jess, knowing she would understand this comparison and calming my tones to a more understanding nature.

She cheesed and nodded. "No one has better ball-handling skills than me?" Jess said, a bit on the cheeky side.

"Right, well, women have their own rhythm, or handles, if you will. They are one with their shoes, one with the sound it makes when it hits the floor, one with themselves as their hips sway when they walk. You don't have to walk far for me to know if you got it or not. Just take one step." I stepped forward with the same sway of the hips I saw the princess do earlier today. Jess' eyes were wide and focused on my hips. Then she looked up, horrified. I sighed; this is what worked for me when Kiki showed me how to do it! Why was this so hard?

Kat sauntered over to where we were standing. "Can I try?" She asked me, then looked to Jess for her approval. Jess wasn't giving it. I cut my eyes at Jess and stepped out of Kat's way.

"Be my guest," I said as I plopped onto the bed.

Kat moved from in front of Jess to behind her; this scared both of us. What was she about to do to my friend? Kat got in real close to Jess' ear, and Jess jumped out of her skin.

"Well, there's your first problem. Relax! It's not going to hurt you or kill you or make you a different person. It's what is already in you. There is nothing to be afraid of, nothing at all." Kat gave these words of encouragement in a thick silky voice that felt of lavender and honey as they rolled off her tongue. Where had I heard that accent before?

At that moment, I realized what was happening, and I felt as if the world had stopped spinning completely. I looked at Jess and saw none of the Jess I knew. Instead, I saw a small, scared girl who had also found her mother's high heels and makeup, prancing around the house until her father came home. Who listened to the whimpers of her mother all night wondering why she was created to be something that would hurt her mother so much and begging to be a boy if not only for her mother's sake? I saw the 12-year-old Jess standing in front of me, arm hanging lazily, trying to explain why it was okay and that I shouldn't make a big deal about it. I saw the Jess that wanted so bad to be a girl but didn't know how... didn't understand that it was even okay to do so. One that felt hiding it and suppressing it would make it go away somehow. I saw such a beautiful, confused, and humble mess. Humble was such a stretch for Jess, but Kat's story had reminded me of one thing—you must look deeper than the surface to see what people truly are. I hadn't been truly looking at Jess for a long while. I had been so focused on my own short-comings and decisions I wasn't myself ready to make. I felt compelled to let her know I saw her, to let her know it would be okay.

I stood up quickly and moved right in front of her before they knew what was happening. I grabbed her by both hands, tears in my eyes, and really looked at her, deep in her eyes. I stepped back, holding her confused gaze.

"It is okay to be the you that is on the inside." I got out over a couple sobs. "Even if only while we are here. You will not hurt anyone by doing so. I see you for who you truly are every day, and sometimes I forget that you don't. But it IS okay, Justina. Don't lose yourself trying to appease others. Even if it's only in private." I finished by untucking the bangs that she was trying to hide. Jess flinched under my movements. She looked at the bang and then back to me.

"You knew?" Jess asked, no louder than a whisper.

Bonnie Baraka

"Take a deep breath and close your eyes," I told her, giving no response to her last question. I let Jess go, my hands falling to my sides, but I did not move.

Jess obeyed the command and closed her eyes, tears now streaming from them. Kat, still behind her, was in shock. When she saw the tears on my cheeks as well, her grin disappeared for sure; but when she heard the words I uttered, she was almost paralyzed. What was that on her face? Admiration? I couldn't tell for sure. The shock was draining from her face when she put her hands on Jess' hips to guide her. Again, Jess tensed.

Kat cleared her throat, trying to get herself back to reality, no doubt. "Okay, let's see... do you like to dance?" Kat asked in a light, airy tone.

Jess shifted her weight, not even trying to answer the question as if to say, "be realistic."

"Alright fine, we will just stick with basketball then." Kat rolled her eyes. "In your mind, visualize a basketball court and a basketball in your hand. Now dribble it."

Jess moved to dribble an imaginary basketball, as she had done so many times before. Her imagination got the best of her, and before we knew it, she was doing tricks. I giggled.

"No, no tricks, no between the legs, no extra movement, just dribble. Dribble on the left pass to the right, one dribble on the right, pass back to the left. That's it, okay?" Kat instructed sternly.

Kat moved Jess' hips as she passed from right to left. When she had given all the directions, she let go and stepped back to let her try it out. Jess swayed her hips with each pass of the imaginary ball.

"That's good; now slow it down just a little."

Jess changed her speed, and I couldn't believe how much this looked like she might get the hang of a strut! A very awkward strut, but a strut all the same. We just needed to tweak a couple things. Kat was still behind Jess. I knew she couldn't see what I saw. I dashed for the vanity and grabbed a red-tinted gloss. While her eyes were closed, I squeezed a little on her face, chiming in to help with the positioning of her hands so she knew I was still there.

"Ok, now. Don't let the ball go quite so high, keep your dribbles short." Jess repositioned her arms to stop her imaginary ball short of a full bounce. Kat came around and stood next to me to see Jess' progress.

"Open your eyes, Jess," Kat said, her voice thick of honey again. Jess opened her eyes and looked at us, searching for approval.

"Well, nothing left... but to try it!" I said, eager to see if she could pull this off. We were running out of time. "Can you walk over to the mirror like that?"

Jess closed her eyes for a second and took another deep breath. When she opened them, you could see the determination on her face. She was ready to master something new and foreign to her. She turned around with a short glide and then strutted her stuff right over to the mirror. When she made it there, she paused. I watched her face light up as she took in her reflection. Her newly outed bangs that curled slightly from being tucked behind her ear fitted her face perfectly and brought out the mossy green and hazel swirl in her eyes. She looked to the mauve blouse that cinched in on her tiny waist and accentuated her growing breasts that she chose not to tape down today. I blinked. She filled out my skinny jeans from last year perfectly. It was like she knew exactly which ones to choose out of that top drawer. Like she had chosen them before but never had the courage to wear. I hadn't seen that pair in months, I guessed, now knowing there was a reason for it. Her toes wiggled as she looked down at them in the mirror. Painted. I looked up in shock at what I was seeing—her smiling. How long had I not noticed this transition?

Seeing the shock on my face, she blushed and explained, "Mom did them."

I could see the warmth of that memory behind her eyes. As she basked in it and let it fill her with all the womanhood she needed, she started to prance around the room without her imaginary basketball. I smiled to myself; finally, the

Jess I know. I looked over at Kat, who was doing everything in her power to stay out of the special moment between the two of us but watching every movement like a hawk. I could see the yearning in her eyes. Two sides of a coin were Jess and Kat, similar to what she said about her own Star and me. No more different than alike, and yet you would never know unless you looked deep within.

Bonnie Baraka

"Well, I guess you're ready then!" I said with excitement in my voice. I looped my arm in Jess' and we pranced around the room to our own beat. We giggled to each other and made a memory I would not soon forget. Kat stood by, not wanting to interrupt. I'd assume from remembering what happened to the closet door earlier. When I looked at the clock, I almost had a heart attack.

"Is this clock right!?" I screamed, and both girls froze in alarm.

All at once, without answering my question, we all started to move frantically. We bustled around the room, grabbing shoes and clothes and anything we could think we might need. Out the door we went all in a heap as we ran down the street to the Studio that was marked as our pick-up location. As we got close, I grabbed out for my companions to slow them down.

"It has to look like we are coming out of the studio, guys. We can't be coming from up the street walking with Princess Tina beating us." I looked to Jess with a grin. "Ready to play some ball?"

She grinned back. "As ready as I'll ever be," Jess said with total determination.

We circled around the back of the station to make sure the car service was not there yet. They weren't.

"Let's go in, ask a couple questions, pretend to be interested in coming back and when we see the car, leave," I said while the wheels were still turning in my head.

"It's closed," Kat said flatly. I looked at her, confused, so she explained. "This station has been closed for months. I'm not sure why, but there was a big thing about it on the news." She shrugged her shoulders to show, implying that she really didn't know. She was not a particularly good liar. As I turned to address her lie, I saw the car pulling into the back of the parking lot.

"Welp, it looks like we will just have to go stand at the door then, and fast because the car is here. Jess, stand behind us. Don't stare too long, and if you choose to, make sure your face is either curious or disgusted. Let's go!"

We hauled ourselves up over to the front of the studio and got into position. I prayed the driver didn't see us up until that point. Kat walked over to the car to make sure everything was secure and in order. Then nodded for us to get in.

"Good evening, Princess, and thank you for trusting us with your security and discretion," the driver said with a smile. Jess smiled back and spoke as if she had always been a slinky princess that got everything she wanted.

"Yes, of course. Please do not make me regret this in the near future. Your ultimate discretion is necessary in this matter." She patted the driver on the hand and stepped into the limousine.

I must have worn a hint of shock across my face because the driver beamed at me like he was the first person Princess Tina had ever talked to, and with a wink, he was rushing around the car to pull off and get her to her private plane. I giggled softly to myself and got into the limo next to Jess.

Kat positioned herself on her other side of Jess, keeping up the charade for anyone looking. When we got into the car, I noticed Jess' shoulders sag a little. I shook my head slightly so only she could see and positioned myself in front of the driver so he could not get a good look at our dear Princess. This was a small feat that she had passed, but the real test was yet to come. I wanted to congratulate her and tell her she was doing great, but, in my gut, fear was spiraling for her instead. She was doing great, but what if she did too good of a job? This was beginning to be a trip I wasn't so sure I was excited about any longer. I reached out and gave Jess' hand a squeeze. Then I turned back to Kat to see what we should be ready for next.

12

I would have thought my first ride in a limousine would have been more exciting. Unfortunately, this was not a moment to remember. All three of us were nervous and on edge; and scared to say anything that would be out of place in the presence of Royalty while in earshot of our driver. I was looking for something to say that would be less mind-numbing when the driver alerted us that we were close to the private airport and that he would have our belongings brought directly to the plane.

"Splendid," Jess said without a second thought.

I looked over to see if she had even noticed her response, but she seemed to be deep in thought about something. I couldn't take the time to focus on that now, though, as the door opened for us to exit the limo. I went first, then Jess, and Kat brought up the rear triple checking our surroundings. I did the same, scanning for any threat, but also scanning to see who our audience was and if we were going to have any trouble. There was just one attendant there waiting for us as we walked into the private terminal.

Kat and I walked in, looking around and taking everything in. I witnessed Jess jerk at the urge to do the same but stopped herself. Good girl. That was our job today. Once she put herself back into character, Jess sauntered through the lobby of the Terminal with such grace, I could no longer see where there could be room for imaginary bouncing basketball. Jess reeked of imperial delight, taking no interest in the people or things around her, but being aware of it all. I was impressed. She was so far into character at this point that I felt we had lost her to the princess.

"Why are we still standing in this atrium? We do not have time to waste here, or to be seen," Jess said, sounding both bored and stern at the same time. Now that was something I knew she had learned from her mother. I personally had heard her mother use it time and time again on Jess when she needed her to do something... like clean her room or take out the trash. She shifted her weight and looked at Kat.

Kat took that look as her cue to spring into action. She drew in close to Jess as if to protect her. Following her lead, I did the same.

"Something is not right here. It shouldn't take this long," Kat said in a low tone that was loud enough for only the attendant and I to hear. At first, I was nervous that we had been found out. I took a step closer to the attendant and then scanned the room around us. The attendant was frightened, but mostly by our actions in front of her.

"You!" I said with a low snarl. "What is taking so long? And you better have a damn good answer for keeping the princess waiting." I looked her in her eyes, daring her to say anything other than what we wanted to hear.

"I um... I'm sorry, ma'am. The plane was delayed in another city because of the weather. It. It should be here any mu-mu-moment." She struggled to keep herself from passing out. She was so nervous as she tried to deliver this information.

"Where will it arrive? We will wait there," Kat said from behind me in a short and choppy voice that reminded me of an old Russian militia movie.

The nervous attendant pointed to a small waiting area right in front of the airplane door. I nodded to her and then turned to wait for Kat to move out. Kat took a second to scout the area before she moved, and we went over to take up the comfortable looking couch in the waiting area. No one said anything until the plane arrived. The same attendant, now with her nerves slightly under control, smiled and assisted us with boarding the plane.

Bonnie Baraka

After first meeting the pilot and then his co-captain, we finally made it safely and securely onto the plane. No one breathed until the wheels went up. Finally, we were off.

Once we made it into the air, Jess gave out a long over-dramatic sigh that made me giggle. I looked over at Kat as she fell into an oversized chair in her own fit of giggles. Relief had set in for all except for Jess, who remained in character.

Jess looked at both of us, confused.

"Oh, still in character, are we? You do realize there's no one here but us, right?" Kat said to Jess with a smirk.

Jess' shoulders sagged as she took in the rest of the plane and felt relieved of the weight Kat had just removed.

"Oh?" Jess asked no one in particular in almost a whisper as she shuffled past us to the back of the plane and found a cozy place for herself. As she stared out the window, I could see Jess smile to herself. Had she not only pulled off the charade but enjoyed it as well? I was deep in thought about this when Kat pulled me back to reality.

"Give her some time to recalibrate her thoughts and actions," Kat said, pointing to the seat across from her. "At least, sit down, you can still see her from this seat. I mean, or don't, but I don't suggest you just stand there and watch her like a stalker," Kat said teasingly.

I hadn't even realized I was standing in the middle of the aisle at the front of the plane, staring Jess down like a hawk and not saying anything. I took a deep breath and slid into the seat across from her that Kat had pointed to and attempted a dry laugh out loud.

"I am no such thing. I'm just hoping there isn't a backlash explosion like last time." I made a point to emphasize how bad that would be if we had to deal with that in the moment. Really bad.

Kat nodded in understanding. "Well, I would still give her some time to herself. After hearing, I mean like really hearing what you said to her, I understand better where she is in her head and sometimes... we just need a minute to wrap our heads around what is really happening in life. She needed this trip;

she needed to know how good it feels to be herself and understand that it wasn't a mistake when the Creator made her exactly the way she is." Kat looked at me with knowing eyes, and I had a feeling that Jess wasn't the only one who had gone through a lot growing up.

I stared at her, "We just normally deal with these things together." I shrugged, feeling a little left out by Jess. "Also, I get you have a back story, I do. I understand that it may have been hard for you. Hell, I wouldn't be surprised if you were still living it right now, but you don't know her, and you don't know her story. All of your words are assumptions and implications of what you think is happening." I choked the words out at Kat. Who does she think she is?

Kat nodded. "That's the problem now. She knows how much you care. She trusts you, far more than she should. So, instead of figuring out how she wants to feel, she allows you to tell her how she should feel. She doesn't believe it as much as you do. Although she may feel like you're right, she doesn't think you understand the seriousness of what's happening. She doesn't know where you get your belief in her, because she doesn't feel like she's worth it. SHE has to feel it. You can't tell her."

I clenched my jaw and balled up my fists. It was all I could do to keep from standing up and smacking Kat right across the face. I leashed my anger as much as I thought I was capable of. "I know exactly how it affects her mom; I know exactly what's wrong. I have been there, right in the thick of it all when the yelling commences. I have laid next to her and listened to her dad beat her mother for the 'painted nails' and the 'Christmas dress.' I have seen the black eyes and bruises her mother sports to her games when she has the strength to make it. I know she feels personally responsible even though none of it is her fault." I stared Kat down like a hawk and saw surprise and shock in her eyes. She didn't know.

I continued with my rant because the words wouldn't stop coming, "I'm not just some outsider trying to tell her what's right. I live it with her EVERY DAY, and I would continue to do so with whichever decision SHE makes, and THAT is what she knows. You don't even know what is going on by any measure. You have never even met the real Jess, so I would say the only person who shouldn't speak on it is YOU." I slammed my fist down on the side table. Both Kat and Jess jumped.

Bonnie Baraka

I startled Jess back to reality, and she called from the back of the plane, "Everything okay up there?"

I looked over to Kat then back at Jess. I hadn't meant to startle Jess in my anger. I agreed that she did need some time to think things over, but I hated Kat for making me feel like I didn't know what was going on with my own best friend. I glanced from Jess' confused face to Kat's startled one. Realization came flooding in and hit me like a ton of bricks. How could Kat know anything about what was going on with Jess? The words she was using, the emotions she was feeling, were not geared towards me at all, but towards my double. I looked up to answer Jess in a much calmer tone after realizing what was happening.

"Everything's fine, just hit my elbow on this table thingy. Sorry!" I said with a smile. "You..." I paused to let Jess know I understood and was okay with her distance. "You want to rejoin the group? Or are you working on a plan for when we get there?" I made eye contact with her to alert her that I knew she was not working on a plan but planning on a task for when we returned home.

Jess caught the look and said, "Yea, I will join you guys in a minute. Trying to work out the kinks in my plan," and turned back to the window.

I looked away from Jess, satisfied with our clear connection, and said to Kat smugly, "She's not even thinking about her mother. She's laser-focused, which is normal for her. I don't even know why I let you get under my skin." I smiled at Kat and nonchalantly pulled my pack up on the seat next to me, preparing to do some research and work on the actual plan that we didn't yet have.

Kat sat across from me with her head down in thought. We sat in silence for quite some time. I wondered if she had bought our charade, but as I watched her, my thoughts changed completely. How could she be so hellbent on being alone? It had taken me longer than I would have liked, but I finally saw that she was speaking on her own flaws and her own home life issues. So, why had no one else noticed? What was happening in her own home that she felt not even her best friend could possibly understand? Surely, Star had been to her house and seen whatever it was. Right? I took another deep breath that made Kat look up from her thoughts.

"What?" Kat shifted in her seat, noticing my eyes on her.

I shook my head. Better to keep this information to myself until I needed it. I looked away to throw her off about what was really going on in my mind. I instead decided to turn my energies to something that was a better use of our 4hour plane ride.

"I was just thinking you must be really good at meditation or something. You're always so calm; nothing really gets to you. I mean, that's what it seems like. I was just envying you, that's all," I said, letting my voice trail off.

Kat was definitely not expecting that response. Was it that I knew little or that I envied her for knowing so much, I couldn't tell anymore?

"How did you get so good at it?" I asked coyly. Even if I didn't trust her as far as I could throw her, I felt compelled to get into her head. To learn from her. I knew she was a levy of information, and I was just standing at the threshold, trying to figure out how to pry the gates open.

She gave me a sideways look that showed me she was determining whether to tell me what she knew or keep it to herself. I prayed she chose the latter. After what felt like a good minute or two of holding her gaze, I looked away and continued to pull Gran's letters out of the pack, pretending to abandon all hope of her telling me what I wanted to know. That one movement unnerved her.

"Why do you act as though you don't care if I tell you or not when we both know what I have to say will change your outlook and probably your outcome on what happens next? I can tell you really feel like it doesn't matter, but you know that it does. That is so aggravating!" Kat crossed her arms and turned to look out the window.

I chose my next words very carefully, knowing there was a fine line of information I knew and the information I needed her to know, and I was about to walk it like a tight rope.

"Why do you let the actions of others sway you so much? I mean, seriously. I picked up my bag, and now you're upset?" I dug at Kat in the areas that I knew would send her over the edge. "I know I just said you were good at keeping calm, but I can tell that's only on the outside. So, what do you do with all that pinned up anger that you keep bottling up? Where do you think it goes? What do you think happens to it when you don't release it? You think it just evaporates or what?" I finished my remarks and turned to the pages in front of me, completely ignoring Kat at this point.

This sent her to rage. "You know, I thought you were different than her. I thought 'double' or not, there is something that is really different about these two, but I guess I was wrong. You are exactly the same. You know, she said the same thing to me just last week before she took off!" Kat's eyes got big as she realized she had just given away some information that she was trying to hold on to.

Jess was on her feet before Kat could take it back. "So, you knew that I wasn't her."

I cut my eyes from Jess to Kat. Kat's poker face came crashing down right before my eyes, and she snarled at me. I blinked unfazed. Jess sat down next to Kat, pinning her into the corner and trapping her in our conversation. Kat went from anger to anguish before Jess had completed her motion.

"No, how could I have known!" Kat yelled, exasperated. I could feel her emotions sway and turn like a tide. Her vibration was starting to pick up in her panic. Every emotion that came over her was like a merry-go-round in my tummy.

I put my hand out onto the table to steady myself and looked up at her. "Could you stop, please?" If her eyes could get any wider, they would. I thought they might pop straight out of her head. Jess scooted to the edge of the seat, putting a little distance in between her and Kat to better access the situation.

"You can feel that?" Kat said in an airy voice I assumed was shock.

I looked at her, confused.

"Well, you're flinging your emotions out like a spinning top with water caught on it. Everyone is getting wet, and I'm getting sick." I sat back to try and relieve the pressure in my stomach.

"Star of V is not an empath. Are you an empath? I mean, she used the same language as you do and she always knew when I was not feeling the best, but she wasn't... Was she? Did she have things she didn't share with even me?" Kat was abuzz with questions that we couldn't tell were for herself or for us.

I looked at Jess, trying to understand what was happening. Her face was grim, and she looked as though she understood what Kat was feeling. I had never hidden anything from Jess. How could she possibly understand? I looked back to Kat and cleared my throat to get her attention.

"Would you mind sharing with us what you are jabbering on about?" I tried to use the nicest voice possible to coax the information out of her. She stopped jabbering and decided to explain what was happening, or so I thought.

"What does your Gran do?" Kat asked curiously. I looked at her with a curious gesture. What angle was she playing?

"She's a Travel Agent," I said with no hesitation. Gran had been retired for years, but her last known job was, in fact, as a travel agent.

Kat sat in silence for a long minute before she decided the information was probably valid and began her story. "Well first off, no, I did not know that you weren't her. I knew she was up to something and that she left, but I thought she was back. I had been covering for her for days when you ran into that kitchen. That is why I was so anxious to find you and talk to you after you left school. I thought something had to be up, and I needed to find her and make sure everything was okay. Now it makes sense that you were uneasy and guarded when I asked you at first. You were feeling my emotions of anxiousness and that something was off with me."

I shifted in my seat, remembering my mini explosion when she walked into the kitchen.

"Secondly, you are an empath. One that I'm going to assume is untrained and immensely powerful. So, the way you view things is a little different from others. That means when you approach people, you can feel their joys and pains. Some powerful empaths can even send feelings back up this connection to help ease the things happening to those people. I don't know if you can do that or not, but I do know that you are smart enough to know when to try and when not to, like earlier with Jess. That's not something that was taught, that's what you were born with. Like me, I was born with this poker face, and I can most often always use it to my advantage." Kat paused, remembering the most current events at the airport.

I interjected, remembering the same. "Lately, have they been harder to control and manage?" I asked, raising my eyebrow.

"Lately, as in the time that Star has been missing?" Jess turned from me to face Kat directly.

They were sharing a connection that I couldn't understand. I shook my head, trying to remove the feelings of hurt and jealousy that were starting to form in my gut. I now knew what Jess was feeling earlier, seeing me having fun with Kat. I said a silent apology to Jess in my head and looked back to Kat to see her response.

She was looking at Jess with watery eyes and replied, "Yes."

I felt a sharp pain in my chest and knew it didn't belong to me. I knew that the hurt and anger that Kat had showcased earlier had been created from this pain and that there was no curing it with the snap of a finger. It would take time—more time than we had. I slowly reached my hand across the table between us to grab Kat's hand. On first touch, she pulled away. I wasn't sure if she was scared because of the touch, or the mere fact that she thought I would have access to her emotions. Once my hand locked on hers, my skin began to crawl and protest us touching. Alarm bells went off in my toes. As I tried to release her, I looked into her eyes. I found darkness there, trying to swallow me whole. I found pain and sadness so unbearable that I begged for release. Had she felt this all along? Noticing that I could not release her touch, I panicked, and a low agonizing growl came from my throat.

Jess' eyes widened in my peripheral. I soon felt her cool touch on my arm. I felt her presence radiate strength and understanding from beside me. I was trapped inside my head with Kat's emotions, but I could feel the sunshine in Jess just outside the barrier. A thought sparked in my mind of something my Gran used to say. Emotions are like flowers. Water them or feed them, and they will grow. Talk to them or soothe them, and guide them to the sunlight, and they will transform into what you want them to be. If you're really good at whispering sweet nothings to them, they will conform to your will with ease. Was this the right time to use that advice?

I figured I didn't have a choice, seeing the horror on Kat's face. She was no more able to sever the bond than I was. I took a deep breath and closed my eyes.

Slicers

I was already locked in; I might as well look around for something to help me. I found memories of Jess and me as small children with my Gran. A beach day, where we played and played and played in the sun until we were tired and withered from all the water. I coaxed my memory to change from Jess and me to Star of V and Kat. Altering it like putty and hoping I would still be able to one day remember it as it was. I peeked out to where Kat was sitting—to where the dark agonizing despair was sucking away at my will to live. I balled up my memory in my mind and threw it towards the darkness. It inched back. And I felt my fingers loosen from her grip. I hurled another memory and another and another until I decided to just throw myself glowing with all my happy moments against that darkness and watched it wither away into nothing.

I released a breath; I could finally feel my fingers able to let go of Kat's. Before I let go, I looked at where that dark cloud used to be, and I saw her heart. Veins pumping, sludge through it. Spots so black that there was no way she could feel like herself or even want to be herself anymore. I mentally reached my hand out to touch it. Gooey in those dark places like it wasn't just dying, but it was dead and feeding off the rest. I caressed those dark parts and tried to mold them back together. My breath quickened, and I felt a stabbing pain in my own heart.

But beside me, Jess was there. Under the table. I felt her grab my hand to sturdy my now swaying torso and bring me back to reality, covering the pierce in my heart with her own memory of that beach day with Gran. Feeling the tug of the world, I turned to leave the dark clouds in Kat's heart, but before I went, I reached with both hands as far around that decaying heart, and I gave a tight hug. I thought all the happy thoughts I could think and said a couple things I had always heard my Gran say to those mourning. I'm sending you light and love in your time of pain and darkness, to fill every dark space that was once attacked and bring back every happy time you have had the pleasure of being alive for. I said those words and released Katiyah's heart, simultaneously releasing her hand.

Jess' hand, I held for much longer. Shaking and confused and needing her strength that I had always felt through that bond. She was there with no hesitation and no concern as to how this might affect her.

Thinking that I had said those words in my head, I was oblivious as to why Kat stared at me like she did. Then she asked me, "Your Gran is Jinny Roi?"

I nodded, not wanting to speak anymore.

Kat got up and went to the minibar. When she came back, she had chocolate bars and coca colas for the table. "Caffeine helps when you use your gifts. Empaths take on a lot, so they use themselves up fast. Sliders do too." She nodded to Jess at the last part to alert her that this was knowledge she would also need.

"Why did you ask about my Gran?" I asked after taking a shaky drink of my cola.

"Because I saw her in your memories." She stopped and looked at me as to say she saw more than she was supposed to and that she was sorry. I saw her wage in her mind whether she was going to share the rest of what she knew.

It took her a few minutes, but I could definitely see a real change in her. She was no longer using her poker face with us. Her breaths were short but steady, and the anger that usually daunted her face was minute in stature to where it had been when we met her. I could see the change happening right before my eyes. She noticed it herself as well, I could tell. She finally made her decision, and with a deep sigh, she began to divulge some jewels I would have never guessed and much more never known without her.

"The memories that you chose, they were of your Gran, you and me and your Gran. I saw them. I could see them through that cloud. I'm just not sure where the cloud came from. I have never been inside emotions like that. I have only met a couple of empaths, and they are very skilled in the art, so they rarely have events like the one you just had." She paused on the next bit of information. "Now, I know why they always refuse to see me, though." She looked glumly at this. Shaking off this memory, she stopped to look at me to see if I was understanding her.

I wasn't. "What do you mean like the one I just had?" I giggled a bit. "I sent happy images that I thought would help you... that dark cloud was a part of you. I was merely trying to change the storm to a rainbow; the memories that I used were of Jess and I," I said, turning to Jess, hoping she wouldn't get mad.

Jess beamed. She had felt the anger boiling inside me. She had willingly reached out her hand to be there with me. Jess was elated that her memories were the happiest that I had. I could read it all on her face.

Kats brows furrowed. She didn't know. She had no idea that her heart was damaged and that her emotions were so black that I was stuck there with them until they could be tamed. I felt bad for Kat, genuinely. I wondered if her emotions had affected my double in the same way. Kat wasn't sure if she was an empath or not, so it could have been nothing, or it could have been everything. Time would tell.

Kat started again. "Well, I'm not sure, but I was able to see your memories. I was able to see you work against that cloud to create a pathway for us to escape and break the bond. That's really good, considering you haven't had any training. Then again, it seems like you actually have and just didn't know it." She sat a little closer. "Your Gran is an empath for sure. She has mastered many gifts, to be honest, and hasn't told anyone about them, but that much I am certain of. She has mastered and forgotten more gifts that others will possess in their entire lifetime. She is immensely powerful, and if she kept you in the dark about what was transpiring until now, there must have been a good reason that even I will not question." Kat looked lost in a memory out the window at the recalling of Gran and her abilities. "That also means, if she kept you in the dark for so long that she is now risking putting you in the field without being trained, something major is happening." She would not look at us as she continued to talk. "Your gifts are awakening in this place. You've probably always had them, but here, the vibrations are higher with so many gifted people. Well... that, your bracelet and now actually knowing certain things are possible. You are about to experience things that are much different than what you used to."

She finally looked over to see both Jess and I were wide-eyed and hanging onto her every word. She smiled.

"Look, what you need to know is that your gifts are not common, and because of that, they require a lot of attention. You will need to study them and practice and make sure you are always aware of your surroundings." She stopped talking as the plane started to descend.

Jess was not done yet. "What about me? I don't think I'm an empath. I mean, I guess I must be a Slider, but what about my gift?" She almost sounded whiny.

"I don't think you are a Slider," Kat said blankly.

Bonnie Baraka

I turned to her to see the yearning on her face. All she wanted was something just for her. I turned my head to buckle my seat belt. I knew what she was; I knew she stood for those who couldn't stand for themselves and that she could mend the spirits of anyone who wasn't feeling the best. I knew who she was, and it said as much on my face, but I also knew that Kat was right. I couldn't continue to tell Jess what she was or who she was; she needed to know and experience it for herself.

Kat gave me a look of warning. "We all have to discover our gifts on our own. No one can tell us what they are or how to use them. Either you have them, or you don't, but even if you have them and you don't know what they are, you can't use them. It's for you to find out." She turned and stood to get to the airplane door.

I looked out the window to see the busiest airport I had ever seen and the most unique one too. With its World of Worlds decorations everywhere. I was slightly confused when we flew over it and kept going. Then looking at Jess, I remembered we were with Princess Tina and could not risk a landing with a crowd of that size. Jess was remembering too. Getting back into character, she took a few deep breaths and arranged her face to be more solid but carefree.

"Almost done," I said to her with a pat on her leg. She looked at me with her shoulders back and a somber face.

"I think that's what I'm afraid of most." Jess said, blushing, and she rose from her seat next to me to head for the door.

I got to my feet, shouldering on our pack, and did one last check of the cabin before I joined them both at the exit. We reached our destination! We had finally made it! I was amazed at how far we had gotten, but I couldn't shake the butterflies in my tummy that told me this journey was just beginning. When the door opened, we walked out to meet the world.

13

It sounded easier than it was. When we got off that airplane bridge, there was a host of Royal guard and important figures there waiting for us, all seeming a little too eager to get to the princess. With Kat in the front of the pack, we kept our heads held high and alert and moved through the crowd like nothing was amiss. They all watched Jess saunter through without a care in the world, most of them calmed, and some of the tension in the room evaporated. I felt the breath creep from my lips a little easier. I was thinking it was a good thing she looked like the princess. Because of that, they weren't paying attention to details. At a glance, they missed the sturdiness of her jawline or the way she still walked like there was a basketball in her hand at times. For all intents and purposes, she was Princess Tina, and she might have just been in a bad mood. Most of them shrugged and went back to their posts, without a glance back after confirming that for their judgment, it was the princess and not someone trying to scam their way into the festival. All but two of the people in that hallway disbursed to go back to their jobs and posts. All but two. I guess we would need to fool them a little more than the rest. We stopped short of where our welcoming party stood waiting for us.

"Well, good morning, my Princess. How was your trip?" One of the gentlemen said in front of us.

My breath caught in my throat as I peered down the hall at the sender of the well wishes. He was shining so bright it was blinding. Not in a literal sense, though; it was his aura. So bright that it seemed to continue to grow and envelope us as he got closer. Smooth olive skin, pearly white teeth shining, and a thick

British accent to go with it. He cheesed at Jess with a look of love and excitement that almost always meant trouble.

She looked over at him. "Exhausting, actually," Jess replied in a lazy tone that felt as if she would pass out right there on the floor.

I looked over to her. To the outsiders around our small welcoming party, she was doing amazing at pulling this off; and as much as I wanted to high five her and give her an encouraging smile, I couldn't because warning bells were going off in my head. Something was not right. I broke my gaze away from Jess to look over at Kat. She was busy marveling at our new friends. I looked at him again and finally realized what that hint of trouble in his eyes really meant when he looked at Jess. He knew her, and very well at that. Not like a guard, but a friend or family member. He cared for her. Well he didn't know her at all, he knew Princess Tina, and though Jess looked like her, she was no princess underneath it all. He knew Tina's mannerisms, her sarcasm, and he would certainly know if this was her standing in front of him or not.

I turned to look back at Jess and let her in on my newfound information when Kat stepped up to shake this strange shining boy's hand, giving me a chance to fall back and get Jess out of the line of fire. I grabbed her by the arm and pushed her back slightly. "He knows you," I mouthed to her in the process. Her eyes glazed over slightly. Then she was back into character like nothing happened.

"Hello there," Kat purred in front of us.

I spun around to see the transaction. The boy's face changed from true happiness to snide uncertainty.

"Well, well, well. Hello to you too, miss Kitty," he said with a low growl in his throat.

"I don't think you have had the pleasure of meeting Charlie's daughter. She was the one showing the princess his project, although they are unable to yet transport it here and will miss the festival. This is Starla." Kat was using her strengths to her advantage and toying with this newcomer like a ball of string. She commanded the attention of both suitors, and as she spoke, they had completely forgotten we were even there. She grabbed me by the arm and slung me up into the face of the guy with the aura of gold. After regaining my balance, I extended my hand to shake his.

"Um, hello, I'm Starla. It's nice to meet you," I said coyly.

His eyes bloomed into golden sunrises and beautiful blood orange moons all in a split second. He extended his hand as well, a bit shakily.

"Good to meet you as well, Starla. I am Royalti, but you can call me Roy."

His voice was as dripping with Sugar. We shook hands for much longer than necessary, neither one of us wanting to let go. I finally broke away, feeling my cheeks turn red and hoping that no one saw.

"Welcome to London. Is this your first trip to our country?" Roy asked, sounding like this was something he asked often. Nothing special then, this is his job, and he would be welcoming to anyone. Understanding sunk in, and I began to remember what was happening around me.

"Um, yes. This will be my first. My father is under the weather and could not accompany me, so I was gracious enough to be able to travel with my best friend. Obviously, at the graciousness of your Princess Tina, this would never have been possible without her." I made sure to make clear what was happening without divulging too much of anything important.

"Awesome." Roy smiled; eyes still planted on me. He began to turn around and say something to his companion, who then nodded his head and left us alone with Roy. I wasn't sure if that was a good sign or not until Roy spoke again. "Well, Tina, you still have other projects to view and approve for entry into your contest before the day ends, so we might as well get started now," Roy said with a wink to Jess that made me wonder; was he trying to out her?

She nodded, but displeasure was written all over her face.

"I guess we should get on with it then," Jess said in her fake British accent.

It really didn't sound too bad. Roy looked her over once. Assuming that he decided it was close enough to a response the real Tina would give, he offered me his arm, and we strode down the hallway.

Bonnie Baraka

"You ladies will have to join us. I'm sure there is plenty that you will want to see anyway. We will have to go through the World of Worlds Festival to get to the portion where all the projects are being housed right now anyway," Roy said, fixing his face so his smile was painted on and unwavering. We strode arm in arm as if we had known each other for years as we headed straight out of the private airport and right into the craziness of the festival traffic.

I was immediately accosted by the various smells and noises. Roasted pecans and fried Oreos covered in chocolate wafted through the air to my nose. I stopped at a corner to take a good look around. Ferris wheels, makeshift Eifel towers, goats running the streets, games and prizes, children and teenagers alike; all of this was here to create an experience that happened only once in a lifetime. But that wasn't all; there were men on stilts and women with beards; children with no parents racing through the crowds without a care in the world and couples enjoying each other's presence a little too much. Dancing was everywhere around us. In the streets, there was salsa. To my left, I saw them nodding their heads to a solid beat while the ones in the middle spun on their heads, and to my right, there was a line dance going to a song I had only heard in the corner store about ex's in Texas.

We missed the light for the crosswalk twice because I was unmoving, taking in everything around me. I was gaping at every little thing I noticed. I had never seen a place where so many different cultures and so many different groups of people felt comfortable enough to be themselves around others. I was elated to see how different this dimension was from my own. Jess was doing a much better job of keeping herself together. I could tell she was excited, but her face said something different completely. It was more like 'This is the smile everyone expects, so this is the smile I will give them.' She hid her excitement well.

I finally let Roy lead me across the street and fully into the World of Worlds to witness the full effect of the fair. I couldn't stop grinning. My first trip to London! Was this really considered a trip to London, though? This isn't even my dimension; did it even count? I didn't care; I was enjoying the sights far too much.

Besides that, there were the obvious variables to consider. Cute boy, arm in arm, showing me his prized possessions with a smile that could melt butter. This was by no means a date, but it was beginning to feel like one. I couldn't stop myself from thinking about how my first date was with a cute boy in London. Top that, Susan! I beamed on the outside, and Roy caught me.

"What are you so happy about?" He asked jokingly.

I smiled up at him with eyes that sparkled in the lights around us. His features softened at my grin.

"I was just thinking how wonderful it is to see all the different..." I paused. Were they still called cultures? Was that even a thing here in this dimension? "...kinds of people coming together to celebrate. I mean, it's one thing to hear about it. It's completely different to actually get to see it happen." I chose my words as carefully as possible, but there was still a hint of confusion on Roy's face when I finished.

"I keep forgetting how different it is over there," Roy retorted, explaining. "It's hard to think that we are ready to help others in other dimensions and time frames, but that we still have places here in our own back yard that need the help, and we overlook them." His face was saddened as he spoke the blind truths of most countries. He must have heard something about what was keeping Charlie away.

I tried to look a little misty-eyed about the disappearance of my family and home life I was supposed to feel. It didn't work well. I just ended up looking like there was something in my eye, but I wasn't sad about it. I turned away so Roy wouldn't catch it. Then looked back to see how Jess and Kat were taking everything in. Jess was searching the crowd and attractions around her out of her peripheral, and Kat seemed to be bored with the whole show. We stopped at the entry gate, and Jess nodded to the guards to let us through.

They bowed and obliged, pulling a horse-drawn carriage out for us to all climb into. You would think at this point that Roy would check on the Princess, glance over at Kat, or seem interested in his surroundings in some way, but he wasn't.

Roy jumped into the front of the carriage where the driver had sat and reached for my hand. "The view is better from up here; would you like to join me?" He asked slyly.

Bonnie Baraka

I glanced back at Kat and Jess whose faces read the exact opposite message. Kat, seeing that Jess' face was of warning and jealousy, pushed me forward into Roy's grasp. The moment our fingers linked; I was exploded into a cocoon of emotions. These emotions, however, did not leave me frozen but made me want to dance. Roy's emotions felt like they were going to burst right out of his chest. I looked up at him and immediately knew he felt my presence. As I slung myself up onto the top of the carriage, I reeled in my emotions as much as possible to keep him from noticing too much, praying that I was doing this right. When I was safely planted in my seat with a blanket on my lap, I turned to see that Jess and Kat were assisted by one of the foot guards into their seats and given a warm mug of hot chocolate. I could still see the steam coming off the mugs. The girls looked cozy and safe.

Deciding I was satisfied with the seating arrangements, I turned around to get back to my view of the excitement that was beginning in front of me. With a flick of the wrist, Roy sent us into motion through the crowd and towards the back of the fair where he told us they were setting up the specific projects to show off in an exhibit before Tina made her ultimate selection. There was chatting between Kat and Roy behind me, and I felt the tension shift immediately. Oblivious to their quarrel, I was busy looking into the crowd dancing to the concert on the big stage to the left. Alternative rock was one of my favorites; I mean, who could not appreciate Creed? Laughing at the comedy show on the stage to my right, although I didn't think the comedian there had done stand up in my dimension in years. That made me smile reflectively.

I looked at all the wonderful things around me that I was able to be a part of without even trying. I was highly favored and where there were so many times I chose not to see it but, in this moment, I knew it to be true. I looked back out the side of the carriage to glance at Jess without anyone noticing. She was genuinely enjoying herself. As the princess, she was responsible for greeting the people and making them feel appreciated and warm. She would stand and wave, touch a hand or two on the way past and blow kisses out of the side of the carriage. She was eating the attention up with a ladle. To see her like this and truly know how empty that well was broke me a little. Seeing it being refilled and knowing how much of this attention she needed brought me back to contentment.

When the chatter behind me stopped, I knew it must be time to finish our journey on foot. I turned back to the front of the carriage to see that Roy was waiting with his hand extended to assist me with my dismount. Jess made a gargling noise behind me and covered it with a yawn. I cut my eyes at her forgetting our audience. Roy laughed and grabbed me by my waist, carrying me down to the ground and placing me softly on my feet. My cheeks were getting tired from all the smiling I was doing.

I turned and walked deeper into the hall that our carriage stopped in front of. From behind me, I heard Roy explain to no one in particular that we had to walk through this hall to get to the back stadium where the exhibition would be. I was probably the only one who heard a word he said.

He turned to Jess to reiterate the message he was trying to get across. "You are unguarded out here; they will try to grab you if you venture too far from the group, T. Stay close and make sure your presence is known." Roy looked Jess in the eye to alert her that he was serious.

I walked back and stood next to Jess to block her in the center of our small group. She let out a sigh of relief and mocked Roy in an amused tone I had never heard her use before.

"You worry too much. These are my people; we will be fine." Jess smiled at Roy.

Roy looked taken aback as if he were seeing a ghost. I kept a mental note of this look as we began to stroll the aisles of the hall. This space was massive, with no shortage of high ceilings and tall windows. Fitted with plenty of space for the pets and children to run and play, there were wall-to-wall stalls set up everywhere. It was like a farmer's market almost. Fresh fruits and handmade jewelry were being sold or bartered for at every turn. One lady was selling fresh egg rolls that smelled so good I wanted to follow her around all day just for the smell. I didn't bring any money, and I couldn't be sure if it was the same here anyway, so I didn't make a fuss as we passed her on our journey. At least I didn't think I did.

Roy must have read the longing on my face before I could remind myself of where I was because he stopped at the next cart we saw and offered us lunch.

"You ladies must be starving by now," he said, elbowing Kat in the side.

She rolled her eyes but stepped up close on her tippy toes to see what the buzzing truck had to offer.

"Anything good?" Jess asked.

I looked to see the same eggrolls as the ones the lady we passed was toting around. "Egg Rolls for the gods," I said, my mouth watering and my heart skipping a beat. I was starving.

"Let's grab some rolls to hold us over, and then we will have a formal lunch when we get to the Stadium," Roy said, pulling money out of his pocket. It was the same as back home for sure; the only difference was...was that President Obama on that bill? I tried not to stare as he ordered eight egg rolls and paid the gentleman behind the cart. Taking the egg roll, I was ready for an explosion of gooey vegetables and chicken, but it never came.

At first taste, it was like no egg roll I had ever eaten. Warm and salty at first, but sweet in the middle. I could tell there was meat in the roll for sure, but I couldn't tell what kind. I could taste the veggies and all the normal things that belong in a traditional egg roll, but what stuck out most was the sweet chewy fruit that bloomed in my mouth. Cold and sweet meshed with warm and salty inside the crispy fried wrap. It was a battle of the taste buds to see which portion would be enjoyed the most. I was on the fence about whether I liked it or not, but the more I ate it, the more I craved the cold fruit in each bite until without noticing, I had finished both of my rolls and was looking at the group for more.

Jess was eyeing them with distaste. I knew she would not like the concept of something healthy in her egg rolls. Between her and Gran, she could practically make them in her sleep.

Kat, on the other hand, was all smiles as she slowly demolished her rolls. She looked at Roy, who was watching us all with curious eyes.

"I thought those were your favorite, Tina?" Roy called over a smug smile on his face. Was he toying with her again, or did he truly already know that this girl standing in front of him was not the friend he knew so well?

I let that thought go. If he thought that Jess was an imposter, we would not have made it this far. I looked over to Jess, who was trying to hide her disgust in the morsel she held at a distance and think of a way out of eating it. I gave her a sidelong look and decided to interject.

"It's your favorite? Oh, wonderful! My Gran used to make egg rolls, but nothing as fancy as this." I turned to Roy drawing his attention from Jess and back to me long enough for her to pass the uneaten rolls to Kat, who happily stuffed them down her throat. "Are these special to London? Or did they maybe come from somewhere else?" I held his gaze and attention to make sure he was not aware of the plot unfolding behind us.

"I thought they had them everywhere, actually," Roy said, amusement setting in. "You are such a ball of questions. No wonder your father sent you. To scout out the competition and use that sweet face to get the inside scoop, I bet." He cheesed, pearly whites showing bright. That was the last happy moment we had in the Hall of Shops. At that moment, our connection was broken by someone far behind us yelling and a stampede breaking through the tight aisle we had chosen as our path.

"PRINCESS TINA IS IN THE HALL TO BRING US GOOD FORTUNE AND BUY ALL OUR ITEMS!!!" I heard it as clear as if the person speaking were standing right next to me. I turned to see where the commotion was coming from as Roy forcefully grabbed Jess and almost threw her behind me. Out of the shadows slithered a boy with jet black hair and pale skin. He wore rags, and behind him came a mob of homeless men and women thrashing against each other in the hope of getting closer to the front of the pack.

I stood frozen, not sure what to do. From behind me, where everyone else in our group had apparently moved to, I heard Roy yell to me.

"Starla, LET'S GO!" He shouted.

I turned to run to him and was grabbed by the wrist. I instantly felt pain and anguish under this person's grasp and doubled over.

Trying to look up and see who held me, I heard him speak. "Let us speak with the Princess, and we will let her go!" It was the tall boy from the front of the pack. I felt the rest of them circle me.

"We just want food and money!" Another one shouted.

"Help us!" I heard from another.

I looked up and locked eyes with Roy. The pain on my face was evident, and he was not happy about it. Within a flash, Kat was there in the face of my offender with a tongue that I had only imagined she could have.

"Let her go RIGHT NOW!" She pushed against his surprisingly strong build. For a slim, slimy, and frail boy, I would have never thought he was strong.

I looked at her with warning in my eyes.

"No, run, save yourself!" I whispered to her. She took her eyes off the boy to see the pain in my face and realized what was happening. I was emotionally connected to the boy, and it was not pretty here. Her face changed from anger to surprise, then to understanding. Kat took a step back, but it was too late; the boy grabbed her wrist and forced her into the same doubled-over position.

"This is who you bring to protect our Princess?" The boy mocked Roy.

Kat didn't seem half as frazzled as I was at the sight that was unfolding in front of us. She whispered to me, "Don't let any of the darkness in. Focus on your breathing and building walls of sunshine around yourself." I looked from her to Jess. She noticed my glance. "She will be fine. He is trained to protect her; it is you that should be worried right now. We need to get away from this mob." Kat was pleading with me at this point.

I accepted her reasoning and closed my eyes. The bond between her and I on the plane was much more force, but the feelings inside of her were nothing compared to the ones I felt here in this boy. I didn't have any memories to throw at the darkness, so I just thought of beaches with hot sun and waves to wash away the past. I sat down in my mind and placed each memory around me like a wall. Soon, the pain inched away little by little, and I could tell the boy was feeling it too.

He looked at me with a grin so evil it made me shudder. "Learned a new trick, have we?"

I looked up at him, confused. Did I know this boy? Surely, I didn't. That could only mean that my double did.

I looked around to access our chances of getting away. The mob had almost made it to Jess and Roy. I didn't like our odds. I looked to Kat to see if she had anything up her sleeve. She was squirming under the boy's grasp with no luck. There were no objects close to hit him with to break free and run. We were out of time. Objects, I thought again. We didn't have any objects, but Kat said a powerful empath could sometimes alter the emotions of others if close enough. What if I sent something else instead of a memory through that connection? I didn't feel like I knew enough about what I was doing to change the anger that lay in this boy's chest, but it was worth a try to send an object that would scare him enough to release us. I didn't even know if it would work, but I knew I had to try. I looked at Kat, making eye contact to alert her that I had a plan.

She nodded and continued to thrash. I closed my eyes again and returned to my sitting position, where the darkness had begun to creep under my wall. I took one of the memories of the beach and filled it with all the light I could find in my memory. I filled it with hugs from Gran, wrestling with Trey, playing with friends. I filled it with love scenes from movies, places I wanted to go. I filled it with the warmth I saw in Roy. Then I shaped that memory into a knife. Standing up again, I imagined myself in the Olympics. I had one shot, and I would need to make sure I was aware of what was going on around us so we could make our immediate getaway. I opened one eye to see the mob had made it to Roy and Jess, and they were backing down the aisle. Time to go. I looked to Kat, her eyes were on me, waiting. I closed my eyes and threw that knife as hard as I could into the darkness that was now on my heels.

It struck, sending sparks and flames throughout. The boy yelped and jumped, loosening his grip. It was just enough for us to snatch away. I did. I looked to Kat; she was already on me, pushing me towards the rest of our group. I turned to run, hoping Kat had done the same. The boy was on us in a flash. Navigating the mob in front of us was harder than I thought.

"Split Up!" I yelled to Kat.

Without a word, she darted in another direction ducking down and getting lost in the crowd. I prayed she made it back to our group. I ducked and dodged, and finally, I was able to see them again. Why hadn't they run? If I knew Jess, she wasn't going anywhere until she knew I was safe. Having me in her sights, she lurched herself on top of one of the food carts and began to try and calm the mob. Bad Move. I could hear her trying to reason with them, but I was still not close enough to hear what she was saying. Roy was below her, looking for us and making sure no one slipped past to grab her. I saw Kat in the crowd making it to them much faster than me and quickened my pace. With no time to think about anything but dodging the crowd, I put my head down and weaved through as fast as I could. I finally reached the cart to hear her say something about caring for them all and that she would be back with gifts before the mob pushed into Roy, and the food cart came crashing down. I grabbed her arm just before she hit the ground. She was about to pull away when she looked up and saw it was me. Thankfulness washed over her face as she stood to run. I stopped her.

"Where is Kat?" I asked, turning around to look over Roy's shoulder. He had gotten up and made himself a barrier between us and the mob. The crowd kept pushing us further and further away from where this all started. I scanned the crowd as fast as I could until I laid eyes on that Blonde head of hair and pressed black shirt. My stomach dropped as soon as I did. "He has her!!" I shouted to no one in particular.

"Shit!" Jess spat from behind me. This drew the glance of not only Roy but the rest of the crowd. Their princess would never use such language no matter what was going on around her.

In that instance of confusion, Roy had let his guard down, and the mob moved through his barrier like water, advancing on us. I looked from Jess to Kat and back to Jess.

"Run!" I yelled at her, pushing her further down the corridor. I pushed past Roy, prepared to wave back to where Kat had been captured.

Roy grabbed me. "You will be trampled and captured too," he said, his eyes sad and pleading. He knew I would go after her anyway.

"Stay with..." my breath caught as I stopped myself from calling her by her true name, "the princess," I yelled back as I waded through the crowd. I had almost made it to Kat when he took her. He slung over his shoulder and turned away from the angry mob he had just created. Her eyes were bright with terror as she saw me approaching. She shook her head to tell me to stay back. I was too late. Kat had been taken, and I felt responsible. Hopefully, Jess had better luck.

I turned to run back toward the direction Roy and Jess had gone and noticed the crowd had stopped its advance. That can't be good. I finally made it back to the overturned food cart and kept going. I looked up just in time to see Jess being pulled through a trap door. I barely saw his face, but I could have swarm it was the only person I knew with eyes like a cat and a Running backs gate. It did help that he was wearing the same clothes from this morning. Ken was here? I took a deep breath, thinking at least now she was safe with someone we knew. No, my mind said, it couldn't have been. Then reality set in. We were in another dimension, nowhere near our home. If that was Ken, that was the Ken of Dimension V, and I couldn't be sure if he was friend or foe.

I went back to the overturned food cart and sunk down next to it, prepared to have a good cry. Before the first tear had a chance to fall, Roy hoisted me up onto his back and ran in the direction of the Stadium. I hoped he didn't notice the wet spot that was forming there on the back of his shirt. It had been such a long day, and I couldn't hold back another emotion. The tears were for Kat, for Jess, but most of all, the tears were for Gran.

The Stadium was quiet. Too quiet, considering what just happened. Roy sat me down on a bleacher close to the field where they were working on fitting it with a large makeshift stage in the middle. I sat in silence as he stormed off to order a couple of people around. My thoughts were jumbled. In a matter of minutes, I had lost my best friend in not only one dimension but two. They were gone, neither of which I could be certain would ever come back. I cried and cried until my wrist was ablaze with blinding lights. I looked at it, expecting to see the thermostat glowing. It wasn't just one jewel, but all of them. Something was different with this glow. It didn't hurt, it wasn't to take me somewhere, and it didn't vibrate. I probably could have been more interested, but I wasn't. Regardless of my current state of dampened emotions, I noticed that it was the stone that was identical to both girls I had just lost that shone the brightest. I felt the glowing gem with my free hand. It was cool to the touch, comforting almost. It was as if the stone was trying to soothe me—to tell me that they were okay. I closed my eyes and tried to reach for them through that bond. I could feel them both there. Kat, a little shaken up and angry, but intact all the same. A small weight lifted as I felt her there. I kept reaching until I came to Jess. Her emotions were different somehow. She was scared and worried, but she wasn't upset or in any pain. It wasn't happiness completely that I felt there, just a tidal wave of jumbled emotions that I couldn't sort through. It was more like yearning, and reservation. I calmed a little more. They were okay for the moment, and that was all I could ask for. I looked up just in time to see Roy storming back over to me.

"Come on," was all he said as he passed me on his way up the stadium stairs to what looked like the scoreboard room.

I followed quietly. I wasn't sure how to take his new mood, except to confirm that I didn't like it much. Was he upset with me? Did he blame us for what had happened to Jess, or who he thought was Princess Tina? Did he blame himself? This had gone so wrong. I felt like such a terrible person for not being honest with him. I wondered if he would have treated us, treated me, the same if he knew the truth.

At that moment, I knew I had to tell him. But how? How do you tell someone that you lied to them to get what you needed and that everything that he might have felt was a lie? We made it to the scoreboard room, and he kept going through to one of the attached private skyboxes. When we got there, lunch was already set up for us. Just for two, though, like they somehow knew the rest of the group wouldn't make it to this point. I put my head down now feeling worse than ever for dragging Jess into this mess. Roy sat down with a grunt and put his head in his hands. I slowly lowered myself into the chair across from him so as not to bother his thoughts.

"I... I'm sorry," I stammered as calmly as I could muster. I didn't know specifically what I was sorry for, but I was.

He looked up at me, confused. Some of the blatant hatred dissolving when our eyes met. He shook his head.

"You couldn't have known that Sin would be in that Hall waiting for us." In a flash, his features reverted to something much colder than I thought he could muster. "Or did you?"

My face must have read surprise and hurt because his features immediately relaxed and softened to regret, as he put his head back down before I could even respond.

"I didn't know anything about what was happening here. I don t know this Sin guy; I have never been to this place before. Ever," I said, being honest, and judging from what I just saw, I doubt he had ever left.

He looked up swiftly with a puzzled expression this time. Alarms were going off in my head as he turned away, not sure what to believe.

"I mean, someone that looks like me may have, but I... I haven't," I stammered, trying to make it make sense without sounding like a loony bin.

"However, your friend Kat has. Many times." he said as he turned away.

Information I had not known. Honesty. That's what he was giving me. I cocked my head to one side, not sure what to say. So, I started with whatever came to the forefront of my mind instead.

"Question: What do you do when you know what needs to be said, but you don't know how to say it without sounding a little crazy or altogether insane?" I said in a low voice that was meant mostly for myself.

Roy looked up at me. His face read understanding, but I wasn't sure we were understanding the same things.

"I felt it too, our connection. It was almost instant. The moment I saw you, I knew you were special," he said, with spots of color popping back into his face. "That is why I was so upset with myself. Letting him capture you, not taking Tina away when I should have. I was torn between what I felt for you and my duty." He hung his head again.

"How can you feel anything for me?" I turned away, not sure how to explain my jumble of feelings.

I knew there was a connection between us, for sure. I felt it. Coursing through my body whenever we were in proximity, but I couldn't shake the feeling that there was something going on between him and Kat. Then there was the fact that Kat came out and told me that they had spent the night together. She didn't say they were intimate, but their actions when they were around each other were obvious. Her playing Kat and mouse, him the perfect gentleman. Smiling at her extending his hand to assist, all the things I wanted him to only do for me. I felt jealousy boil up in my throat as I spat the words at him.

"I know I was just in your way when you were trying to reach her. I know you just couldn't leave the beautiful Kat behind." I instantly felt guilt with the anger in my voice and felt apologetic.

"What are you talking about?" Roy said with confusion and desperation on his face.

"Kat told me you guys spent the night together and that she has been with you many times. That is why she wanted to come with us on this trip. Well, that, and we are looking for her friend."

Roy took one look at me and blew out all the air he could muster, shaking his head.

"Little Star, always so trusting and genuine. I think you may have been played." Roy moved to pour some tea.

"Did she say she was coming to see me, or did she say we saw each other while she was working? She is a tricky one, that Kat. I mean yes, we have spent many a night together...working on your father's project, but we have not laid together. Not ever. I stayed when I should have left for fear of what might happen to you." He took a long drink from his tea with a pondering expression.

Hearing this made me queasy. Was Kat playing me this whole time? Or was she just jealous of the attention Roy was showing me? I thought back to the emotions swimming in Kat's gut from the plane. Yes, jealousy was a constant in Katiyah's life. For an exceedingly long time, it seemed to me. I took a deep breath, trying to release the jealousy that had tethered itself to my vocal cords. I needed to think clearly; I needed to exist above the emotions that were swarming me at that moment, which was an exceedingly hard task. I focused on my breathing and tried to tune out the other sounds around me. I saw tendrils of white smoke escape my bracelets and almost screamed. I watched as they slithered up to my neck and settled around my throat, where I could feel the venom I had spat at Roy a moment ago. It soothed the ache, and I relaxed. I debated with myself on what to say next. Telling him would put me in a vulnerable position I wasn't sure I was ready for.

"So, you trust me, and I can trust you? Right?" I asked, a little uneasy.

Bonnie Baraka

Grabbing my sweaty palm in his, he nodded slowly. I know better, I do. I can't trust anyone; Gran already told me this. I am in a different dimension for Christ's sake! But something in my chest vibrated with excitement when I stared into those big blue eyes, and I found myself taking a leap of faith.

"Welp, okay then, here goes nothing," I said and took a large breath. With his eyes trained on mine, I blew out the breath and gave the craziest explanation I could muster. "Things are not as they seem with my group, if you haven't already guessed. Tina is not who you think she is, her name is Justina, and she is from another dimension." I stopped to let that sink in. No response. Not even a flinch from him. I continued on so I didn't lose my nerve. "She came here with me on accident. I am Charlie's daughter, just not the Charlie of this dimension. Kat, on the other hand, met us when we got here and was helping us get here to the World of Worlds. Not by choice at first, I might add, but this is where we thought we needed to be. My Grandmother sent us here to... well, umm... I'm not entirely sure why she sent us here right now," I said, blinking.

I know Suzie had said one thing, and it felt right, but I couldn't shake the feeling that it might be wrong. Why had she sent us? Was it to find Trey? To help my double instead? Were we really here to stop the destruction of the whole multiverse? I realized I was having an internal conversation with a silly look on my face. When I looked up and saw that Roy was now staring at me hard waiting for me to finish, I tried to hurry and quickly complete my speech.

"I was told that it was to stop the destruction of the whole multiverse, but on our way, I have been noticing other reasons she could have sent us. Something I will have to, for sure, sift through later. However, we need to stop the projects from leaving this place before the festival ends, and I know I need to find Jess. Like I said, she wasn't even supposed to be here, and I don't know what to do!" I threw my hands into the air and sat back as far as I could, bracing myself for his undeniably angry reaction. I finished my statement, realizing I hadn't finished my speech. I crossed my arms anyway to alert him I was done. I probably wasn't as sure of what was going on as I thought I was, but when our eyes met, I saw something different there.

Roy laughed a real, joyous, genuine laugh. Hearing his laugh made me guess I wasn't the one who was insane here.

He took my hand from within my crossed arms and placed it in between his and with a look that was sopping in apology as he said, "I know your friend isn't Tina. Princess Tina is my first cousin. I am Prince Royalti." And he laughed again.

I couldn't believe what I was hearing. I snatched my hands away, and Roy immediately stopped laughing. Before either one of us could say what we were thinking, the Royal Guard stepped into the room with their hands on their holsters. I looked from the guards to him and back. Was he going to lock me up for treason? Was this all just a show to get me here? To get a confession? I felt emotions creeping up my belly again, at the ready. Not of anger or of rage, but of pure disappointment and sadness.

Roy stood and addressed the guards without a word to me.

"As planned, me and a Decoy princess took a stroll through the Hall today, and there was indeed an uprising. The princess's decoy was ambushed and taken, and her guests were assaulted. They are still missing. Go to the hall and make sure it is a safe place for our travelers to shop, aid the sellers with cleaning the area where the angry mob congregated, and make sure that any of our hungry citizens get food to eat. Listen to the whispers in the shadows for any clue of where our friends may be. Report anything and everything back to me immediately." He was firm and powerful in his words as he saluted them, and they bowed, then backed out of the room.

I was still upset until I heard what he said. "As planned." He knew the entire time that Jess was not his cousin. He knew that we were coming. We were bait.

My mind was on the fritz, trying to calculate what was happening around me. So much so that I hadn't noticed Roy retake his seat across from mine. I jumped as he touched my hand again.

"My apologies for the dismay, beautiful Star," Roy said with a voice that was charming, yet withdrawn. I couldn't tell if he was talking about scaring me or about lying to me. Noting the confusion on my face, he began to clarify and make his case. "I was alerted that you were on your way here, once the plane was at its peak in the sky. Your arrival was no surprise to us; we had arranged for your family to come months ago. That was not the suspicious part at all. The fact that you were with someone who the people could not tell was not the true

Princess. That was a problem. They were terrified of your partner's sassy pants and put in an alert to make sure everything was okay with Tina. Although she is poised in public, people who know Tina outside of the famous eye know she is caring and joyful; she is full of life and fearless. So, when your friend went into a panic and made everyone think it was at the alarm of Tina, well, they put in a call to check and make sure everything was as it should be. When I alerted my cousin that something was going down, she saw an opportunity to kill two birds with one stone. A, we would see if there really was a mutiny happening in our own streets as people often try to throw at Tina; and B, we would get a chance to see who this imposter was and what she was trying to do in our own back yard." He stopped and looked me over as if taking in the last view he would see in his life. It took everything in my power not to blush. "I never expected to see you get off that plane. Never expected to like you, to see those light brown eyes pour over my soul and let the flecks of gold there drag across my heart as if they were put there just for me. Not to mention how much it kept throwing me off that your friend was just like my favorite cousin. Right down to the filthy mouth that seems to blossom when she thinks no one is listening."

This made me giggle. Jess didn't care who was listening when her sailor ancestry kicked in. I said as much to Roy through my fit of silent laughs.

"Well, she played the part extremely well, especially to have never met Tina before. You know her name is Justina also?" Roy cocked his head to the side, remembering. "But when her mother named her, our King felt Jess was too strong for his delicate princess. He felt that Tina sounded more elegant and trustworthy. He believed Tina suited a Queen much better." Roy recalled.

I laughed at this outright. Polar opposites.

"Jess' father wanted her to be a boy. So naturally, he treats her like she really is one. Actually, this was her first time getting to be a real girl. I think she really enjoyed it, but she would never admit it," I said, smiling to myself and remembering Jess' genuine smile while waving at the crowd just earlier.

Roy's eyes widened. "She could have fooled me. I mean honestly, if I didn't know my cousin was safe and sound in her room, I would have thought that it really was her." He laughed back.

It was starting to make more sense why he was not surprised at so many turns; and why he stayed and waited for me in that hall. Princess Tina was not in any danger, and he knew it. I put my head down. Although the princess wasn't, Jess and Kat still were, but they were my responsibility, not his. My fault, and my mess to clean up somehow.

I looked up to see Roy looking me over with those smiling eyes again. I watched as he slid a hand through his sandy brown curls and wondered if the connection I felt was the same as his. I brushed that idea out of my head swiftly. I would be returning home soon, hopefully sooner than later, and Roy, he would stay here right by his cousin's side, no doubt.

Regardless of the connection or the feelings I thought I felt, no matter the lazy daydreams I saw in my mind's eye of the love we could share, we were two souls passing in the night. There would be no happy ending for this lust that filled my gut. I shook off the feeling of disappointment for not even letting myself get the chance to try for that ending. I was here for a reason, a purpose, and love, however alluring it may seem, was not it. I fixed my face in a somber calm as I looked up at Roy. I picked up one of the finger sandwiches that had been left out for us to eat as my tummy grumbled louder than I had expected. A giggle snuck from my lips.

"I guess that's one way to break the silence," Roy chided back to my belly, poking it promptly like the Pillsbury doughboy.

Another giggle escaped. I lowered my eyes to avoid his stare as I put the corner of the sandwich in my mouth as politely as I could muster. Roy, obviously feeling a little hungry as well, picked up a sandwich of his own and dug in. Once I had finished my first sandwich, I slowed down a bit to ask my host some questions that I was hoping he could answer.

"So, you knew we were coming?" I asked, looking at him from the edge of my vision as I carelessly picked up another sandwich and took a bite. Play it cool, I said to myself. He won't give me the information I really need if he thinks I'm here for something other than the same reasons he is.

Bonnie Baraka

Roy looked me over a couple times as he nodded his head, his eyes went glassy for a second and I was immediately unsure of how much information he would share with me. So, I leveled with him.

"Okay, so you knew we were coming... you knew Kat, and you knew me, but you don't know where they are now?" I regurgitated before I could stop myself slouching in my seat as I realized none of that mattered if I could not find Jess. If I didn't come home with Jess, what would her parents think? What would Pops and Trey think? How could I face life at home without her?

Tears began to wet my cheeks again as the pain finally took over, and the events of the day came crashing into my memory. All of this started over a fight with my best friend. A fight that meant nothing now. I felt him move before I could look to see what was happening, and then Roy was there squeezing me tight in his strong built-for-combat arms. This made the tears come even faster. What was I doing? I needed to keep it together for Jess, for Kat, For Gran. I needed to keep it together for myself. Pushing myself reluctantly out of his grasp, I stood and looked out onto the stadium field.

After a while, Roy joined me at the glass. "We will find them. That I can promise you. My men are out scouring the streets as we speak." He turned and grabbed my hands to pull my gaze to him. "There will be no stone left unturned."

I searched his features and found comfort in his strong jawline that told me of clenched teeth and his tight smile that made me believe he would search until his last breath.

I sighed. "I believe you," I finally managed to get out. "If only there was a way to see what actually happened in that hall," I murmured, leaning into the rail to watch the crew assemble the stage and angle the cameras in just the right way.

15

Into the Shadows

I sat up abruptly. The gears in my mind churning.

"What if we can!" I almost screamed into Roy's face. He took a step back, a little thrown at my sudden change of heart. "This morning, I was at school with Jess. We had a fight. Before we made it to lunch, everyone knew, and I was sent to the principal's office for skipping class. When I tried to assure them that I would never skip class, they showed me on camera, slipping into the BFS class to watch Jess and Ken arm-wrestle." I paused, trying to remember every detail of how they had gotten that video. I caught a glimpse of the goofy smile that had replaced the look of horror smeared across Roy's face at the thought of Jess, or probably more accurately, Tina, in an arm-wrestling match with a boy. "We can discuss how she beat him to a pulp later. Right now, we need to find all the cameras that may have picked up what went down today and get clues as to where we can find them." I looked up and around, finally taking notice of the mini discs that plastered the ceiling and awkward corners of the building. "Of course, Security Cameras! We can use the security cameras to see which way they took them! We can review the tape for clues! We may have a real chance at finding them!" I jumped up and down in place as I spoke the last words. Only to be stopped dead by the look of disappointment in Roy's buttery, inviting eyes.

"Unfortunately, we don't have any working security cameras in that hall," he said through gritted teeth. "Every time we try to put them up, they are broken. When we try to replace them, something happens, and they are again knocked down or rendered out of order." He punched his fist into his palm. "You know, one time I even found GUM covering the lenses? GUM!" Roy was fuming, and

Bonnie Baraka

I wasn't sure which part was making him angrier at that point. "Now I'm starting to think this may have been the plan all along. NOW, I am even more convinced that there is a Splice Market in my own back yard." Roy plopped in the closest chair and put his head in his hands.

I sat down on the floor in front of the picture window, scanning the field. "Spliced Market?" I asked, confused. That can't be good.

"Well, yeah. It's like a market for Slicers only, almost like a black market. That boy Sin, they say he is the one who runs it. Those rags he was wearing; they were most definitely for dramatic effect. I mean, he's not rich, but he is definitely doing well enough to afford new clothes. No rags necessary. I heard he got into the market business because his mother wants to go back to her home dimension. I haven't been able to confirm anything yet, though," Roy explained.

I heard what he wasn't saying. Spliced Market here where they are planning on unveiling a project that carried masses across dimensions is not a good thing at all, and if it's anything like any other black market, it's probably pretty hard to find or infiltrate.

"Well, I guess there may be other ways we can find them," I said glumly.

In one swift movement, Roy was turning to slide down the glass to sit with his back facing the stadium next to me. "What do you mean? Like another camera somewhere? Maybe one without the gum?" Roy huffed, tension in his voice still gripping me slightly.

I blinked. I hadn't thought of that at all.

"Well, no, that's not exactly what I meant, but not a bad idea. Maybe someone took a video of it on their phone. I do remember seeing a picture booth when we walked through as well. What about your other cameras'? And I mean, gum isn't that bad, we can still hear what is happening with those, right? Maybe we can't see, but at least they aren't completely useless."

We stood at the same time and almost knocked our heads together.

"THAT'S IT! Oh, you go first," he said, noticing my face full of ideas also, and in a rush to get started on our journey. I slid down next to him to see if we were on the same page.

"Do you guys have social media outlets also? Like I mean, can I search the events of the Worlds fest on the web? Is that a thing here?" I asked, hoping this would be something that was the same as home.

Roy, thinking hard, only said, "let's go to the libraries to see if I can get you someone who can help you with what you're asking for." Roy rose from his place next to me and grabbed for my hand. I stood up, and he led me out back through the maze of the box and out of the stadium. We walked through a garden and right up to the most glorious castle I had ever seen. I stopped in my tracks, taking in the monument.

My face must have given me away because Roy paused and said, "She is a beauty, isn't she? Equipped with a draw bridge and a moat too!" He was beaming.

"I have never seen an actual castle up close and in person before. I mostly have only seen pictures," I answered honestly. "Most castles back home have been traded in for small homes and mansions. Sign of the times, I guess." I shrugged.

We continued into the castle and up the second floor, where we found the library Roy had told me about. It was like I just kept getting thrown off by all the different things in this dimension. I began to wonder what my own home dimension had looked like before I left it. As we walked in, I chose the seat closest to the door in a quiet sitting that looked like it was made for discussion around the fireplace. Too warm outside for a fire in the middle of August yet, there wasn't one going, but the oversized chair made up for it. I turned to look around and noticed the rows and rows of books that looked like they went on forever to my right. They extended far higher than the top of the second floor. There must be hundreds of thousands of books here, I thought, intrigued.

Rising to my feet to go and see what books were in the forefront, I heard Roy making a call at the Great Wooden desk I hadn't noticed on my left. Behind the desk was a large floor to ceiling glass window that looked over all of the World or World's Festival. Torn between the Window and the books, I missed where I was going and walked straight into a table piled with books where it looked like someone had been studying.

Umph!

"I'm alright," I said, holding my hand up for Roy not to leave the desk when he looked like he was headed to help me up. With the crash and ruckus I had caused, several books had fallen into my lap on impact. I gave them a glance over and started to put them back on the table I had run into. "dimensional traveler – a tale of the Great Traveler King, Dimensional Wars – X, T and in between, Worlds unturned – how alone are we, and The Kings' guide to Slides and making the right choice." I read the titles to myself as I picked them up. The last one had me holding my breath. I looked at the author and almost dropped it again. The Great Charles King the First.

"Are you okay over there?" Roy called from the desk as he hung up the receiver.

"I'm fine. I knocked over some books and was just picking them up. You guys sure are into this Dimensional King stuff?" I said, trying to change the subject from my clumsiness.

Roy turned to see what I was talking about.

"Dimensional traveler – a tale of the Great Traveler King? Dimensional Wars – X, T and in between? Worlds unturned – how alone are we? Seems like a theme, right?" I read the titles aloud for him, keeping the last book title out of the list.

Roy, looking confused, came over to see what I was reading.

"I have never heard of these before. They must be something Tina just got to aid in her new projects," he explained.

As he approached, I turned to pick up another book that had fallen and slid the Kings Guide into the inside pocket of my jacket lent from Gran. Thanks to her for the secret pockets that expanded when I needed them.

I shrugged at his approach. "Makes sense. If you have to judge which is the best, you probably should know that kinda stuff, right?"

"That's right because we want something that won't hurt our own home while we are in the process of helping others," a voice said from behind us. Tina had entered the Library without a sound. I jumped at the strength in her sweet voice. I was just hoping she didn't see me steal the other book.

I turned to face our new guest and was nearly blown away by her beauty. Where Jess was hard and calloused, Tina was soft and sweet. How Jess would enjoy her blemishes that she felt made her who she was. Tina opted to treat and remove anything that would make her look like anything less than perfect. She was a vision of beauty so perfect that there was no way you could call her anything else. But as different as she was, she was Jess to a T.

"Oh, my goodness, where are my manners! It is a pleasure to meet you, Princess." I bowed to Tina and motioned to take her hand.

She laughed lightly and requested that I rise with one small flick of her wrist. Tina took me by the hand and led me back to the sitting area near the entrance of the library.

"So, tell me, Star, have you been enjoying my favorite cousin's company today?" Tina teased.

I blushed, hoping that she didn't already know that we were indeed enjoying each other's company on a level that we shouldn't be. I nodded in response, letting her lead the conversation where she chose. "Splendid," she replied.

"I was alerted that things went pretty badly in the Markets Hall earlier, and your companions are now missing. Please be assured that you have my best resources at your disposal in finding them. If there is anything I can do to get them back from Sin, I will do so immediately." She finished with a reassuring smile that quickly changed to anger and then to confusion as I shook my head.

"Jess was not taken by Sin. Only Kat." I recalled the tussle in the hall, and the color drained from my face. "Jess was taken by someone I remember from somewhere else. I don't know who he is now, only who he was before." I gave the answer mysteriously, not wanting to tell Tina everything about my day, but enough to help us find who we were looking for.

"Oh! I thought they were taken by Sin?" Tina asked, turning to Roy for confirmation.

Roy looked taken aback.

"I never said who took them, Cous, I just said they were taken. I also didn't get a good look at who took your doppelganger, so I am unsure of who she's talking about." He plopped down next to his cousin, deep in thought.

"Well, I did dispatch a few extra undercover guards to the Hall when I got word you were en route there. Maybe we should call them and see what they saw or what they have to report, shall we?" Tina replied with a cool head. Is she hiding something?

Roy strode back over to the desk to make a call, and no sooner did he hang up than three men all dressed in street clothes come into the library and stand before Tina in a row.

"Report" was all she said to them.

I remembered noticing one of the men in the Hall, but I felt like he was working against Roy. I said nothing as I took in the scene before us. The first man spoke, giving his recollection of what happened.

"I saw Sin with the two girls, when they broke free. I was pushed back, and when I finally made headway to them, The Decoy was safely with Roy. One girl was screaming from the middle of the crowd," he pointed to me when he said this, "and the other was running for the group. They had split up in the crowd. At that point, the crowd busted through, and the Decoy was lost in the sea. I did not see where she went. The two girls running from Sin were lost to me also until I saw Sin haul one over his shoulder. I assumed at that point they were both taken and tried to effect crowd control at that time to get to the Decoy." The man stepped back into the line to let the next speak.

"I saw much of the same as he. I tried to help the other girl in the crowd, but she tore away from me, heading back in the other direction." He shrugged and stepped back as well. I frowned at this recalling. Why would Kat run back towards Sin?

The third man stepped forward. "I was at a different vantage point than where they were positioned. I saw the fight ensue between the two girls and Sin, but Ken and I were too far away to get there. We made a path for Roy to leave with the Decoy, but when he didn't, it was futile." The man then turned and nodded to Roy to alert him he saw his hesitation in the field. "When the stand collapsed, and the Decoy fell into the crowd, it was this girl that caught her and turned to fight off the crowd so the Decoy could get away. I gave space for the Decoy to continue past us, but she was stopped short. So, Ken went in and got her out. I believe they used one of the old passageways to get her to safety and are probably in a safe house in the city awaiting orders now." He finished his recalling and stepped back with a smirk on his face as to say, Gotcha Prince.

I blinked. Jess was okay! I felt all the tension I was holding in with each story given escape my body. Jess was with Ken, that I knew, but Ken was not a bad guy here, that was news, and this news was the best news all afternoon! Jess and Ken were friends back home; she wouldn't be scared or in trouble. I took a deep breath and let it out, just as Princess Tina relayed the last bit of information that set me right back on edge.

"The safe houses are empty. I checked them already, hoping that this was the case instead of the latter," she said as she waved her hand for them to exit. "Also, please do not think that I missed the point in your story where you accused my cousin of being more concerned about people he barely knew than me—his Princess. I was safely waiting on him back here, and his orders were to bring all three girls here. Waiting for the other two instead of getting the decoy out, again not me, does not have anything to do with his loyalty, Sam." She rolled her eyes at the third man. "You should probably be more concerned about where your partner is right now." Then she added, "Find him!"

The men shuffled hurriedly out of the room, and Roy looked from the door to his cousin with shock.

"Why are you being so mean, Tina?" Roy asked with surprise deep in his voice.

At this, Tina straightened and turned her charming smile and voice back on to answer.

"He clearly was trying to insult you! I will not stand by and have my cousin's loyalty questioned."

She batted her lashes, and I saw right through that act. She put on a good show for Roy, but I was beginning to think Tina wasn't the nicest person to work for.

"One down, one to go!" Tina turned to me and said with a genuine smile that made me want to give her the benefit of the doubt.

Internally I didn't agree, but my hope for finding Jess was restored by the news we just heard. I reached for my stone matching Jess' and thought I could almost feel her delight. Whether it was real or I was imagining it, I was unsure, but that didn't matter.

"Kat ran back towards Sin?" I turned to Roy quizzically. "Did you see that happen?"

"I was a little busy fighting off a hoard of angry people and praying you two made it out, so no, I must have missed it. What I saw was both of you running for the cart, you split, and she got to us first, then the crowd surged, and she was gone again. I can't say how she made it to Sin's hold, but he definitely left with her over his shoulder." He finished confidently. I agreed—that was what I remembered also.

"Well, I guess we better start to scour the cameras to see if we can find her, maybe traffic cameras or something?" I asked him.

"We can start there, maybe the web thingy you were talking about. We don't really need the cameras in the Hall when we know they left." Roy stood to go back over to the desk, beckoning us to follow him.

We followed his lead and watched as he tapped into the cameras and looked vigorously for Kat.

"Stop! There! On the next corner! This one!" I yelled, pointing to the video on the corner of the screen. "That looks like her blonde hair right there!" I was excited.

"No, that's not her. This camera is the farthest away from the Hall at the back of the grounds. They wouldn't have made it there that fast unless they teleported or something," Roy said, turning away from the video I was talking about.

I focused on this video until it was over. The video showed a blonde walking into a church, ragged men in front and behind her. I understood that there was no way, but I knew it was her. Wanting to be sure all the same with all the other factors against it, I reviewed all the other camera videos with Roy. Coming up with nothing. We found a few others who looked like they could be Kat, but when we followed them, they turned out to be someone else completely.

"This is boring, we haven't gotten anywhere, and I would rather read a book," Tina said, rolling her eyes. "All my scouts are out searching for them, so I will be over here researching this in the meantime." And with her last declaration, she walked back to the stack of books on the table where she was studying. I plopped down in the desk chair next to Roy as she walked away, feeling defeated.

"She has to be here somewhere," I sighed. "She didn't just disappear!" Unless she did. Seizing the controls from Roy and maximizing the video I initially thought was Kat to full-screen size, I went back to just before I thought I saw her on the screen. I turned the camera to further down the street in the direction of where the group came from. Nothing.

"Star, there's no one there. This is pointless; I told you there is no way." Roy stopped mid-sentence when he saw Kat materialize out of nothing onto the street corner. I jumped out of my chair in surprise. "Where did they come from? How could they just?" Roy was in total shock.

"Far more advanced than you initially thought I see." I turned to Roy with a solemn look. "They are Slicers. Apparently, that means pocket travel as well, not just large dimension to dimension."

"What travel?" He asked, a look of horror streaked across his face. At the commotion we were making, Tina looked up from her reading. At the same time, 'Sam' walked back into the library. Good news, I hope.

"Good news, we have located Ken & the Decoy. They are in the safe house just outside the stadium in oldtown," Sam said cheerfully.

"Well done, friend. We will be to retrieve them shortly; I believe we have found all we need to find here and will be to move out. Please alert Ken that we are on our way and to hold tight.", Roy admonished as he strode over to the guard and clapped him on his back in thanks. Sam, beaming at the praise, left the room as quickly as he had arrived to go deliver the message.

"Found something then, have you?" Tina said from beside him.

"I believe we have! Looks like they are in the old abandoned church, right here in our very own back yard. I think it would be better to go and retrieve the decoy first and then proceed to get the other. The more time it takes, the less Sin will be expecting us. We can use that to our advantage." Roy shared his plan with Tina and me.

Still standing at the desk, I continued to watch and re-watch the camera video until I was sure there was something going on I did not like. Kat didn't seem to be in any danger. Her body language said she knew these people and judging by the fact that she had been here before many times, I was willing to bet she had. What troubled me was how she had met them, and what was happening now.

"Very well then, cousin, as you wish. I will wait here for an update on the outcome," Tina said as she strode back to her studying. Roy looked to me. I hadn't moved from my spot, deep in thought.

"Time to go, Star!" He shouted as if we were not standing in a large room with just the three of us.

I moved toward the door with a final glance at Tina. She had her head down as though she was engrossed in reading, but the expression on her face was nothing of inquisitive. She looked far angrier that I waged she should be with finding the two people she had just vowed to use every resource to locate.

16

"**D**on't think I missed what you said in there about pocket dimension travel," Roy said as we left the castle. I turned to look at him, trying to determine if he was upset, or simply confused. His face said nothing to alert me of either direction.

"Did I say something wrong? I asked before giving him anything more. I can't be the only one giving away information today, especially when all this stuff was brand new to me.

"Probably not. You are probably correct. I just didn't know it was even a thing. We know some stuff about Travelers, but we are not all-knowing, and ever since the LA disbanded, it's hard to recover much of anything. The only people who seem to know anything around here are the damn Slicers." Roy pounded his fist into his hand. So that was anger I spied.

"Ah, well, before today, I didn't know much of anything, or even believe this was possible, But after the day I am having, I am quite sure the people who truly believe anything is possible are spot on," I mumbled, feeling slightly grumpy myself. "What is the 'LA' anyway?" I asked.

Roy led us down a town street going away from the festival. The noise was not any less, but you could tell this was a different part of town completely. There were more drunk men outside of bars and in the streets and women in their home washing clothes. There were no children to be seen, but crying babies were heard through open windows. Not to mention the smell that was burning through my nose. Whiskey and BO. This must have been the area where people worked to earn their living instead of frolicking all day. As I realized this to myself, the people around me confirmed it with sneers and discomforting looks at Roy's uniform. I was just wondering if he had noticed when he put his eyes down, trying to look away from the unkind faces. He noticed alright, and he hated it.

"LA or LAO was the Legacy Acceptance Organization. They were a group of Sliders who gave their lives to ensure the safety of the multi-verse," Roy said with pride. "My father was in the LAO, and I wanted to one day be a part of it too until I found out they disbanded, and there were only a few left. That's when the Slicers got stronger. I don't know if they have an organization like the LAO or if they just share knowledge, but I have heard that most places have a Spliced Market and that most Slicers have at least one student that they choose to teach their crafts and carry on their own ancestry. Which is why they thrive where we don't," Roy finished.

"So, you are a Slider? Didn't your father ever teach you anything about Sliding?" I asked, curious.

"I am not a Slider. I am a Soldier. I was not born the same as you, and my father was incredibly sad when he learned of it. He loved me, but he hated that I was not like him and that he could not teach me the ways," Roy recalled gruesomely.

"Where is he now? Shouldn't he be helping in stopping whatever is happening? I mean, if he was a part of the LAO and all," I asked, confused as to why I was even here if there was a trained LA member living right here.

"He passed away, stopping the last Slicer event," Roy bowed his head in remembrance. Lost in thought and not paying attention to where we were going, Roy missed our turn. "Shit!" Roy swore. "I don't come down here enough, I guess. Let's loop here and go around."

We turned into an alley just as a commotion started behind us. I turned just in time to see Jess and Ken fighting with some men I did not know.

Then he was there, dressed in black jeans with a black shirt that had red wings embroidered beautifully on the back. Jet black hair tucked behind his ear and hanging long down his back, Sin was an embodiment of a demon himself. He had the 'bad boy' look down pact, and I doubted he had ever veered from it.

Even in his earlier rags, he looked like someone you didn't want to cross. I knew from experience I didn't wish the emotions rolling through his soul on anyone.

I turned to look at Roy, who was already on his way to help. He made it there too late. The three men that were flanking Sin had overpowered Ken and were headed to grab Jess.

"Jess!! Look Out!" I screamed in a dead run to get to my friend. Jess spun around at my voice and right into her attacker's arms. Her eyes locked onto mine and she pleaded for me to run the other way with them, but I would do no such thing! I launched myself at one of the men, feet first, and landed right on top of him.

"Look what we have here," came a voice of burning, liquid metal from behind me. It was Sin, and he was advancing quickly.

I sprang to my feet, backing away from the voice and grabbing Jess as I did. The instant we locked hands; I was given a glimpse of her day with Ken. Walking through the festival, getting away through the hidden passages together, all the knowledge she gained, like a picture show in my mind's eye. It was like she was pushing her visions to me through her emotions. Along with a message.

'You have to run; they want you, not me. You are what they need to complete their Voyage home. I will be ok! I have learned a few things this afternoon, but you have to go!!' Jess' voice sounded strongly in my head. She made eye contact to make sure I understood her message and then turned and threw herself at Sin.

"Ken! Now!" Jess said to Ken as she took out Sin's second lackey. At her command, Ken sprang into action, jolting Roy and grabbing me. He slung me over his shoulder and bolted for the alleyway we were headed down when I started to protest not to leave Jess. Roy, confused and clearly not in on this plan, tried to stay and help Jess as well.

"No, you have to go! NOW!" She said, and she pushed Roy behind Ken. I felt the tears fall as I watched Jess' body fall to the ground with a piercing blow from Sin.

Bonnie Baraka

"NOOOOOO!" I yelled until I was hoarse. "We have to go back! We must get her! We can't just leave her!" I was sobbing.

"Shhh... it's okay," Ken soothed as he sat me down against the Alleyway wall and grabbed Roy to make sure he didn't turn around. "I will explain everything, but we are running out of time. They will be on us again in a minute." Realizing he was right and everything Jess just did would have been for nothing if we let that happened, I calmed enough to think about what to do next.

"Where do we go?" I asked them both, searching their faces hoping they would know. Neither said a word, looking from one to another, hoping the other had a plan. I reached up to brush the hair out of my face, and the tiny mirror brushed against my cheek. Well, he wanted to know about pocket dimensions, didn't he? I sighed to myself and grabbed for the mirror.

Ken, seeing what I held in my fingers, immediately asked, "Do you know how to access the door?"

I looked at him, shocked. How did he know what I was holding or that it had a door? I shook my head—both in disbelief and acceptance that I didn't know how to open the pocket base.

Reading my face for both, Ken instantly raised my wrist mirror aimed towards the wall and punched me in the gut.

"UGGHHHHH!" I yelled in pain. In my yell of pain, a door shown on the wall where the mirror shone. Right where red brick and green moss used to be, now stood a deep purple door outlines with Gold crown molding. The purple had flakes of silver in it, giving it a shine like no other. It stood before us only where the mirror shone on the wall, as if it had always been there.

Roy, turning from the approaching thugs to the wall, almost fell back in shock. Ken grabbed me and hauled me through the door, pulling Roy with him. He shut the door tight and locked it behind us, as bells and alarms started to blare everywhere.

We were in a sort of uncomfy entryway that I did not see the last time Jess and I were here. Doubled over, clutching my throbbing stomach where Ken had just punched me, I looked around for the source of the alarm. Seeing a password reader on the other side of the room, I slunk over to it, still grabbing my stomach to see if I could turn it off.

"Intruder! Intruder! Intruder!" The system called, not in Suzie's voice. I wondered where she was and why she wasn't here to confirm it was me.

"It's me. Starla King. I have two guests with me. They are not intruders. They are allies." I yelled at the alarm system. Nothing happened. As the pain in my tummy lessened, I stood up and put my hand on the panel to try and turn it off. Reaching to touch the enter button, the panel pricked me, and blood started to blossom on my finger. I yelped again. Why is this such a painful process?

"Put...The Blood...ON THE READER!" Ken called from behind me.

I turned to see the color draining from both boys' faces as they were frozen in place. Literally. Ice was forming at their feet and threatening to freeze them whole. I turned to the panel and saw a place to deposit my blood and apparently confirm that it was, in fact, a King who was in need.

"System confirmed, Welcome Starla King. Thank you for your deposit. Please proceed." The system called back, and two more panels appeared next to mine. I turned to see if they were still stuck to the floor, but Ken was rushing to the panel farthest from mine and depositing his own sample without delay.

"You need to hurry and do what she did, Roy, or you're in for a world of hurt. Hurry! There isn't time to explain right now!" Ken was coaxing Roy to follow his lead. Roy was still frozen in place, but it was no longer by the floor or the ice—it was shock. I went over to Roy and grabbed his hand, leading him to the panel and pushing his finger up to the keys. He let me lead him and did what was necessary with no fuss, but you could tell he was still in a daze.

"Thank you! Welcome Royalti Mathews of Dimension V and Kendarough Conners of Dimension C. Ken, we have been expecting you," the system said in a delightful voice and opened the door to our actual base.

It looked different than the last time I was here. Things were scattered in places I didn't remember leaving them. The chairs were moved and arranged in a sort of conference meeting style, and my big squishy chair was missing altogether. I walked to the back of the room, where there were refreshments to hydrate myself. I turned to Roy and Ken and threw them bottled water also. Hopefully, that would give us some time to figure out how Ken knew about the pocket base, why Suzie or the Pocket System or whoever was expecting him, and why Roy looked like he was about to throw up.

I took a seat at the large table and offered them both to do the same. Not sure where to start, I was hoping one of them would do so instead. Neither did, of course, and we sat there and drank water in silence until my bottle was empty, and I was debating on getting another. I wonder if I have to like, restock the cabinets and stuff here like we do at home, or if it just happens? I was thinking when Ken finally spoke.

"Roy, are you okay? You look like you're going to be sick man, are you alright?" Ken asked in a tone that made me feel as though these two had known each other for a long time.

"How did you know how to get in here?" Roy slammed his water down on the table, sloshing a little on the floor. "How did you know how to get past the security? What made you so confident to leave the Decoy?" Roy asked Ken in a rush of questions with a look of anger and disappointment on his face. "I thought you were reporting back everything you found out about Sin's operations," Roy finished and tuned away from Ken, who looked not only confused, but hurt at the assumption.

"I am, I mean, I have. I told you everything I learned from Sin, the Spliced Market, all the others over there. I told you everything. What purpose would it serve me to hide information like this from you?" Ken responded.

"Then how did you know?" Roy retorted, not backing down an inch from his first accusation. He didn't care about their friendship; he wanted answers.

Ken, clearly feeling the tension, sighed deeply and sat back. He started to tell us of the day he shared with Jess and how he came to know the base.

"Did you know this was the LAO Office?" He looked at Roy and asked with wonder in his eyes.

Roy sat back and looked around, a little slower this time, taking it all in a little more. I guess he hasn't realized that we got here with my mirror. I held up my bracelet to show him the mirror and the engraving on the back. 'for a Legacy in need.' I didn't know what it meant at the time, but after him giving me a history, I knew the Legacy they meant was the Legacy Acceptance team members. Roy looked at my bracelet, and the color slid from his face.

"You are in the LAO?" He asked, flirting with the anger in his belly.

"Look, until you told me on our way here, I didn't even know what the engraving meant. I didn't know how to get in here, and before this morning, I didn't even know any of this existed." I shot a glance over at Ken. "I'm assuming punching me in the gut was completely necessary for us to get in here?"

Ken paled sheepishly.

"I am really sorry about that. I am. You should definitely ask your AI how to get in here without that option because it's really bad. I mean, I get it's a distress thing if you can't perform your entrance sequence because you're hurt, it's good, but if that's the only way you can get in, that's probably not a good thing." Ken shrugged and continued before we could interrupt him again.

"Anyway. If you let me tell you what happened today, I think you will have a completely different set of questions." Ken cut his eyes at Roy, who was trying not to let his anger get the best of him.

"When I got Jess out of the hall earlier, we used the old passageways, and we made it to the big Ferris wheel. I was headed to the safe house in Moorestown when we were intercepted by some more of Sin's gang. Jess got a little banged up. I mean, there were five of 'em and I was doing my best, but that girl will not just leave it to the experts, will she?" Noticing my stare, he wiped his face and continued with the story.

"Sorry anyway, I didn't think we were going to get away, but she put her hand up to block a punch, and I saw the door appear in the mirror like yours. I didn't realize that it wasn't a real door until I pushed her into the wall. After she yelled in pain and punched me, she fell into the wall, and we tumbled in. She didn't know how to access it either. I almost didn't make it in time to deposit my blood for sure, but Jess is a very smart girl." Ken winked at me. "She figured it out, and we made it here. That is why I knew how to get in, that and I asked a few questions once we were in." Ken gave Roy a look that said 'told you so' before turning back to finish the story.

"When we got in here, Suzie was waiting for us, asking all sorts of questions. Taking inventory of what we saw and learned and asking where you were. Jess thought you would meet her here, so we waited for a bit, but then I asked her if you knew how to get back in here, and she said no, so we went to plan B." He turned back to Roy. "That's when I called Sam to check in and make sure the other two ladies made it out. He told me only one and that Tina was combing the streets looking for the others. So, we arranged to meet you all here. As far away from the commotion as possible. That meant we also had to travel across town from where we were. We got Jess a disguise and tried to blend in with the crowd."

Ken blushed, obviously leaving something else that must have happened around that time out. I would be sure to ask Jess about that later. I knew she would tell me, so I let him finish.

"About halfway here, we ran into Sin and the other girl. It looked like they were on a date or something, but I couldn't be sure. They were having dinner at that little Italian place you two used to go to all the time." He paused to let that set in.

Roy turned away looking taken fully by surprise at that last bit of information. So, they did do things other than work! I noted.

"So, Jess and I found a table close enough to hear what they were talking about but far enough away not to be seen. I'm thinking if I can find an opening in the convo, or one of them goes to the bathroom or something, I can get the girl, and we can make a dash for the safe house. But that's not what happened. We heard everything. Their plan, what is about to happen, who is in on it, everything. So, we slipped away from the restaurant and kept going to the safe house to meet you. Hoping that Jess and Star could come up with a plan to stop the inevitable and then make a break for home before Jess starts to get sick."

"SICK?" I stopped Ken mid-story to confirm what I had just heard. Jess was fine; she wasn't sick. She was fine. Both Ken and Roy turned to me with concern on their faces.

Slicers

"Wait, so how did you get into a fight all the way over here near the safe house if you saw them at the Italian spot?" Roy turned back to Ken, clearly trying to change the subject.

"Good question, and one I would like to know the answer to as well," Ken said, slamming his fist down on the table. "I thought he might have seen me leave, but that place is at least a 20-minute walk away from where they caught up to us. I was intently careful not to be seen, and they knew exactly which one was Jess."

"Pocket Travel!" Roy and I said together. Ken flinched. He was clearly familiar with the term.

"Pocket Travel? You mean like going into a pocket dimension and using another door to come out somewhere else?" Ken looked bewildered.

"Well, obviously, you have heard this term before to have defined it perfectly," I said to him rolling my eyes. Were they trying to get me off the fact that they just said Jess was sick? "Back to this Jess being sick thing," I said to bring the conversation back.

"So, you don't know then?" Ken said slowly. "I didn't think you would, you know, since she didn't either. I didn't want to be the one to tell you, but it looks like it's going to be me." He turned to Roy, hoping for a way out.

Realization had set in on Roy's face, and he looked to Ken with a nod to show him that he would deliver the news. Roy took my hands in his and faced me straight on.

"Princess Tina's mother is sick; do you know why?" Roy started, hoping background information would help. I shook my head. "Her mother is sick because when people told her that she should not Slide and that every time she hopped from one dimension to the other, she was hurting herself, she did not believe them. She has O negative blood." He stopped to let the words sink in.

"What does that have to do with Jess?" I pulled away from Roy angrily. Ken looked at me in shock. Roy put his head down. "What is it!?"

"Jess is also O-, Star. Didn't you know that?" Ken said, anger creeping into his voice now.

Bonnie Baraka

I looked at Ken, startled at the fierceness in his tone and the fire in his eyes. "How could I have known that?" I retorted quietly. Tears welling up in my eyes at one single thought, Did I kill Jess by bringing her here?

The emotion wasn't lost upon Ken. He reached out a hand in comfort and turned to Roy to continue. As another thought crossed my mind, why is he so angry about it?

"With Tina's mother, it wasn't immediate. She did in fact go on many adventures for many years and help an abundance of people, with no problem. I guess it affects some more than others, and it probably has to do with the gifts the Creator has given and how well you can master them. After a while, she would get sick after every slide. Then she would just get sick randomly, until it came to the point where she is now, where she can't even get out of bed. She once told me the longer the trip, the sicker she would be when she made it home."

Roy hung his head at reliving the conversations he had with his Aunt.

"I believe that is why Tina is so hell-bent on finding a way to get masses through the barrier without harming the way things are. If she can, then she thinks she may be able to help her mother or make it to a dimension where all the healers are and bring one back. I won't say her efforts are futile or ill-placed, I will say the worst part of watching all of this, is knowing that If she makes it to the place where she wants to go, her efforts may be in vain, since her mother probably won't make it that long," Roy finished and put his head down on the table in thought.

"So, Jess isn't sick, but we want to solve this mystery and get her home before she is sick, which could be anywhere from now to never." I threw my hands in the air and pushed back from the table, standing up to pace. "Kat is on the side of the bad and dangerous, no surprise there if you know her. We are stuck in a pocket dimension until we figure out what else is going on and how to get out, and the only one who has a clue just sacrificed herself for me to get away. Have I got everything?" I asked, slightly pissy.

"Wait, I haven't even told you what we learned yet, why would you say she's the only one who knows what going on?" Ken beamed in front of me, clearly proud of himself.

"Sorry, well, I guess that true. I just assumed she was since she told me to run and that they were looking for me to finish their project and push off in their maiden voyage." I shrugged, sitting back down.

"When did she tell you all of that?" Roy asked, confused.

"When we were out there trying to fight off Sin." I looked at him with my own confused face. He was standing right there; didn't he hear us talking?

Ken pushed back from the table to get a good look at me. "Star, the only thing she said to you out there was to run." He blinked.

"No, she didn't. She said I was the one they wanted, that she would be fine, and that she had learned some things on her trip to the safe house. I mean, she didn't go into detail, but she did say that!" I looked from one boy to the other. Both were looking like they had seen a ghost.

"She is an Earth Dreamer," Ken said blandly as he stood and started to pace, himself.

I had no clue what that was, so I didn't even move. I turned to Roy to see that he had gone a few shades lighter at the words.

"She can't be! Can she? I mean, there are only like three that we are aware of ever being created. EVER. In any dimension! She can't be." Roy was shaking his head and coming to his final decision.

"If what she told you is true, that would make you the slider with a heart of Gold," Ken said, stopping his pace to look at me. It was almost as if he was trying to look through me to see my heart. "That also means they already have the other pieces they need. A balancing heart of differences, and a heart with the innocence unfound," Ken stated.

"Am I supposed to know what ANY of this means!?" I yelled, finally coming to my breaking point. "SUZIE! WHERE ARE YOU!?" I searched, finally taking notice that Suzie had not come to check on us at all. I looked around for her to show her face. Suzie didn't so much as hum. "I will reboot you if you don't come out here right now! I can do that, you know!" I yelled at the air.

S uzie never showed. I walked over to the computer and slammed my fist on the keyboard. Nothing happened. I walked around to be sure it was plugged in. It was. I held down the large button that looked like power in the center of the console and listened to the computer whirr into action and then stop. Not sure what else to do, I turned to Ken to see if he knew what was happening.

"You said you saw Suzie when you were here last, right?" I asked him, slamming my fingers into the keys.

Yes, she met us at the door. Asked all kinds of weird questions to be honest, but she was helpful in the end." Ken shrugged. "She helped us with the plan to get back to you, and then she and Jess had a conversation about how pretty she looked and some other stuff I tuned out."

"Then, where the hell is she now?" I said under my breath. Shaking my head, I sat down in the large chair and shook the mouse hoping that would at least wake the computer up so I could do some research. I turned back to Ken to get him to continue talking. "Well, get on with it then, we will have to figure out what's happening and how to get Jess back, and soon I would guess," I said, pointing to the clock. "They are taping the projects tonight, right?" I asked Roy.

"Mmmmhmmm," Roy said, deep in thought. "Wow, an Earth Dreamer, and I didn't even notice." I couldn't tell if he was talking to us or himself. "I mean, you, I noticed for sure. Your training is shotty, and your emotions spill all over the place when you're happy. It's only right. But an Earth Dreamer right in front of me?" Roy shook his head and looked up as we stared. He must have completely forgotten that we were here because he blushed. Ken, listening to what he said, turned to me.

"Empath, of course. That's why you stood between me and Jess this morning. You could feel her emotions building up," Ken said with enthusiasm.

I blinked twice and then whirled to face Ken.

"I KNEW IT!" I exploded out of the chair, forgetting the computer completely. "It was you this morning in BFS! Everyone knows ESPECIALLY Ken Conners, the boy who has been on Jess' team since she was 3, not to ask her that dumb question." I was walking towards Ken now. I didn't know what I was going to do when I got there, but I was on my way!

"I know," Ken whined. "But I couldn't help myself. I saw her, and she was confident and beautiful and hiding the best qualities of herself, and I wanted to see her in action! I just couldn't help it!" Ken was blushing. It was hard to think anything could taint his beautiful mahogany skin, but he was standing in front of me, cheeks as red as a fire engine. "I drew too much attention to myself; I know. Especially since the real Ken Conners moved away a week ago." Ken slumped against the wall behind where he had been pacing. He had been going to school with us for a whole week, and we didn't even know it wasn't the same Ken.

"Wow. Just WOW!" I said, backing away. I had never heard anyone talk about Jess in such a feminine way. Well, except that one kid that she pulverized in 3rd grade. This was becoming more interesting by the minute. I was going to need to get the details of the afternoon from Jess later.

"So, you were what, spying on us?" I asked, confused. "Why were you in the Various Dimension at all?" I couldn't understand why Ken would be there watching us if we knew nothing about him. Ken was fading into the wall behind him as much as he could manage with every question.

"Jin asked me to watch you," Ken whispered.

At the mention of her name, I sank to my knees. My Gran. Ken knew my Gran? I sat in silence as Roy tried to spark another conversation around me. He came over and hoisted me back up in the oversized computer chair while asking Ken if he had learned anything else of use from the Slicers.

"We did learn of their plan from sitting at the restaurant. It was weird. It was like the girl, Kat. I felt like she could see us. She looked directly at Jess a couple times, and she kept egging Sin on to talk to her about their plan. But she was definitely not in any distress, and she was not leaving his side. So, it was hard to tell if we should leave or not." Ken shrugged. I was only half-listening, as I was thinking of my Gran instead.

"So, all this stuff is going on here, and you travel to another dimension to babysit someone's granddaughter?" I asked angrily. I couldn't believe what I was hearing. I also couldn't believe that these two tried to change the subject AGAIN.

"It wasn't like that. I got a tip that something was about to go down with Sin and his crew. I didn't know if it was true or not, but I knew I couldn't blow my cover. So, I went to see your Gran. That's when I found out she was sick, and her replacement hadn't even been properly trained. She begged me to keep an eye on you. Said keeping an eye on you would be a better use of time, and now I know why. If you are the last piece of the puzzle for them to execute, well, we better keep you safe then, shouldn't we?" He hesitated to say the rest; looking at my face and continued on. "She told me to bring you straight to her once all of this was over, she said she wanted to be the one to help you through the transition, and she wished she could be with you, but she is sick, and it is weird. She is sick like Tina's mother, but she is not of O- blood. Leads me to believe there is foul play somewhere. But I think we will need to deal with one crisis at a time." Ken sat in the chair closest to the computer and turned towards us.

"I supposed you're right," I said with sorrow in my voice. Hoping my Gran would make it that long. "Let's lay out what we do know and see if we can come up with something to trip them up." I took a deep breath and recalled what I knew. "They are going on a maiden voyage. Sounds like some sort of ship. Is it a boat-like ship, or is it like a spaceship?" I asked aloud, not expecting an answer. "Well, you were pretty solid with that guess, weren't you?" Roy said with no enthusiasm. "The contest is full of both."

I put my head down. I couldn't work with all the emotions in this room and most certainly not mine. I put a pillow over my face and screamed at the top of my lungs. After a full minute of doing so, I pulled the pillow down to see both

Ken and Roy on their knees filled with emotions. Ken weeping and Roy laughing, both uncontrollably and begging for it to stop. I shot to my feet and grabbed Ken, raising him up to his feet and helping him back to his chair. I followed suit with Roy, who was still laughing.

"What happened?" I asked, feeling more confused by the minute. "This is no time for jokes, and I mean seriously Ken, I'm sad too, but weeping?" I looked from one boy to the other. They had stopped their emotional fits and were looking at me with venom dripping.

"You are apparently an extremely powerful empath, who has never been taught how to use their gift. You just screamed EMOTIONS into a pillow for a full minute straight, and you're going to ask us why we are having a fit?" Ken looked like he might punch me in the gut again.

I giggled. How was I supposed to know what was happening?

"I would laugh with you, but my abs are sore from the laugh fest I have just completed. Apologies," Roy said sarcastically. He turned and walked over to the computer screen that was dark and used it was a white board instead. "I'm going to dismiss that all together and move on. I am going to insist you get a hold on that sooner rather than later, though. We are lucky you didn't choose rage to be let out instead."

"I'm sorry, guys. I didn't know," I started, but Roy put his hand up to stop me. I sat back down in a flop and angled my chair toward his makeshift whiteboard. I turned to see how Ken was doing and noticed that he had genuine tears in his eyes that I didn't think belonged to me.

As he noticed my watch, he wiped them away and moved to a better position to view Roy. Ken started to tell what he knew, as Roy wrote.

"I am willing to bet it's probably a ship as in a boat. I heard Sin talking about his mother's dimension. I believe it is mostly covered in water there. So, disguising a boat that will help them there in the contest to get insider knowledge would be smart, and Sin is definitely smart," Ken finished confidently.

Bonnie Baraka

"Agreed. There are very few boats in the contest. Sunshine Kaster's of Switzerstill, Charlie's and Tina's project actually." Roy nodded. "So, should we just go ahead and assume that it is Sunshine's?" Roy asked.

"No," I said flatly. "I wouldn't do that at all." I shrugged. Charlie was sad about something, and I didn't know what. I wouldn't rule him out.

"Are you implying that the project could belong to My cousin or your father?" Roy asked in an insulted tone. I was beginning to see what Tina was talking about when it came to his loyalties. He was completely devoted to her, and it showed.

"I am merely saying that just because the project belongs to someone we can trust or THINK we can trust doesn't mean that Sin hasn't decided that project is the one he will steal or use." I shrugged again. "Besides, Charlie is not my father. My father is back at home in another dimension completely, and the Charlie here is sad beyond repair about something, and I have no clue what it is." I wouldn't put it past anyone at this point. Ken turned to me with pity in his eyes.

"He is sad because they took his son," Ken said quietly. "I couldn't figure out who took him or why, but now I know both. It would be wise to assume that Charlie's project is the one they plan to use." Ken paused, questions clearly swirling across his face. "Roy, have you seen Tina's project?" he asked curiously.

Roy shook his head. "She won't let anyone in or out. She is hell-bent on keeping it a secret even from me." He looked a little hurt with the news he shared with the room.

Ken sank back, defeated.

"I think we're going to have a bigger problem than I originally thought," he said directly to me. I could read the despair in his face when he voiced his next opinion in the room. "I have seen Tina's project when I was investigating for Sin. It looks exactly like the boat in the picture behind you and Jess in her BFS locker." Ken turned to me, hoping I read what he didn't say. I did, and I wasn't the only one.

186

"What are you trying to say?" Roy said angrily, turning on his old friend once more. This wasn't going to go well. We would need solid evidence to convince him that Ken wasn't making it up.

"Tell me more about the boy. What exactly happened?" I jumped in between them to move to something a little more pressing.

Roy, who looked like he was filled to the brim with fire, backed off slightly, like a bobcat waiting for the perfect time to pounce.

"Charlie reported that he would no longer be a part of the competition. He said it was too risky and that there were far too many things that were unknowns. He dropped out of the race on national TV," Ken started to tell the story. He looked at Roy for help in recalling the event sequence.

"That's right, he dropped out, and then he went in his house, and he never left. Closed down his TV studio and neglected his kids," Roy said viciously.

I couldn't believe that would be the case. Ken rolled his eyes at the last part also. Charlie would never neglect his children or anyone's children for that matter. I found it really hard to believe that even across dimensions that his core traits would be that much different.

"How different are people across dimensions?" It was the only thing I could think of to cool the water. If we could convince Roy that things were not right, we didn't need to convince him it was Tina. Was it Tina? I couldn't be sure of anything at this point.

"Most core character traits are the same, names very rarely are. Same person looks-wise and stuff, but its thoughts actions and stuff that's different. Like in one dimension you could be a painter, and in another you could be a truck driver who hates art. Just depends." Ken gave an example to get me in the right direction.

"So, if Charlie was a father to not only his children but also others, like say one Justina Mathews, in one dimension, then he would probably not just randomly neglect his kids in another, right?" I asked intently, interested in hearing the response. My question and the honesty in it got Roy thinking.

"No, that is not what that means, but if I'm being honest, I never thought he neglected his kids. There were many pictures of him and the boy in the studios when we first went to visit the project. He was attached to his son. I also remember that he fell ill shortly after his son was taken, and then the rumors came of neglect. He just never recovered from losing him," Roy said, exasperated and plopped down in a chair close to the board. We were getting nowhere with this line of questioning, but it did get him to thinking.

"Okay, so it could be any of the three. Let's move on to other things we know," Ken said, hoping to change the subject to a lighter mood. "Jess is an Earth Dreamer. I am hoping that they don't know that, because if they find out, they won't need you anymore." Ken looked over at me.

"I still don't know what any of these things are, but okay. I'm an Empath, she's a Dreamer, and we're all one big happy family," I said, throwing my hands in the air. I shook my head, and Ken busted out laughing.

"Well, you're both empaths. She's a Dreamer, you're an Emo. She can manipulate dreams like you can manipulate emotions. Don't you get it? She can see the barriers, she can see the tares, and if she's powerful enough, she can repair them." Ken beamed bright. I wasn't sure if it was because he was excited to have figured it out, or if he was just excited for Jess—either way, he was giddy. "We will have plenty of time to teach you both about all of this AFTER we get this situation handled. Deal?" He asked.

"Fine. I mean, that is awesome, though!" I let the excitement of Jess having a purpose wash over me. "She's going to be so happy." I smiled to myself. "Okay, so yea, let's talk about Jess for a minute! So, she was showing me dreams? It was crazy, for sure! So exciting! But back to what she was saying. What do they need me for?" I asked.

"Heart of Gold, you will sacrifice yourself for those you love without a second thought. Probably those you don't even know?" Roy looked at me longingly. He was probably right; I can be a bit over the top, but I have my moments of anger too. I wasn't sure they had chosen the right person for this one.

"Makes sense, though. The boy with innocence pure and unfound has a big sister with a Heart of Gold? I would say that is a definite reflection of how you protect him. He is innocent beyond any other," Ken said with a sunny disposition that made me uneasy.

"But again, my baby brother is safe and sound in another dimension. So, it has nothing to do with me. Plus, the Star in this dimension is missing. So, I don't think we are the same in that right. Just from being around Kat, I can assure you we are quite different. 'but the same' is how Kat described it. Finding her was the actual reason Kat agreed to help us get here in the first place. Now I'm beginning to believe that was probably a lie too." I shook my head. "She probably already has her tied up somewhere, or they are working together or something." I shrugged. "That's what would happen if it was Jess and me anyway."

Roy rose to his feet. "Shit." He hit himself in the face. "They probably already do have her." He spun around to Ken with hysteria on his face. "Did they say they already had all the missing pieces? Or did Jess guess at that?"

"They never said. They said there were three pieces needed; they called them Heart of Gold, Innocence unfound, Balancing Soul. Said they would get the Heart of Gold today, and they would be ready for their voyage tomorrow while everyone was busy watching the show. Kat and Jess made eye contact a few times, and after Jess was different. Maybe that's when she found out she could Dream ride. Maybe she had a conversation with Kat, and that is how she knew the 3rd person needed was Star." Ken stood from his chair and walked over to grab another bottle of water. "Jess definitely knew more than was said from that small encounter," he said, remembering.

"What are you thinking?" I turned to ask Roy.

"Well, if Kat willingly came with you to find her friend, but she already knew where she was, she would try to break away from us to go save her, right? You remember the detail guy told us he saw her running back towards Sin, maybe she thought she could get away. Then there is the fact that she was helping you guys get info out of him. I mean there is something fishy going on there, and I wouldn't put it past her, but you said it yourself, if it were you and Jess, either you would be doing it together, or neither of you would be." He cut out, still trying to unjumble his thoughts.

"So, you think the other Star is the Balancing Soul of Indifference they need? You think the reason Kat came here was to help her, and she relayed that message to Jess so she wouldn't let me be taken?" I asked. "Well, if that's true, we need to hurry up and find her. Didn't you say if they knew she was a Dreamer that they wouldn't be looking for me anymore? Well, if Kat knew to have that conversation with her, then I'm sure someone else knew too!" Ken shot back to the front of the room in a panic.

"We have to figure this out now. We are running out of time," Ken said, the panic in his voice rising.

I wasn't sure if I was more worried about the panic in his eyes, confirming my discovery, or that Jess was out there alone again. I grazed over our matching stone and fell to my knees. Jess was in pain. She was not doing well, and she was calling out for help. I pushed as much happiness and healing to the stone as I could, hoping it was making it to her and went back to the conversation at hand.

"That is an understatement," I said, looking up at Ken from my knees. "She's hurting. We need a plan."

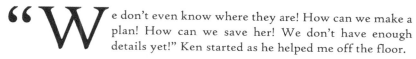

18

"**W**e don't even know where they are! How can we make a plan! How can we save her! We don't have enough details yet!" Ken started as he helped me off the floor.

"Well, we don't have much to go on now," I agreed. "But we have enough to be dangerous." I smiled. What was I getting myself into? I looked over to Roy. "We already figured out where they are hiding." I looked back to Ken, not wanting to share my thoughts with the room. One thing at a time. "We can go there, use those tunnels you guys keep talking about, and case the place. Roy, maybe you can distract them while Ken and I grab Jess and whoever the other two people they are keeping are? That's the best I got on this short notice." I checked to see if they were up for the challenge only to see them headed for the door without another word. "Wait! Aren't you guys going to say anything? I mean, Ken, you don't even know where we're going!"

"Doesn't matter," was all he said.

"Your plan works for me. Get in, find the captives, create a diversion, get out. I make plans to keep the suits happy around here, I almost never follow them anyway." He tipped his head in a bow and turned for the door.

I stood up and looked around at the base. I wonder, how many others have access to this place? A question for another time, I decided. I gathered myself up and headed to follow the boys at the door. They were standing there waiting on me. Awesome.

Bonnie Baraka

Stepping out of the base, I expected to see the alley where we entered, but we were far from that alley now. We were discarded directly in front of that beautiful castle in the same place Roy and I had entered it earlier that day. I turned in surprise to face Ken and Roy, hoping they knew what was going on.

"Pocket Travel," they both said to me at once. I giggled.

"I know what it is; only I'm not sure as to how or why. Did one of you wish us here?" I looked to see who the guilty subject was. They both stared back at me, puzzled.

"If I had to guess, I would say once you decided where we were headed, the Slicers Den, then as it is your dimension to wield as you see if, that is where we started to drift. It's close to here?" Ken asked with confidence.

"I'm sure there is more science behind it than that, but yes. Roy, didn't you say it was at the back of the castle?" I turned to Roy to confirm. I had no clue where the place we were going was. He nodded and turned to Ken for clarification.

"Old condemned church in the back. The one that has been closed for about a year or so now." Ken gave me an uneasy look that I returned with a knowing one.

We were on the same page, but it hurt my feelings to think that I could not trust Roy with what I thought. I knew his loyalty would get in the way at this point, so I said nothing. We continued down the path around the castle in silence. Alone with my thoughts, I was able to ponder some things that had happened today. Jess was a Dreamer, whatever that was. Gran was sicker than I had originally thought, and I might not only run into myself in this church, but also someone who looked just like my baby brother. I was shaking at the thought. I knew it shouldn't matter to me because my own brother was home with pops, but could I really just sit there and not do anything for the boy who wore my brother's face? I didn't think I could. I would need to be confident and smart and get him out too.

When we finally approached the Church, I could tell why it had been closed. There was a fire on the side closest to the forest behind it. It looked like a big one. The front of the Church that faced the castle still looked to be intact, which led me to wonder if this fire was deliberate. We crept over to what looked to be a wine cellar and plunged down deep into darkness. I wasn't scared of the dark, but the dark here was thick and unsettling. Ken lit a lantern to my left as Roy hopped down and closed the doors above to my right. There was one path, and it led even deeper underground.

"This will take us to the back of the church where we should be able to see what is going on inside without being noticed," Roy directed us.

Ken nodded without a word and gave the signal to head out. I followed behind Ken as we walked hunched over and slowly so as not to be heard or bother the growing mold around us in the little hallway. There were pictures on the walls down here. Pictures of travelers and tales of love. I stopped in front of one in particular with shock and awe.

"Who is this man with my great grandmother?" I asked before I knew what I was saying.

Ken stopped and looked mortified.

"Your grandmother?" Roy said aloud. "That is your grandmother?" he looked confused. "That is Jin?"

"No." I shook my head. "That is Jin's Grandmother." I tried to remember the story Suzie had told me of her origins and realized she hadn't.

"That is my father, and his lover, before my mother," Roy said. "She gave her life to save the world in the War of Dimension D. He told me stories of this war often, of the curly red-haired girl that was resilient and determined to save her family. I have often dreamt of her after his passing. Hoping they are together now." He bowed his head.

Interesting that Suzie gave her life for a war and for the creation of the base. Could they be one in the same?

"How fancy your father loved my Great Grandmother, and now you're looking at me with those big brown eyes." I fluttered my lashes at him, teasing. He liked me because he saw her. I joked with him to deflect how it made me feel to know the connection I thought we had was none of my own making.

"It's not like that." Roy shook his head.

"I'm sure," I said flatly.

We continued through the hall in silence, only stopping when there was a fork in the road. At this fork, we stopped and listened for any noise or movement. There was plenty coming from both directions.

I looked at Roy and said, "I think this is where we part. You go to the left. Find a good place to make a scene away from the people, and we go right, to the back, and hope the captives are close. It's quieter here to the right."

Ken nodded in agreement, not saying a word. Roy nodded as well, then pulled me in close.

"I have fallen for the Heart of Gold you wear on your sleeve. Not the bedtime stories my father told me. It's the smile in your eyes and the genuine north arrow that has knocked me off my feet." He released me and backed away slowly. "And don't you forget it."

I let the emotions in my tummy roll over me like a warm breeze before opening my eyes to look at Ken and face reality. Ken had his head bowed in the same conflict with himself. We were going to have a major problem on our hands before all was said and done.

"How deep do you think Tina is in this whole thing?" I asked, getting Ken's attention finally. We walked in silence for a while before Ken finally spoke.

"Deeper than I would like to admit," he said solemnly. "But if she has Charlie's boat, chances are she also has Charlie's son, which means she could be the one holding the cards if all goes bad here."

I thought about what he wasn't saying. This whole time we thought Sin was in charge, but was he?

"Did you ever get a vibe from Sin, like he was working for someone else? Like he had to check with someone before making any major moves?" I asked curiously.

"Well, yes, but I thought it was just his mother. She is the one who is from the dominion with all of the healers. She left there in search of a place where her own dark gifts would not stand out so much, but now she is miserable and depressed for her home. She will stick out anywhere she goes, though. She was a part of the war in your dimension. She helped wage a war on Love. Do you know how twisted your brain must be to think the world would be better without love? She never loved Sin; she tolerates him, and he craves her love. So, he has been trying to find a way to get her and their clan back to her home since she brought it up." Ken sighed. "There was a time when he wasn't as bad and cold as he is now, but she has twisted his thoughts into believing the pain in his soul will go away if she loves him. It will not. He was born with the gift of death. Many manage it, more go insane from it. It has a hunger for things to die. There are those that manage it well. They take up jobs of walking old ones who are in pain home, of caring for the dead, of removing life before pain is unbearable. There are those that see the beauty in the process of ending and beginning. He did once. He wanted to be a doctor to the old. Assess their struggles, move those that could be fixed onto someone who could help, and help those who couldn't have a peaceful ending, but she has changed him. There is no coming back from where he is now." Ken kept walking as if he hadn't just called Sin the angle of death. Taking it all in, I moved to assess our other enemies.

"And Tina?" I asked. "Is she like that also?"

"Tina is everything Roy said she was, in an endless search for whatever will keep her mother away," Ken muttered. "They are probably playing off of one another, Sin knowing she could be his way of getting his mother home, giving Tina false hope that her mother will survive." *What a withered existence that would be*, I imagined.

"What do you think of Kat?" I asked, going down the line of bad guys I knew of. "Is she in on the whole thing too?"

"That one is puzzling to me. She gets you here, helps you get away from Sin, and then goes back. She is clearly a part of the situation, you should have heard her talking to Sin in the eatery, but something is off about the whole thing. Why help you if she didn't even help her own best friend? What is her motive?" he asked.

"Well, she did ask me for a favor. That was the deal I mean; we shook on it. She would give me information and accompany us here, and in return, she could ask any morally sound favor of me when she needed," I said. Ken stopped dead.

"You shook on it!?" He said, terror and shock in his voice.

"No, Jess stepped in between us and shook with her before I could," I said, now feeling more uneasy about the deal I almost struck. "When Jess shook her hand instead, she nearly passed out."

Ken sighed deeply.

"Well, she defiantly needed something from you. I'm just wondering if it was to take the other Stars place or something in that nature or if it is actually something to come. I'm sure she will find a way to twist you back into the deal if she asks it of Jess. Since you bound the deal, if Jess can't supply what she needs, there will be repercussions from your stones." Ken started walking again.

We came to the opening to hear people shouting and moving fast. Stopping to see if we could make out what was going on, I heard myself loud and clear from the room in front of us.

"How could you do this to us, Kat? We are best friends. I would never harm you no matter what, and yet..." I was sobbing. Well, The Star of this Dimension was sobbing to her best friend. Who was doing her best to tune her out?

Ken reached for a trap door in the ceiling, and we climbed up to the rafters to see what was unfolding below us.

There was the boat, with Trey tied to the front like an ornament. Arms outstretched and sleeping. The boy who wore my brother's face was bruised from head to toe and sleeping. My heart sank down to my stomach. Jess was there, caged and lying on her side next to my doppelganger. Who was tied to the outside of the cage? Jess was half-conscious, calling my name. There was blood dripping from an open cut on her lip. She was alive. I reached for my bracelet again and felt for her. I sent as much happiness as I could, then watched as she tensed a little before relaxing into the glowing stone at her wrist. I looked back at Ken; whose eyes were fixed on Jess. I looked straight ahead to see if there was anyone else, I knew here and noticed something moving in the rafters across from us. Roy had joined the party. Catching my eye, he nodded and counted down with his fingers from 5. I had just enough time to warn Ken and get in position above the helm of the boat.

"I'm going for Trey; you get Jess and get her out. Untie the other Star; she looks like she might be okay enough to trail you," I said to Ken as I moved.

Ken snapped into action and was on top of the cage just as Roy jumped down and screamed from the other side of the room.

In an instant, Sin's lackeys were everywhere. Roy was fighting them off with an intensity I had never seen. I paused to watch the scene. Wrong move. Kat was on Ken as soon as the fight broke out. Altering my trajectory, I jumped right on top of her. Not today!

Ken doubled his efforts to get into the car and finally ripped the door off entirely. Moving swiftly, he had Jess hauled in the air and over his shoulder, slashing the binding on the other Stars in a flash.

"We have to go now," he said to her, but she was not listening. She ran for her brother and woke him with her touch.

"Starley?" I heard her say. Starley? Distracted, I missed the punch Kat threw and was hurtled backward on my butt.

"Why are you here!? Why don't you listen? Why am I even surprised?" Kat said through clenched teeth.

I stood, back against the cage, and attached myself to the rage she was letting out. With her rage flowing through me, I launched myself at her again, knocking her down in the process. She looked up at me in shock.

"I don't know why you are surprised! You knew I would come for my best friend. Just as you should have!" I yelled at her. The other Star was untying Trey, and I was doing all I could to keep Kat busy, so she didn't notice. One hand. I punched at Kat, not connecting to anything as she ducked away from the blow. Two hands untied. I pushed in further and slid her view away from Trey then started my second decent. Kat was quicker; she knocked the wind out of me with her blow to the stomach. I doubled over in a heap on the ground next to the metal cage. From the ground, I saw Star pull Trey down and hand him over to Ken, who was now empty-handed. Where's Jess? My eyes pleadingly asked him. He gave a tight nod and slid back into the darkness. Star number 2 prowled over and knocked her friend in the head.

"How could you let them feed on him like that!" She said as she swung again and again. "How could you!"

"I didn't have a choice," Kat begged from under the storm of punches. "I swear! I didn't have a choice! You don't understand!"

Regaining my breath, I stood to reenter the fight ensuing when I heard the growl of a wounded soldier from the other end of the room.

Roy was holding off as many as he could, but he was getting tired. He was losing. I looked to where Ken had escaped and did not see him there; he had again taken the ones I loved and left. In a quick decision, I rose to my feet and sprinted down to check on Roy. I managed to get through several Slicers before he noticed me coming. He shook his head for me to turn back, but I was in the thick of it all now. I did a running jump over the last of them, and he grabbed me out of the air. Tired from holding off a mob of them at once, he slouched under my weight.

"We still have a chance if we can make it to that wall," I whispered to him.

I turned to look at the fight ensuing at the other end now, praying the other Star would have time to get away when I saw him again. Sin had entered the room from the other side and was on Star before she even knew he was there. "STAR!" I yelled, but it was already too late. He had her. I turned to Roy, hoping he saw what I was seeing. He had. He backed away from the fight slowly, still fending off Slicers.

"Spin me!" I winked at him, and he complied. I ran in a circle to pick up some speed and then launched myself at our attacker's feet first as Roy held onto my arms for dear life. They fell, and those that didn't back off just enough to wait out the kick, that was all the time we needed. I grabbed Roy's lagging body and half-dragged him into the shadows back to the tunnel where we had come. We didn't get far before they were on us again, but I didn't care—this time, I was ready.

I punched myself in the gut and pulled the mirror out to shine on the wall in the candlelight. I pushed Roy into the pocket dimension and was about to go in myself when I was caught.

"I'm stuck!" I yelled for him, but he did not move. I shifted just enough underneath my attacker's grip to see that Roy had passed out on the floor in the entryway. "ROY HELP ME!" I yelled, fear in my throat. Roy's eyes fluttered at the desperation in my voice, but he did not budge. How could I blame him? Roy had single-handedly taken on seven or more men to ensure that the rest of us made it out safely. I should feel bad for putting him in this situation. Serves me right to get caught, I thought through the despair I felt.

As I watched the rest of the attackers come back to help their companion, I was almost ready to let go, and at least give the others a chance to make it safely. I pulled one arm down as far as I could reach to see if I could pry my attacker's hand loose before giving up completely. I couldn't reach it if I tried. Giving one last look behind them to see Sin approaching, I gave a hard tug, and a whimper escaped my throat, remembering the pain in Sin's chest I knew he would delight in inflicting on me. I struggled aggressively against the hold.

Kicking and pulling against him, I found no relief. I stopped struggling, as I had abandoned all hope and instead decided to come to terms with my situation. Strong hands gripped around my middle and sent me launching deeper into the entryway with one last fling of power. Roy fell back to the ground in a heap completely drained of any reserve energy or power. I scrambled to my feet and ran back to the door to slam it, just as Sin was approaching the threshold. Locking the door, I slid down it to the floor, trying to catch my breath. Finally remembering our last encounter with this hall, I looked up in search of the key reader. It was there on the wall, but there was no need for it as the door to the base had been left ajar.

Rushing to the open door, I peered in to see Jess and Ken leaning over Trey, who they had put on top of the table, scattering papers and bottled water along the floor in their desperation.

"Ken! It's Roy; he needs help!" I called over and slacked my legs as I heard a pound from the outer door. Ken sprang into action as he heard the noises from outside the door as well. "Why hasn't the door disappeared? Are they going to get in!?" Fear crept into my voice, thinking about who was on the other side of this doorway.

Ken grabbed Roy and hauled him into the base, dragging me along with him.

"Who is out there? Is it someone who should be in here?" Ken asked with intensity. I didn't understand what he was asking me. "Has Kat ever been in here?" He asked a follow-up question.

I thought about it hard, slamming the door to the entryway and praying we moved far away from our current location.

"Not with me, but" I thought out loud, "MAYBE with her own Star! She's still out there; she was fighting Kat and Sin grabbed her! He is the one who was banging on the door. Do you think he is using her to get in?" I was sad and thinking of home. I felt a jolt and heard the pounding stop abruptly. We were moving. Was it because we were no longer in the entryway? "He has her," I said again, defeated all over again.

Jess grabbed my shoulder, and relief washed over me as I saw her. She was hurt and leaning against the table, holding onto Trey for dear life, but she was alive, and she was here. Mini victory, I guess. As Ken continued to aid Roy, I embraced Jess. She met me halfway with open arms. I reached up to squeeze her cheeks and make sure she was really here. Standing in that uncharted space, we giggled to each other until it hurt. In that moment, it felt like we were back in our own environment, having a normal day, just the two of us. Like everything was back to normal. I wanted to stay fixed to that spot with her forever. We were brought back to reality when Ken tried to put Roy down on a couch, I had never noticed in the corner next to the table. Roy moaned in pain and exhaustion as he eased down. Realizing our fight wasn't over yet, I went to get chocolate and water for the room. Roy, in one peace and exhausted, accepted the chocolate and stretched out fully on the couch. He was asleep before his head hit the pretty decorative pillows. I pulled a chair out from the table and tried to give tiny bits of chocolate to Trey.

"He is drained. You two will need to do far more than just give him chocolate to wake him up," Ken said, sorrow filling his face.

"What do you mean? He needs more energy?" I asked Ken, then turned to see Jess' face. There was pain there. What does she know that I don't?

"They were draining his life force to power their boat," Jess said, hands shaking as she grabbed his. "That is how they thought they were going to be able to make it move through the barrier without shredding both the barrier and themselves. They were to disguise their boat as a person slipping through it instead, but to do so, they needed someone who was innocent, as their soul would not lie. They tried other souls in the past and failed. They said it was because their souls were tainted. I heard them talking about it when they thought I was unconscious."

I shook my head in disbelief. Would Kat do such a thing to the kid brother of her best friend? For what price? I was confused and stricken with grief at the predicament we were in. I looked at Jess, hoping she had more to tell. If she did, now was not the time to tell it.

"You guys can help him, but it has to be now. He is on the brink of giving up, and he will soon be gone from us," Ken said, head bowed. I looked at Jess, hoping she knew how to help. Ken nodded to her to go ahead and start, but Jess' face was that of confusion and frustration.

"What can I do to help him? I do not have any gifts!" She said, angry.

"Don't you?" I asked, looking at her with uncertainty.

"You are an Earth Dreamer, Jess," Ken said. "You can find the wicked dreams he is caught in and change them to beautiful ones. You can help him find us again. You can guide him back to himself and hold his hand, so he doesn't falter on the threshold. You alone can see that he is almost gone, you alone can change that." Ken put a hand on her shoulder. Jess flinched away from the loving touch and looked to see if I was paying attention. I glared at her and nodded to Trey.

"Try it," I said, knowing there was more pain in my tone than necessary.

She was a terrible liar. Jess looked over to Roy to see him sound asleep and drew closer to Trey. She sat down in a chair closest to the table he was not perched on and put her head on his arm. I moved to sit across from her and grab his other hand when Ken stopped me.

"You need to be at the head of the table. I will be here for him when he wakes up," Ken said as he guided me to the computer chair and swiveled it, so I was watching the scene from a higher vantage point.

19

Y ou will not be able to see what she is doing with your eyes, but you will feel the emotion, and you will hear the difference in the sounds. You need to recognize what that emotion looks like to you, so you know how to combat it. Trey will be an emotional wreck when he wakes up. You will need to know how to help him calm himself and battle the emotions that will consume him if he does not fight back. If he doesn't, he will be in a state similar to Charlie's, maybe far worse." I sat back and watched as Jess' entire body started to vibrate. Not a physical vibration, but an emotional one. There were swirls of colors around her, hidden to the naked eye. I saw them only when I looked away or when I looked at her at an abstract angle. The colors were there and then gone in a flash. I focused on them and watched as they slowly faded into Jess like a mist. She was sweating. Ken went over to her and wiped her brow. Jess flinched and then leaned into the touch. Trey's body started to convulse. I looked at Ken, who altered his position from next to Jess to the other side of Trey, holding him down and pouring water on his brow to cool him. Tears welled up in my throat, and Ken immediately turned to me with cold eyes. "Now is not the time Star. Be strong for him. Do not take pity, take pride."

"Starleyy!" Trey sang from the table.

I doubled over. That name again. I rose from my seat and went to the head of the table. In my mind, I imagined a beautiful garden with flowers dancing in the breeze to Charlie's old saxophone. I imagined chasing Trey down the rows and rows of large sunflowers that were reaching down to give him a high five as he passed. I poured the warmth of the breeze into the image and wrapped myself in the airy emotion it gave me. I then put my hands-on Trey's shoulders, pushing them out with a deep breath. The moment I touched Trey, I wished I hadn't.

Bonnie Baraka

There was a storm waging deep in his belly, and I was now caught in the center of it. I looked over to see Jess there too. She was yelling for me to turn around, but there was no place for me to go. So, I ran to her. Reaching her, I saw Trey, stuck to that boat and screaming. I looked over to see her losing hope. She had no clue what she was doing, and Trey didn't know her. I stepped closer to Trey and was almost swept off my feet by a huge wave.

"I need to get closer. Can you get us closer?" I asked Jess, who was shaking with anger. I looked in her eyes and saw she was having a hard time not losing herself here. I grabbed both of her hands in this place and let the emotions I was holding for Trey fall through her. I pushed images of us, playing basketball, of Charlie fishing us out of the creek, of building sandcastles with Gran. I pushed the image of us, normal, plain old us through our bond, and I hoped it would last. When I opened my eyes, Jess was staring at me with clear eyes and tear-stained cheeks. I nodded. "Get us closer."

"I can't," she sobbed. "I have no clue what I am doing. I am not the one he needs; you are!" She shook her head, defeated.

I sighed. I couldn't tell her she was capable; I couldn't do it for her, and I was pretty tired of building her up and her not believing me. She needed to trust herself. So, I let her go. I knew I could trust her; I just needed her to know it too.

"WHAT ARE YOU DOING!" Jess protested from behind me. "You will drown! This isn't a real ocean, you know!" She spat.

"Then get us closer," I said, annoyed. "Make a boat; find a way. I don't know, but I have to get to him, and we need to get out of here before we're stuck forever." I turned and continued to wade into the deep waters. Another wave came crashing down on my head, and I barely made it back to the surface.

"Stop this! I can't do it! You're going to kill yourself!" Jess pleaded from behind me. I wasn't stopping, and I wasn't dying here. I turned to look at her as my head went under again. "Star, get back here now!" she stomped her foot.

"Stop being crazy. Sit down, deep breaths in and out, calm yourself, and get it done! Imagine what we need and call it to you. Breathe through it. You are in control! I am fine. Get what we need, and let's go home already." I called as another wave hit me hard, and I went under. This one was going to be my last if she didn't do something. I felt tentacles of anger and sorrow wrap around my ankles in an attempt to pull me deeper. I couldn't lose myself here, lost in Trey's emotions. This could not be the end for me!

Deep breaths were out of the question as I continued to drop to the bottom of this sea of emotions, but I followed the other directions I had just given Jess anyway. Noticing the darkness around me, I focused on the bright sun and warm breezes from earlier. I let the happy emotion of being with my family roll through my body and heat me up as I opened my eyes to see a glowing gold light start to radiate my body. Heart of Gold, indeed, I smiled to myself. Feeling the tentacles loosen around my ankles, I pushed up. Just as I felt like I was running out of air, I felt Jess' fingers wrap around my outstretched wrist and pull me up onto a raft. She had found a raft. I choked as I tried to suck in air and got water instead and rolled over on my back on the raft. I knew she could do it!

"DON'T YOU EVER DO THAT AGAIN!" Jess yelled at me as she turned around to paddle towards Trey. I coughed a little more from the water in my lungs but gave her a big smile.

"Don't act like a helpless ninny again, and I won't have to." I chided from next to her. "Things are hard enough for us with no training; we don't need you to be second-guessing yourself at every turn of this thing also." I sat up and folded my arms.

Jess scoffed.

"So, what do we do when we get over here?" She asked, clearly ignoring my disposition.

I hadn't thought about that part. I looked at the obstacle ahead of us and cringed. The angry tentacles were back and snipping at the raft. I shook my head. He always was a little on the annoyed side. I looked up at the mast that Trey was tied to in his mind and tried to guess how high it was. Too high to climb and cut the ropes.

"I'm gonna need you to sit on this raft and imagine being a really big person. You need to be HUGE, cause you're gonna need to reach both of those at the same time," I said.

Jess looked at me like I had six heads.

I shrugged. "Someone has to be here to catch him and hold the raft steady. You are the dreamer, use your imagination, and cut the ropes. I don't really care how you do it! Just do it!"

Jess glared at me, but she sat down and closed her eyes. The winds picked up, and rain started to fall hard. The boat started to rock, and I looked over at Jess to see if she was growing. She wasn't.

"Jess," I said uneasily. I was looking at a huge wave that was about to pull us under that I knew she didn't see.

Jess put her finger up for me to hold on.

I rolled my eyes as I fought to keep our little raft in place. "JESSSS!" I screamed as the wave got closer.

Jess brought her hands up, palms facing the sky, and opened her eyes. Noticing the typhoon size wave coming for us, she quickly brought them down, and with a crack, lightning shot down from the sky, singing the binds holding Trey in place. He fell in a dead drop for the open water.

"We haven't made it there yet, Jess!!" I screamed from the back of the raft as I started to run for Trey. I stopped mid-way through the front of the raft as a heavy wind carried him right into her lap, leaving it to Jess to imagine the easy way out! As relief passed through me, I tipped my head back to wipe the rain out of my eye. As I did so, I realized that the Typhoon was still coming. "BIG WAVEEEE!!!" I yelled and went back to my paddling.

Jess looked over her shoulder at me with a quirk to the corner of her lips, as the wave slammed into us and carried us back to the bank. She had thought of everything in that big beautiful brain of hers. Crashing into the bank, we rolled in a heap onto the grass.

"THAT," I coughed uncontrollably at the water still stuck in my lungs, "WAS AWESOME!" I said, checking Trey's pulse and smiling over at Jess. She was in action and didn't even hear me yelling in delight.

Jess sprung up from her position under Trey and slid him to me fully. Scanning our surroundings and taking in anything that could be a potential threat, she circled us in an at ready stance.

"Wake him up, get him moving. We are not alone here. We need to get going and fast," Jess said in a whisper for my ears only.

I looked around, confused, and saw nothing. I was just about to ask what she was talking about when Trey shifted in my grip, and something else shifted behind the Tree next to us. I surged into my own emotions of happiness and fun and pushed as many of them to Trey. His eyes sprang open, but the rest of his body was unmoving.

"Get up, little boy!" I coaxed into his ear and rubbed his shoulders to warm him up. He shivered against my touch. I looked over at Jess, hoping she could grant some assistance. "It's not working!" I pleaded. Jess rolled her eyes.

"Treyson Anthony King, son of Charlie um, King Brother of Star King. GET UP NOW!" Jess yelled. The boy's body stood as directed, but I could tell he was not in control.

I started to weep and hug my little brother tight. Feeling overcome by emotion, I remembered what happened the last time I was in this position, giving me an idea. I took him in my arms and screamed all the happy memories I could muster into his belly. He giggled and cried and roared all at once. It was like an electric shock to his system, and he jolted awake, blinking his eyes to make sure this was real.

"Starley?" he looked at me for the first time with confusion of not where I was, but who I was. I looked back, hoping he saw comfort there.

"We have to go. I will explain it to you when we have a moment, right now I need you to run. We need to get out of here before we can't anymore." I whispered. Looking around mortified as I pushed him forward, he looked back at the boat where the bindings still hung and went sheet white.

I picked him up in my arms and stood. "Let's go, gonna have to carry him. But we gotta move." I looked at Jess. She was giving me a strange look of uncertainty.

"I don't think we can. I can see..." she paused, looking for the right words to explain what she saw and finding nothing to compare it to. "He is tethered to that ship somehow. I know I 'should' be able to break it, but I don't think I can do so without his permission." She sighed and sat back down in the grass. I set him down next to her and took up her position.

She took him from my hold and looked him in the face. "Do you know who I am?" She asked curiously. He shook his head no.

Not my Trey then. I sighed deeply, feeling the tension in my limbs loosen a bit more. I didn't know what I would do if this was the little brother I had sworn to protect since the day he was conceived.

"I am a Dreamer and a friend of your sister," Jess continued. "And I am trying to get you to safety. You have to trust that I will do as I am saying and want to be rid of the things binding you here. If you are not fully and intentionally leaving this place with us, we cannot take you with us." She looked at him sternly as I had seen her do with our little brother many times before, but this time was different. I could see the emotion in her eyes as she told him to be strong, not for her or out of importance, but for his personal safety and wellbeing.

The boy with Trey's face nodded his head at her.

"You know my sister?" he asked shyly and then looked from her to me and back. "Not her, but you know MY sister?" He asked again, trying to clarify. How could he know I wasn't his sister?

Jess grinned at him with mock understanding and shook her head.

"Yes, smarty pants, I know your sister, and she asked me to look after you until she could make it to us. So, are you ready to go?" Jess teased.

I looked up to see jet black eyes watching us adamantly. I tapped Jess in warning that we were about to have company.

"We gotta go, kid, you ready?" She asked calmly. He nodded and got to his feet, turning away from the boat and towards the clouds. Jess snapped her fingers at the air between Trey's heart and where a direct line to the boat would be.

I looked up at the boat to see if I could see anything change. There was no change to the naked eye, but in my peripheral, I saw an explosion of red light all around the boat as it began to drift from its place. I looked over to Jess to see if that was it as she nodded in satisfaction.

"Can I pick him up now?" I asked agitated.

"Yes but be gentle!" She rolled her eyes and turned to the trees to see about our attackers advancing. "No patience," she said under her breath.

"I heard that!" I yelled behind me as I scooped up my ward and ran top speed up the hill towards the sunshine. I was stopped in my tracks as Kat walked into view. "Jess, I need you to take him and go. I have some unfinished business to attend to," I said in a growl without hesitation.

At the tone of my voice, Jess turned around to see what was bothering me. Seeing Kat in front of me, Jess jumped up and around before I could make it to her.

"Star, don't. It's not what you think. Kat, leave." Jess said, turning to Kat as if they had been having this conversation often now.

I turned to Jess, feeling left out. Were they friends now? Furious that Jess would take someone else's side in a fight, I pushed past her to get to Kat.

"I heard what you said to Star back there; you let them sacrifice her little brother to save your own skin!" I was on her in seconds. Jess grabbed my wrist as I was about to connect with Kat's face. Adjusting the weight so the blowback wouldn't affect my passanger, I dug my feet into the dirt to stop us from toppling over.

"Are you serious! You're gonna take her side!?" I looked at Jess with confusion and anger. *How dare she!* I was halfway back into the fight when she stopped me a second time.

"Starla King! You stop it right now! YOU are better than that! You forgive when people don't deserve it! You look out for people, and you most certainly do not hate." She looked me in the eyes in a cold stare. "Your rage and hate will lock us here forever, and the more you fight, the angrier you will get. We need to go now! She is just the first wave of minions Sin will send in here to get us. Trust Me. If you don't trust anything else, Trust ME," she finished and turned back to Kat, "Go away."

"Umm, remember that favor you owe me? I am gonna need to collect on that right about now," Kat said with a smirk.

I looked at Kat with shock and awe. What could she possibly think we could do for her right now? Jess' face was a picture of shock. She thought she had it all figured out and look at the predicament we were about to be in.

"The deal was nothing morbid and nothing immoral. Whatever you think will work in here will most definitely be just that!" I yelled at Kat. I pushed both my companions towards the exit. I would not allow this disloyal tragedy ruin my friend, and I would not allow this place to ruin my friendship. I took several deep breaths and faced my opponent. "Don't stop until you get out," I said without looking back.

Kat's eyes were as big as marbles when she realized that Jess would not stop to hear the terms of her favor. Without the terms being given, no favor had been requested.

"Wait, I need help! Help me, please!" Kat yelled as Jess continued, cradling the fading boy in her arms.

"There is no help for someone who could be so disloyal that they would trade in their own best friend and little brother for anything, ANYTHING!" I yelled and ran towards Kat, knocking her to the ground. Jess was right. Not knowing how to control the wave of emotions growing deep inside me, I needed to focus on something else. I focused on getting out instead.

"You don't understand!" Kat pleaded from the ground. "They made me!" She sobbed. "Why do you think I didn't fight Star back yesterday, why do you think I told Jess everything. I am not in control here. Please help me! I have to get away!" She put her hands up to block my punches but didn't fight back.

It's not that I didn't believe her; it was more like I didn't care. The people I loved had to get away. We could come back for Kat. Right now, every second we were still here was a second where lives hung in the balance. The little brother I raised or not, he was still innocent. He has 'innocence unfound' actually. I continued my advance and pushed Kat further away from Jess and Trey. I wouldn't hurt her, but I wasn't about to let her get to them either. No sooner did I make my decision than did I see Sin's minions close in around us from behind Kat.

"Funny, you said all that and then brought your lackeys to finish us off, huh?" I sneered at Kat. Kat's face turned from pleading to terror right in front of my eyes. My stomach turned.

"I didn't. I came here for your help! I swear it!" Kat turned to see them approach as she said it. She swiftly turned back to me. "Listen, Sin is not in charge of this; he is just the face. Starley will be safe until they are able to find the other pieces. But please help me!" She begged this time.

"Trying to escape your boyfriend?" I looked around her to count the lackeys. "How did you find us anyway?" I looked over to her, curious.

"It wasn't hard for me, with you using all that emotion. I'm sure you tripped something when you cut ties from that boat also." She scoffed and took up a place next to me, turning to face the rest. "They have my father. I'm sure all is lost now that they have seen me here with you. I might as well run for it. I will have to find a way to get back to him before they execute him." I heard the dread in her voice as my heart stopped beating in my ears long enough to interpret what she was saying.

"Come back with us, maybe Roy can talk to Tina into using her resources to help find him," I whispered to her as my first attacker got close enough for me to kick.

"No," Kat stepped in and fought him before I could. "Tina is the head of the Spliced Market. She is not a friend to you, Star," Kat said through heavy breathing. She pushed me back.

"Go, I will hold keep them busy so you guys can get out. I have other ways of getting out. I will be in touch." Kat sighed from in front of me.

I ran. I cried, and I ran. Deciding between pops and Jess? I prayed that was a decision I never had to make. I made it to where Jess had stopped with confusion and wiped away my tears.

Why did you guys stop? Sin's lackeys are here; we have to get out of here now!" I turned to look at Jess.

"Okay, but HOW?" She screamed at me in frustration. She pointed in front of us to nothing but blue skies and pastures then behind us to the fiery sea that was rumbling.

"Ugh! How should I know? Make a door or something," I said blankly and shrugged. It was as if a light bulb went off in her brain because she made the biggest DUH grin and sat down in the grass with her eyes closed. I turned to look behind to wage our time. Kat was losing the battle. Deciding I needed to give Jess as much time as possible to focus. Turning to check our surroundings, I noticed the boy's face throbbing with pain like he was still fighting to stay away from the boat. "Are you alright?" I asked tensely.

"I'll manage, but I think we need to go before they pull me back down there," he said through gritted teeth. His body swayed under my touch. I assessed his movement to see what was happening and gripped his hands.

"Did you ever play ring around the rosy when you were little? My baby brother loved it when we played together." I smiled at him, trying to run his attention from the things around us to something that would give him joy. His eyes lit up then dimed a little at the memory he was recalling, but he nodded his head. I started the dance and drew him further into the sunny glen as we went.

"Ring Around theee rosssyyyy. Jess, you need to hurryyyy, Ashes, Ashes before we all go DOWN!" I called to her so she would know we were on the move, as we spun slowly in a circle. Jess opened her eyes to see us farther away then she would have liked and sprinted over to us.

"I can't. I have tried MANY times, but I can't make a door! Something is blocking it in my mind." Her words were angry and bitten. She turned to see how Kat was doing, and her face paled. I kept the boy's back to the fight and took a peek myself. Kat was down and crawling out of the way. They were on the move and hunting us. I put my hand up to my face to block the sun as I counted our attackers again and felt the cool slap of my bracelet on my cheek.

"POCKET MIRROR!" I yelled as the first wave of attackers came into view. Jess looked at me with hope as she slammed her fist into my gut. I doubled over in pain and held my arm into the air.

"Hey! Why did you hit her! I thought we were on the same team!" yelled a small voice in disgust as the door came into view. He was ready to attack Jess when she spun him around to the door. Forgetting his previous anger, he ran for the handle just in time as the first guy ran into our circle to fight. Jess pushed us through the door headfirst and closed it. As I felt life come back to me in the pocket dimension, I opened my eye to a sight I was not prepared for. Jess was on the floor, bleeding, the boy standing over her. Roy was at my side with a towel, and Ken was running for the door. Someone was banging on the outside door. But how?

Panicking, I shot up and ran over to the computer, slammed my hand on the button I hoped was the power button, and yelled, "Take us back to the pantry in Charlie's house!" With a jolt, the banging stopped. I slouched back to the chair and assessed our surroundings once more. "Why is she bleeding?" I asked Ken, confused. His return look told me he did not know.

"When she cut the tie from me, she showed them what her own power looked like. Sin can attach himself to power like that; he was looking for her from her power. He probably thinks it's yours. He would never have let her go if he knew she was a Dream Walker." The boy said as he slouched back away from Jess and let Ken come in to help her into a chair.

Dazed and nose dripping with blood, Jess accepted his help without hesitation and let him look her over without complaint. Ken leaned in and gripped her shoulders, saying a prayer over her as he went. He touched her forehead and fell back with a fierce velocity that carried him into the far wall. Jess shot out of the chair to pick him up and catch him.

"What are you doing?" She asked him as she helped him up off the ground. Her hands were shaking as she sat back in her chair and looked around the room. "YOU!" she snarled when she saw Roy. "What are you doing here?" Her words scared Roy, and he took a step back away from the scene, confused.

Why shouldn't I be here? I was the one who helped get Star out of the Hall. I was the one who was trying to get you both to safety! I was the one who went back for you in that Alley when Ken hauled Star out on YOUR orders! Why would you be surprised that I am here!?" Roy said quietly to the room, hands raised palm up in confusion. Jess shook her head and turned away from Roy as I stood up to come between them. I walked slowly around the table and distributed another round of water and chocolate.

"I think we all need to sit down at this table and have a chat," I said slowly. I pulled up the oversized computer chair and ushered Trey into it. I then gave his extra chocolate with a wink. With Trey positioned at the head of the table, I then ushered Roy to the other end. Leaving Ken and Jess on one side and me on the other. "First of all, what did you just do to Jess, and is she still attached to Trey's emotions or to Sin?" I asked Ken as I finished my task and sat down across from Jess. She gave me a strong look of confusion.

"I am a healer," Ken declared. "I cannot heal on a mass level and most of the time, probably because I am so far away from my home dimension. It doesn't work at all, but I can still perform some tasks, like bruises or waking someone up, etc. Jess was stuck between reality and the dream world because Sin had her tethered there. If she did not come out of it before we departed where we were, she would not have been able to. She would have been tethered to Sin forever, or until he chose to let her go. I woke her up, but there was a blowback from messing with Sin's power. No, she is not attached to him, as he is awake, she would only be stuck if he were still dreaming." Ken nodded his head at Trey and then down. Roy's jaw dropped open.

"All this time, YOU were a healer, and you never thought to mention it to me? Or Tina? She has been looking for a healer her whole life!" Roy slammed his hands on the table, denting it. Everyone flinched.

"I think there are many things your cousin is keeping from you," I said quietly.

"I did tell her," Ken broke in before I had to explain further. "She asked me to go and see her mother, and I went, but as I said, I cannot always use my gifts the way others can. The only way I would be able to relieve her would be to take on her sickness as my own, and even then, I am unsure of whether it would come back or not, given the severity," Ken explained, still not looking at Roy.

"Doesn't matter anyway. Tina is...." They boy stopped himself from saying anything more, somehow more interested in his chocolate bar at that moment. Roy was about to stand and yell when I interrupted him.

"We saw Kat in there. That place, it wasn't like a dream at all, it felt real, you know, like another world. And Kat, she was there. She's the only reason we even made it out, honestly." I paused, remembering her crawling away from the men that were attacking and hoping she was able to escape.

"Why are you telling me about the girl who sacrificed her best friend and kid brother for her own safety? I do not care." Roy spat at the table.

"I'm telling you because she told us why she did it," I slammed my own hands down on the table. "You are so devoted to this princess that you are blinded by your love for her and allowing things to slip right past your face without even a second thought!" I was steaming at his lack of interest in all of the facts.

"Tina has her father. She is holding him captive until Kat gets all the ducks she needs in a row. Tina has him. Not SIN, not someone else. Tina! She begged us to help her, begged us to take her with us, and if you could have seen the dread on her face when she realized they were going to see her and her FATHER was going to pay for it? Your cousin is not the sweet angel front she puts on for your benefit." I sat back down, noticing the tension in the room was because of me. I closed my eyes to center myself and just listened for a bit.

"Star, I'm sorry for my reaction, but how can you be so sure that she wasn't just trying another ploy to get you? How do you know she was telling the truth?" Roy said, calmer than he had been showing for the rest of the team, but still on edge of a blow up. I snuck a peek at him and noticed the regret in his eyes. Is that regret for me?

"Princess Tina? Princess Tina is the one who came and took me from my home. She told my father that all the Project Teams got to choose one student in their family to go and visit for a week. Star had sports that she didn't want to miss, and she had already been to London with our father the first trip, so they decided to let me go instead. My father dropped out of the contest because he found some books written by our ancestors that outlined the trouble lurking if this was attempted. When he came to pick me up, she told him that I had chosen to stay and that he should leave his project for me to enter instead. I heard him demand to see me; I heard him say that I would never choose something like this over my family. But she refused to allow it, saying that she was fearful that he was abusing me and that if he didn't leave that she would have to call the authorities in our own country to investigate. He left but sent Star back to get me. That's when I found out that they did, in fact, investigate and had to close down the TV studio because of it. I was locked in a room above the Library when Charlie came to get me. I heard everything." The boy shoved his knees up to his chest and swung in the chair. I opened my eyes and leaned over to touch him, but he pulled away. Not a good sign.

"No way," Roy said, more shocked than unbelieving. "How could you have been in the castle the whole time and I never see you once. Did you see him, Ken?" Roy turned to Ken for confirmation. Ken was shaking his head in disbelief.

"I mean, I heard stories of a young boy that was tagging along with Tina, but I never saw him. I never saw her as an evil person either, though, until I delivered the news that I could not heal her mother." Ken stared at the table relentlessly. "I mean it can't be a coincidence that the place Sin and his gang are holed up at is in the back of her Castle. Her rooms face that church Roy, do you believe she would have seen the lights on every night and said nothing? That is not like her at all." Ken shook his head again.

"Kat showed me what happened to her father. We didn't discuss, just brief pictures in her head when we were tailing them in the Italian place. She showed the guards taking him, showed her screaming and crying in the street with a letter and then coming here and working side by side with Roy by day and Sin by night. I only saw pictures, so I don't know any interactions, but she showed her and Tina in a library also, many times. Tina is the mastermind behind the whole operation. I mean, maybe they have different motives, but she would definitely be the money, and Sin would be the muscle," Jess chimed in. "Plus, I saw Kat again with Sin when I was unconscious in my makeshift jail in that church. She told him I was nothing, told him I didn't have any power and that I was O-, that I would get sick soon just from being here, but if she showed me everything she did, then didn't she already know about my gifts? She hid my gifts from them so they wouldn't try to use me to get through. She hates me, why would she do that if she was a true Slicer?" Jess sat back and crossed her arms, still trying to unravel this mess.

"We need to talk to Gran," I said with finality. "She is the only one who can completely put it all together for us." I sighed. "Kat did mention one other thing. She said Star would be okay for a while because they do not have all the pieces they need. Do you believe that?" I turned to the group to see their answers. I didn't look at Roy, as I was still trying not to be mad at him for missing the pieces that would have helped us through these days. I was drained, tired, and cold. I didn't have a fight left in me.

"I think that is probably true; I doubt they will hurt her too much, because they will need her to be strong to balance the boat through the barrier when the time comes, but who knows for sure," Ken said to no one in particular.

"She will be okay. Kat is with her, and although I do not like her, I think she will do the right thing. I just couldn't imagine having to choose between the only parent I know and the only friend I have ever had," Jess said with pity.

I rubbed my eyes and looked at the boy with my brothers face. He was sound asleep in the chair. I grabbed a blanket and covered him up. He didn't need to hear this stuff anyway. I finally looked at Roy.

"I'm sorry. I asked the computer to take us out of London. I couldn't think of anywhere else to go but home." I looked at him with as much empathy as I could manage. He shrugged it off. I could tell his mind was elsewhere.

"The books you knocked over in the library. They were your family's?" Roy concluded.

I nodded, looking for my jacket and pulling the concealed book out. Ken stood up to get a better look, as Jess giggled. I cheesed.

"Sorry about that also. I left the rest, but this one looked like something that I would want to read." I lowered my eyes from Roy's, hoping he wasn't angry.

"No apology necessary. When I get back to London, I will have them shipped back to Charlie immediately. I won't tell Tina that I am on to her. Until we have more cold hard facts, there isn't going to be much I am able to do to stop her otherwise. I don't think telling her I know of her sinister plan will make it any better," he said with a deep sigh. I felt a swell of emotions for Roy at that moment. Would I be able to do the right thing if I was in his shoes? If Trey was the bad guy? He was my knight in shining armor for sure. I smiled at him to show my thanks.

"You are taking this rather well, mate," Ken said, turning to Roy with a look of admiration.

"The deck is stacked. What else can I do than believe the people I trust with my life?" Roy clapped a hand on Ken's back with a forced smile. Ken returned the gesture. "I'm sorry I ever doubted you. You have been by my side since we were pups."

"Can we go home now? I am beyond tired! And our parents are going to have a FIT if we don't make it home soon. It's later there than it is here, remember?" Jess whined.

"It's been two days!" I said with a look of horror and panic. "Pops is going to kill us!"

"Ms. S, I think that's what you guys call her; she called your parents. Jess, your dad thinks you're at Star's. Star, your dad knows where you guys are. He is not happy at all with your Gran, but he knows you will be home soon. Hopefully," Ken said, bringing me back down from the edge.

I could imagine pops face, waiting for us to come home, hoping that we made it home safely. Then it hit me. The reason he kept taking Kiki back is because she was not leaving and having episodes, she was sliding all around the multiverse. I looked at Jess.

"Kiki," I said with guilt leaking through, "that's why Pops never gets mad at her. She's sliding." I looked in Jess' eyes and saw the understanding there. I couldn't decide how to feel about the information I had just gathered. I was stunned. Jess, however, was not shocked at all.

"There's more Star," she said in a gentle tone that was not her own. "Starley King is not your doppelganger. She is your sister. You guys are twins. Twin flames." I saw a tear fall down Jess' eye as she said the last part. I fell out of my chair and startled Trey, or whoever this boy that was not Trey's doppelganger was. He woke with a jump.

"Starley? Is that you?" Trey said in a scared tone that had me running to him for comfort. The minute he looked in my eyes, he tensed, knowing that I was not his Star. Not the sister that he was looking for, but someone completely different.

"How do you know I am not your sister, Starley?" I asked him as I walked back to my chair. Curiosity had finally come to call, and I was intrigued to hear the answer.

"Your eyes. Your eyes comfort my soul in a way hers never would. Her eyes told me she would teach me to be strong just as she is. Your eyes tell me, I will have no use for that because you will set a match to anyone or anything that would dare try to hurt me. The same, but different at the same time," he said as he dozed back to sleep. I looked over to Jess to see her swirling little stars in the air his way, urging him back to sleep.

"Why did you do that?" I asked her intently. I had more questions it seemed only he could answer.

"He needs to sleep. He was just drained of his life force. Give him some time," was all she said before she turned back to the group. I sat back down in my chair and tried to take in the information that I was just given.

"So, Trey, he is a twin also?" I asked her, completely intrigued by what was unfolding right in front of my eyes.

"His name is not Trey," she said, looking at me curiously again. "They are both your brothers, yes, but they are not twins. The boy in front of you is older than Trey. His name is Titus. They are two years apart," Jess answered without hesitation. My mouth dropped open.

"Is he Pops boy?" I blurted out. "I mean like MY pops, not the Charlie here in this dimension. But my actual father. Are either of them?" I asked with intensity. How could this be happening? Looking over at Titus, I could now tell that he was older than Trey, but I didn't see two years. So much pain, stress, and frustration could add years to your appearance, but not the boy in front of me. I realized that I could also tell them apart without a second glance, but it had never crossed my mind that he would be anyone else.

"I don't really know. That's a question for Kiki, maybe Gran," Jess responded.

"Well, good thing that is where we are headed!" I spat out with exhaustion rolling in. With the wave of sleep rolling over me as my adrenalin wore off, I looked around the room to see where the best place to nap would be. "I think we should all take a nap here first before we do anything, though. Because I am going to be very crabby very soon otherwise and I think there are still a few things we need to work out. Like whether Ken is going to come back with us or stay here with Roy, or whether we take Titus to see Charlie before we take him with us to see Gran. There's also trying to figure out how to even get home. Not to mention we have to come up with a plan to find Sin and get my sister back." I tripped on the words as they came tumbling out. A new brother and sister all in one day. "It feels so weird saying it, not gonna lie." I yawned and moved myself to the huge comfy chair from the first visit that had someone now reappeared for my use and snuggled into it without another thought. Jess and Ken chatted a while longer then both went over to the couch and did the same. Roy walked over and sat on the floor next to my chair and leaned in to get comfortable himself. I threw a few pillows and a blanket from my chair down and readjusted.

"You gonna be okay here?" I asked, talking about in this dimension and not next to me on the floor. He nodded. "I mean, we will have to come up with some sort of dimensional contact just to make sure, but I think you can manage now that you have all the facts." I winked and closed my eyes.

20

I awoke with a start and jumped to my feet as Jess ran over to make sure I was okay. The boys were still sleeping soundlessly, and the computer in front of us had kicked on to a slowly rising sun. I took one look at the computer and turned to Jess.

"I know why Suzie has been missing since we have been here." I rolled my eyes at the blinking screen. Jess put her finger to her lips and guided me closer to the large panel.

"I was wondering about that. She was here when Ken and I came in the first time, but she has not been since. Ken said she wasn't here when you guys got here the first time either. What's up with that?" She asked, folding her arms.

"It's Roy. In the church, I saw a picture of Roy's father and Suzie. They were in the LA together, before she gave her life and his was taken. I think there is something to do with that. If Roy isn't here, she is," I said, shrugging my shoulders. "I don't want to read any further into it though, I mean she is a computer, right?" Jess shrugged back.

"How are you holding up with all of this? I mean two new siblings? That's a lot to take in." She released a heavy breath.

"Tell me about it!" I replied. "I guess I haven't given it much thought yet. I know one thing for sure, Pops is going to be pissed if he didn't already know." I gave a solemn look, wondering if he did.

"I'm curious to know how much he actually does know about it, actually!" Jess responded.

"I guess we will find out shortly. I'm thinking we will have to bother Charlie; I think he can help us get back home with his studio, and I know he needs some emotional healing, maybe a few good dreams to get him going." I looked over at Jess, still unable to wrap my mind around all that had happened here. "Can you believe the things we have been through and found out? This is madness! I wouldn't be surprised if we woke up in the Kitchens or something at this point," I said, putting my hand to my forehead and seeing Stefilia's stone glow. Jess and I both turned to each other and said at the same time, "Kat." But it wasn't her stone. It was Gran's. I looked over at the rest of the room, which was slowly coming to life with the building light of the computerized sun.

"I think it's time we be on our way Sunshine." Jess cheesed at me. Titus shifted in his seat and turned to us with a big smile.

"What's for breakfast?" He questioned without a hint of fear. At least he had his appetite.

I nodded to Ken and Roy as they stood and prepared to leave our safe space in search of answers.

"I will head back to London immediately, the old-fashioned way since I am not a Slider and do not have a pocket dimension at my disposal. Ken and I have worked out that he will send word and how to get in touch if I need him." Roy tipped his head in farewell and headed for the door. I stopped him in his tracks at the entryway, heart feeling like it was being ripped out of his chest.

"Will I see you again?" I asked nervously.

"I sure hope so," he said through the most incredible smile I had ever encountered. I hugged my knight tightly and moved out of his path so he could be on his way, and with a nod, he was gone.

"Ken and I have worked out that he will go back with us, he thinks we may be able to kill two birds with one stone. I will ask my father if we can house him, he knows who he is, and he knows his parents, from games and PTA and stuff. We will say they have moved for work, but he is the up and coming QB and didn't want to leave. Hopefully, that will draw less attention to my bangs and painted toes." Jess blushed at me. "If that doesn't work, Pops will always let him stay with you guys." She blushed harder and quickly added, "I'm just thinking it may be cramped there with a new son and a daughter who will return." I smiled at Jess. I think I am going to like this new softer version of her.

"Sounds like we should be on our way home then!" I said, feeling a ton of bricks lifted off my chest. I was so glad I had a friend I could depend on to be there for me when I didn't have the slightest clue where to go next.

"Pops?" Titus said to the room.

"Did you know I was your sister too?" I asked him as I led him out of the pocket dimension and into the Kitchen of our Dim V home. He looked at me, startled and confused. "Nah, I will let Gran explain it. I don't have enough details, and I'm just finding out myself!" I giggled to him. Sending him upstairs to pack a bag for our trip, I turned to Jess. "I can't wait to see the look on Trey's face when he realizes he has to share a room with a younger version of himself." Jess and I giggled together, sitting at the bar in the kitchen like old times. The troubles of yesterday were so far away we almost missed when Charlie came in to join our group.

Just watching and basking in the heightened rays of sunshine kissed emotions floating around the room, I looked over, noticing him finally. He nodded his head in thanks as Titus ran down the stairs to embrace his father. All was not right in the world just yet, but all was right in this room, and I was grateful to be a part of it.

"Now," I said, turning to our new gang. "Let's go find Gran and kick some Slicer butt."

Bonnie has been writing for 10 plus years for others. Her work includes songs for award winning music artists as well as articles for magazines & newspapers but never for herself. Finally feeling like it was time to let her own stories out to play, she has debuted her writing with her love for Science fiction & fantasy. Growing up as a Midwestern native, her family often frequented drive-in movie theatres & picture shows, bringing the world of wonder and the escape from reality right to her front door. She now resides in Texas where there is plenty of space to dream and sharing those dreams is her favorite pass time. The Flash and The Green Arrow being two of her favorite heroes. She is excited to raise her little boy on Black panther, Miles Morales and all the good in the world she can find.

Acknowledgements

I wrote this book for anyone and everyone who is unsure about who they want to be. It's okay to be something different each and every day! I find myself holding fast to the above advice and wearing many hats on any given day. So for keeping up with the swift changes and being able to shine in the face of adversity I would like to acknowledge a few people who assisted in making this dream come true. First Nicholas Dicker, without whom I would not have had the courage to continue this writer's life journey. Terrance Abraham for always pushing me through the process, from start to finish, even when I was ready to give it all up and hide under the bed. Your resilience and confidence in this process assisted on many fronts to level set my thoughts and help me through to the finish line. Many thanks to Jeffiah Warner at Jae Press, the ever patient Editor for the push I really needed in most times of lackadaisical bliss. Lastly, the little boy who pushes me to be a better person so I can point him in the right direction on his own path Riley, Mommy loves you to the moon and back!

Finally, to all those who have been a part of my getting there most Thanks and admiration for: David Calderon, Shanell Lee, Raykale Troy, Bernard Steplight, Jason Goodes, Dara Snow, Erin Kelly, Sharmain Bonner, and Cheri Evans.

Wanna keep up with Bonnie?

Website: www.BonnieBaraka.com
Facebook: www.facebook.com/ReadSlicers
Instagram: www.instagram.com/BonnieBaraka
Good Reads: www.goodreads.com/bonniebaraka

Don't Miss Book 2 in The Bequested Series Trilogy Coming Summer 2021

MAVENS

Made in the USA
Monee, IL
13 November 2020